Hell and Back

Natasha Madison

Cover Design: Melissa Gill with MGBookCovers & Designs
Photographer: Lindee Robinson with Lindee Robinson Photography
Models: Daria Rottenberk and Garrett Pentcost
Book formatting by CP Smith
Editing done by Emily A. Lawrence at Lawrence Editing
Proofing Julie Deaton Author Services by Julie Deaton

Warning

This content contains material that may be offensive to some readers. Including sexual abuse, graphic language, and adult situations.

Dedication

To my Nanny, who was the first person to read to me and show me love for books. This one is for you and unlike the last one it's not dirty. You're welcome!

Hell
and Back

NATASHA MADISON

Prologue

Walking into the bare room, I look around. A small dresser with three drawers sits up against the plain white wall.

A couple of shorts, shirts, and some socks fill the drawers, but most are empty. The small toddler bed lies in the middle of the room.

Two nails hold up a dusty sheet in the window to block out the light. It used to be navy, but the years of wear have turned it to baby blue.

I look down at my three-year-old daughter curled up into a small ball. Almost like she is guarding or protecting herself from whatever evil is lurking around us. She's seen enough blackness in her three years to last a lifetime.

She cried enough tears and heard enough sobs to fill twenty years' worth of scary movies.

When the doctor placed her on my chest I vowed to love and protect her, but I've failed her. I've failed myself. But no more. From that fateful day I vowed to right all the wrongs I did to her.

I've escaped the horror we've endured. The bruises are starting to fade. The black and blues have now turned into a greenish yellow.

The scars will fade, too, but the terror, the memories…nothing will erase them.

I wake my girl up and grab her from her bed. "Momma, we habe to leabe again?"

"No, baby, I just want to show you the stars outside." I tuck her into my chest and make my way to the porch.

No one knows about this one-story house my grandmother left me. Which is why we are safe. For now.

The yard is overcome with weeds. Something I plan to rectify tomorrow. We've been here for the last seven days, staying inside. Trying not to bring attention to us. I've done my best not to be too jumpy, but every time I hear a car door slam shut, I hold my breath, hoping no one is coming up the steps that lead to the front door.

We haven't even opened the windows. It is almost like we're shuttering ourselves inside this temporary safe haven as if we don't even exist.

Opening up the screen door, the rusty springs make a loud squeaking noise in the dead of the night. Trying not to make it slam shut, I hold the handle till it shuts softly.

The sounds outside are quiet. Serene. No car sounds, no horns honking, no rushing, just crickets. I settle into the swing I know my grandfather hung to make sure my grandmother had somewhere she could sit and watch the stars.

For thirty-seven years, they did it all together until death came and took my grandfather in his sleep. Ten years later, he came and rescued her from the pain of ALS. Her knitting, cooking, cleaning, gardening, baking all came to a halt the minute her hands shook so badly she couldn't hold not even a fork to feed herself.

Settling myself into the swing, I fold one foot under me, pushing off with the other one.

"So many stars, Momma." My brown-eyed girl looks up, pointing to what looks like a million twinkling lights in the sky.

The darkness of the sky makes them sparkle like diamonds. Some are small, some are blinking. All are beautiful. It's peaceful. It's everything I remember it to be.

It's hope, hope for change. Hope for the future. Hope for the end of the nightmare I have been living the last four years. "Look, baby, a shooting star. Make a wish."

She closes her eyes, and I see her lips move, but no sound comes out of her mouth. I lean down kissing her forehead, making my own wish.

I do this for the next thirty minutes, maybe more, pushing myself on that swing with one foot. Once I know she is asleep in my arms, I get back up to go inside.

The whole time I never realized that the neighbor across the street has been sitting in his living room with the lights off just staring out the window at two broken girls sitting across the street.

1

I wake slowly, the sun trying to fight its way through the sheet. I look down to see that we haven't moved since coming in from outside last night.

Stretching carefully, I lean down to kiss her head, making sure I don't wake her. I take a second to breathe in the moment, thinking about how I got to this point in my life.

They say you never know hell until you lived in it. I can assure you I know it. I've lived in it. I've asked to die in it.

I know that you might look at me and wonder what I'm talking about. How can a twenty-four-year-old, who is also a mother, know what hell is?

I can say it didn't happen overnight. It happened gradually, slowly. So slow, in fact, I didn't even know it was happening until I was sitting in the middle of it.

My parents dumped me off on my grandparents when I was eight. It seems partying and parenting don't go hand in hand. Something they thankfully figured out before I ended up dead with the two of them.

They were on the road, following their favorite band from state to state when their car was hit head-on by a semi whose driver fell asleep at the wheel.

I know I should have been sad, but I wasn't. Maybe this is why God is punishing me. I really didn't know my parents. All I knew was my grandmother, who loved me unconditionally. She made it possible for me to grow up being a normal kid. And like any normal kid, I was ready to leave home the minute I hit eighteen. Ready to be my own person. Ready to take on the world.

I was your typical college student trying to better myself. Trying to do things on my own.

Not only did I move away from Nan, I went to a community college some four states over.

It all started like any other Saturday morning. I was doing the breakfast shift at the diner in town.

The diner was filled with early rising families and truckers passing through town. What made this day different was the party of four guys who looked like they hadn't slept yet. Chances are this was the last step before hitting the hay.

I didn't give them a second thought till they sat in my section. I went to their table, asking for their order.

It took a second for my eyes to meet his. It took me a second more to fall for that lopsided smile and lone dimple. That second I fell for him will always be the one moment I wish I could go back and change.

Because from that second on, I was under Adam Fletcher's spell.

Were things perfect? No. I found out he had no job and wasn't attending college either. Instead, he was just living day by day, as if it was his life's goal to do so.

Not every single eighteen-year-old has goals. I was not in it for money. I was in it for love. Boy, was I fucking naïve.

It started with coffee dates. Oh, those sweet first dates, where he just held my hand. Talking about the future he wanted to have, or was trying to have, I should say. He never really achieved anything to make it his goal.

I should have seen the signs in the beginning as well. The times he missed dates, saying, "Sorry, babe, I lost track of time."

The times he didn't call when he said he would call. "Sorry, babe, my phone died."

The fact he always started out the day energetic and hyper, only to end it looking ragged and sleepy. "Sorry, babe, was up late."

A junkie. That is what he was. Something I knew nothing about. Something I would spend the rest of my life fighting or, better yet, running from.

A small voice and little fingers bring me out of the fog of the past and back into the present. I look down at my little girl, who smiles up at me.

"Morning, Momma," she whispers, leaning in to kiss me.

"Morning, baby, are you hungry?"

She doesn't answer me. Instead, she just nods.

"Let's go downstairs and get you some food." I pull myself from the bed. I don't have to turn around to know she is right behind me.

"Momma, can I have more cereal with milk?" Her voice is barely a whisper, a soft voice she learned early to use so as not to wake the monster who was living with us.

"Yes, you can, angel." I fill up her second bowl and add a heaping amount of milk. It's finally time she gets to eat what a normal kid should eat.

We both look malnourished. I'm maybe a hundred and three pounds of skin and bones, and my little girl doesn't look any better. Forced to survive on maybe a meal a day.

I often didn't eat just to make sure she had enough so her tummy wouldn't hurt.

I look around the sparse house. The curtains downstairs are in dire need of replacement, but they keep the sun out, making it feel like we are invisible. Nothing about this place has changed from when I moved in or from when I moved out.

The house was a gift from above. It was our ticket out. I lost contact with Nan when Adam and I got together. The phone calls home became fewer and farther in between.

Most of the time he didn't want me to call her because she was a 'nosy bitch' according to him.

I mean, I suppose if you base it on the fact she cared and worried about me, then yes, she was definitely a nosy bitch.

It was that phone call three weeks ago, the one that gave me hope and showed me there was a light at the end of the tunnel.

I sat there battered and bruised, one of my eyes swollen shut while my little girl sat next to me, making sure she didn't touch my ouchies, and there were many.

I dialed the number I hadn't called in a while. A number he isolated me from. It wasn't her who answered, though, and when I asked for Nan, I was given the news she had passed but had left strict instructions her phone number was to be transferred to her lawyer in case I called and was ready to come back home.

This was the worst beating he had ever given me. But he didn't do all this damage himself. It was more when his dealer took his turn with me.

Each time he would strike me first, right before he had his way with me. I may have been Adam's, but he was more than happy to share me—and my body—if it meant he could keep his high going longer.

That time was the worse it's ever been. My baby girl was thrown in a closet with a pillow and a blanket. The last thing she saw was Adam tying my hands to the bedposts above my head. My last look at her was with tears running down my face. The light in those brown eyes never shone. She was almost as empty as I was.

They left me there, bleeding, one of my ribs broken for sure. My body covered in fingerprint-sized bruises, raised red welts, and caked with dried blood. They at least untied my hands so I could crawl over to the closet to rescue Lilah.

I couldn't breathe as I winced with each movement my body made, but I managed a sigh of relief as I made it to the door, only to painfully gasp when I opened it and found her curled up in a ball and soaked with her own urine. She crawled over to me carefully, making sure not to touch me, but still getting close enough to me so we could protect each other.

A knock on the door has me holding my breath, while Lilah squeezes her eyes shut. No one knows we're here. No one knows where this house is. As the panic begins to rise in me, my only thought is how did he find us?

2

I don't even know why I've come over here. I woke up at the ass crack of dawn, something on my mind, something I couldn't even explain. But then my thoughts went to that scene I watched last night. My mind was running with questions.

Not knowing what to do with myself, I went downstairs to my weight room where I spent the next two hours sweating my ass off as I pounded out a few miles on my treadmill and worked my muscles till they burned and begged me to stop with a punishing lift session.

I stood under my rain shower, the water set on cold, the pressure of the water feeling like ice pellets on my tired and sore muscles. Towel drying my short blond hair, I'm glad it's just long enough on top to be pushed back. My day-old beard is not bothering me enough to take the time to shave it this morning.

I make my way downstairs and fill my travel mug with coffee to go. Looking over at the house across the street, I make a decision I'm not even sure is right.

My feet are moving before my head can comprehend what is going on.

She obviously doesn't want anyone to know she's here since I've only seen them outside at night.

Before she came, the house had been abandoned, the old lady passing away right on the porch. But I know enough about that girl inside to know she needs help. I'm just not sure I'm the help she needs.

When I moved in, the lady across the street would always wave when I came or went, then she started making me cookies. God, did I fucking love those chocolate chip cookies. Crispy on the outside, soft and chewy on the inside, she always brought them to me warm, so I wound up licking the chocolate off my hands. Fuck, but those were good cookies.

She was always outside on the swing. Lonely is the word that comes to mind. She was fucking lonely, looking for anyone to talk to. Her stories could go on for hours. She did hang with the other neighbor next to her in the last four years.

It was during one of those talks when she raved about her granddaughter. She said they grew apart. But the pain in her eyes said something else. I wasn't good at my job if I didn't know how to read people, and she was one of them.

In exchange for her baked goods, I mowed her lawn. Before she passed, I was doing it at least once a week, but lately I'd been slacking. The house looked abandoned, and it was my fault. Something I vowed to rectify the minute I saw that lady rocking her kid outside.

Which is why I'm standing here, way too fucking early in the morning. Hoping to talk to her and let her know.

I knock one more time, knowing she is in there, but also not hearing anything else. The shadow darkens underneath the door, so she must be up.

"Is anyone in there?" I ask, knowing full well she's right behind the door. Probably with her ear pressed to the door, holding her breath.

"I'm Jackson." I lean in so I don't have to yell. "I live across the street. I cut your grandmother's grass." I stop when I hear movement from behind the door. The lock flicks open, the door creaking open just enough so I can see one of her eyes, the rest of her body hidden behind the door.

"Hi," she says, almost in a whisper. "I'm just waking up."

I know right away she's lying because while there are dark circles under her eyes, they aren't squinting at the light that has just invaded her face.

"I didn't mean to wake you. I was just going to let you know I'll be home later this evening, and I'll be cutting the grass then." I put my hand in the back of my jeans pockets, making my T-shirt strain against my chest. I'm a detective for the special victims unit. My job is to look big and mean. The sleeves of tattoos covering my arms from shoulders to wrists sometimes scare people off. By the look on her face, I can see she's not sure what to think. My six-foot-two-inch frame isn't one a lot of men are willing to mess with, so I imagine she must be feeling the same way.

"You don't have to do that." She closes the door a little more, making it impossible for me to see anything but the darkness inside. After Nan died, I saw her lawyers go in with a cleaning company. They basically closed the place up, and it stayed that way until this week.

The first night I noticed something amiss when Kendall was leaving my place. I saw movement across a window. I stood out there staring, waiting for something else, but there weren't any other movements. Until yesterday when the door opened and out stepped the smallest woman I've ever seen. Not only was she short, she was maybe a hundred pounds soaking wet. Up close in the light of day, I can see she's obviously been missing many meals.

But what strikes me the most are her eyes. I see fear in them, someone who is broken.

"It's okay," she tries to say before I interrupt her.

"Your grandmother didn't have a lawnmower, so you have no choice but to take my help." What the fuck am I doing? I'm lying now just so I can cut this chick's grass. A chick I don't even know. A chick who looks like she has more baggage than anyone can carry.

I should turn around and just say I tried. I can't explain it, but there's just something keeping me rooted on this fucking porch. I just can't pull myself away even though I want to.

"I was going to look in the shed today, see if I saw it. I know that Gramps used to have one." She leans into the door a little more, making it hard to see anything but her one eye. But she is now standing straight instead of leaning behind the door, and I can see her body a little bit more.

I notice the bruises on her arms, and she senses the minute I do, because she resumes her previous position behind the door in order to shield her body from view.

"Don't worry about it. I'll take care of it this evening." It is in that moment I know she relents because all she does is nod her head and close the door. Not giving me anything else. Not another word.

I'm not quite sure what just happened, but as I make my way over to my truck, I'm shaking my head, hoping to clear up the thoughts of the conversation.

One thing I do know for sure is she's running from someone, and she's hiding here.

The question is who is she running from? Only she can give me an answer, and it's obvious I've got some work cut out for myself if I'm going to get an answer from her. Something tells me I need to be ready, and I need her to tell me for what. It won't be easy, that's for sure. The woman inside that house looks like she has seen the inside of the devil's playground, and she's survived to tell about it.

3

I close the door, collapsing down to land on my ass. My breathing comes rapidly like I just ran a marathon, sprinting the whole way.

My chest heaving, my hands trembling, my legs still weak, I look down the hall at the kitchen where I see Lilah has hidden under the table. The fear in her eyes matches the fear coursing through my body.

"Momma," she whispers, unable to forget she was never allowed to talk loud. A lesson she learned when her father threw a chair at the wall after she asked him a question one morning.

I nod my head, the tears already running down my face. My hands shake uncontrollably while I try to wipe them off. We are still safe. He hasn't found us.

Making my way off the floor, I walk slowly back into the kitchen, where I bring Lilah out of her hiding place.

"It's okay, just the neighbor. No one is here." I place her back onto her chair where she leans down and continues to eat her cereal.

She's staring into the bowl, not saying anything more.

"Today we should go out and pick up some more food. Would you like that? Maybe we can stop for ice cream?"

The good news is, after meeting the lawyer, I found out the house has been paid for in full. The property taxes paid into escrow for the next fifteen years. When Grandpa passed away, she used all of his life insurance to make sure I never had to struggle. She thought of everything, even putting one hundred thousand dollars aside for me to live on.

Just knowing I don't have to go out and work is a relief. I can heal. We can heal.

"But what if Daddy binds us?" She looks up at me with fear in her eyes. In seven days, she's smiled twice.

"How about we get dressed up and put hats on like we're wearing costumes?" I look over and smile, trying to make her see I'm not scared. All the while my heart is beating so loud I'm sure one can see it through my chest.

"I don't want to go back hobe. I don't like Daddy or his friends, Momma."

I run my hand over her blonde hair that finally looks clean. No matter how much I tried to make sure she was clean, there was only so much I could do. With a bar of soap, sometimes I would use dish soap if I had to.

Every single penny we had went either up Adam's nose or in his veins. He would go out once a week and buy us the bare minimum of food. Butter, milk, bread, cheese, what he said was essential. Sometimes he'd spring for chicken and it would be like I won the lottery.

Since I've made that phone call, it's been a roller coaster. After I hung up, I was picked up by a car in a matter of twenty minutes.

We were then hustled to someone's house, where a wonderful older woman looked after us. She reminded me so much of Nan. Her white hair curly, her soft eyes, and her beautiful smile lit up the room.

She had a doctor come in to check me over. He told me what I already knew; one rib was broken, so he bandaged my side up. My eye would be fine. Nothing ruptured in it, so it would get better with time. He looked over the welts and bruises but nothing could be done with those. Those would heal, was all he said.

The next day, the lawyer whom I spoke with on the phone finally showed up. He had all the papers ready. I signed one dotted line after another before we got in his car, and he finally brought us to Nan's house.

We arrived at night, so no one saw us walking in. He unlocked the front door for us. I walked in carrying Lilah, holding her to my chest. He didn't need to show me around, but he did tell me the fridge was fully stocked and there were clothes in the bags by the door.

There was also a brand new phone with his number in the contacts. Actually, it was the only number there. There was also a new MacBook, which I had no idea how to use.

It was just enough to let us get our bearings without having to leave, but eventually we have to go out there. I have to take my life back. If for no other reason but to show Lilah how to move on. To show her how to live life without fear.

"I say we get up, get dressed, and go buy us some food, maybe even a couple of toys, some coloring books. Oh, you know what else, sweetheart? Maybe we'll get some Play-Doh?" I smile at her, watching her eyes light up at the thought of coloring books and Play-Doh.

"Okay, Momma," she says, nodding her head.

I pick up our plates, placing them in the sink and washing them right away. This is my house, these are my rules.

I look over at Lilah sitting on the couch holding the only doll she has ever had. Saddened, I stare out the window into the vast, weed infested backyard. The shed door is open, showing me we indeed don't have a lawnmower.

I make a note it's the first thing we are going to buy today. There is no way I will allow that man, or any man, to come and save me or help me.

I trusted a man once and look where it got me. Broken, bruised, and scared. Not anymore.

Wiping my hands with the tea cloth, I make my way over to Lilah and pick her up, ready to start our day.

"Let's go buy some toys, yeah?"

She looks up at me with a smile and nods her head.

"It's time."

We get dressed in clothes that are too big for us, but I'm hoping to start filling them up. The next step will be to get a doctor for Lilah. She hasn't been to one since she was born.

I start to panic a little, knowing I'm leaving the safety of the house that has kept us safe for the last two weeks, but I know I have to do it.

Putting our shoes on, I think about how I'm going to get to the store and back. I know there was a grocery store within walking distance. I just hope they have a taxi stand so I don't have to lug everything back.

I think I need to buy Lilah a stroller. It might be too late since she's almost four and walks, but I want her to have it.

We turn to walk out of the house. The sun is blasting down on us. The heat is bearable for now, but I know it's going to get worse as the day goes on.

Locking the door behind me, I grab Lilah's hand and walk toward the street. The neighbor next door that I never met is outside watering her plants.

I try not to make eye contact with her, but I can't ignore her when she shouts at us.

"Hey, you!"

I look up at her and see she has one of those hats that tie under your chin.

"Aren't you Felicia's granddaughter?" She walks over to her white picket fence, the water from the hose still running.

"Yes, ma'am," I answer, pulling Lilah closer to me.

"Is that your baby girl?" she asks, looking me up and down.

I'm not sure if she is sizing me up or passing judgment.

"Yes, ma'am."

"Where are you guys off to?" she asks.

"To get some groceries. Maybe buy a lawnmower."

"The walk is way too far, and it'll be too hot by the time you need to come back. Why don't you wait there, and I'll take you? I have to go myself anyway," she says, turning around, heading to the spout to turn the water off. "I'll just get my purse and keys, and we can be on our way." She is already walking up the front steps.

"I don't want you to go out of your way, Mrs....?"

"Oh, you can call me Brenda. I knew your grandmother. She was very special to me, and I loved her dearly. Just let me get my keys, and we can get to know each other better in the car. All right? Maybe we can even hit up McDonald's. Would you two like that?"

I don't have to look down to see Lilah has another smile. She has had McDonald's only once.

It's a funny thing what one would do for their child. This right here is one of them. My head is telling me not to trust her, my heart is telling me to run, but my gut is telling me it's okay.

"I think we would like that very much, Brenda. Please take your time. We'll wait right here," I tell her, retreating back while looking down at Lilah. "We're going to McDonald's. Isn't that fancy?" And then I hear my girl giggling, which is like music to my ear.

Jackson

I slam the phone down with more force than I intended. My partner, Mick, looks over at me.

"I thought Kendall came over last night. Yet here you are ready to blow up."

I shoot him a glare. We've been partners since the beginning. We entered the academy at the same time, both of us with chips on our shoulders, both hoping to change the world.

Seven years later, there is no one else I would want to have my back.

"Shut the fuck up, Mick, not today." I focus on the file in front of me. Another runaway kid disappeared into thin air.

I look up and stare straight into Mick's eyes. I don't need him to say anything. I know what he's thinking.

"I met my neighbor this morning."

Mick leans back in his chair, not saying a word, waiting for me to finish.

"She had bruises on her arm and a couple faded ones on her face." I close the file in front of me.

I turn around to open up the computer so I can search Nan's name, Felicia, to find something on her.

"So now what?" Mick asks me, but he knows the answer even before I know what I'm going to answer.

"She's running from something. I don't know what or who, but there was real fear in her eyes. There was enough pain in them to break someone straight down to their core," I tell him while I start typing.

"You can't save everyone, Jackson, you know this. It's like you're constantly chasing that same ghost." He leans forward, putting his arms on the desk.

"I don't want to save her." Her scared eyes flash through my mind. "I just want her to know she's safe."

"What the fuck are you doing?" he asks when he sees me type in Nan's name.

"I need to know what her story is, Mick." I almost press enter, but his words stop me.

"It's her story to tell, Jackson. Not yours to find out. If she is the way you say she is, ain't no way in fuck she's going to be cool with you finding out without her telling you."

I shrug at him, not ready to admit he's right. You would think he would shut up, but he doesn't. "Yeah, I know you aren't going to stop searching till you find out those answers. You want to keep her safe." He pauses, cocking his head to the side. "Who is going to keep you safe from yourself?"

"I have no idea, but something is pulling me to her, something I can't even explain. I've got to get home. I promised to mow her lawn."

"Which lawn we talking about?" He ducks when I throw a balled up piece of paper at him. "How are you going to explain Kendall?"

"There is nothing to explain. We're friends, just friends from now on." I go to grab my keys off my desk, not interested in finishing this conversation.

"I hope you know what you're doing, for both your sakes," he tells me right before I walk out of the room.

19

***

I pull up in my driveway to a sight that pisses me off.

Here she is in a long-sleeved shirt, long pants, hat, and glasses pushing a brand-new lawnmower.

I make sure I check my temper before I walk over. Right before I cross the street, the little girl on the front porch stops me mid-step.

She's the spitting image of her mother, just a smaller version. She is sitting at a little plastic table they probably just bought, coloring.

I make my way over to her mother right when the lawnmower goes off.

"I told you I would cut the grass." I try to sound casual, but the blood in me is boiling. It must be ninety-five degrees outside, and she's wearing enough clothes for a trek across the frozen tundra.

She looks up. "I also told you I would take care of it, and I would be doing it myself."

The little girl from the porch makes it to her mother and hides behind her, yanking on her pants leg.

The fearful look she gives me is just like her mother's. I crouch down, getting eye to eye with her. "Hey there, beautiful. What's your name?"

She doesn't reply, and instead she lowers her gaze so she is looking at her feet.

"I'm Jackson." I reach my hand out, but drop it when I know she won't take it. I gesture behind me as I say, "I live in the house right over there. I used to know your great-grandma." I'm trying to draw her into a conversation with me, but nothing I say engages her.

"It's okay, baby, you can tell him your name. Nan used to make him cookies, so you know what that means, she must have really liked him." She rubs her daughter's shoulder.

"I'm Lilah," she says in barely a whisper.

"That is the most beautiful name in the whole wide world. You're lucky to have such a beautiful name."

She smiles at me, right as a car backfires. They both jump up, Lilah yelling and putting her hands to her ears.

Two things happen at the same time. Her mother grabs her and runs toward the house, and the second is from now on I vow to protect them with everything that I have.

"Wait." I rush after them and make it right through the door before it's closed in my face. I stand here inside the house and watch them rushing to the corner to hide.

Two broken girls protecting each other against some monster. I walk up to them. "It's okay. It's just a car backfiring. It was nothing but a car."

"Lilah, honey, it's okay, it's okay. I'm here. It's okay, baby girl, we're safe." She is trying to comfort the little girl, who is sobbing quietly in her mother's arms. "No one is here, honey."

She looks over at me, our eyes meeting for a beat before she lowers them again.

"Look, it's okay, it's just Jackson. There is no one here, baby." She rocks Lilah back and forth. Her back is against the wall while she soothes her baby girl, whose sobs are slowly stopping, her eyes closing.

"What can I do?" I'm now sitting in front of her, not sure how to even start to dissect this.

"Nothing. You can't do anything for us." She kisses Lilah's head. "No one can."

I ignore the last part, not sure how to talk about this now.

"I'm going outside to finish cutting the grass, then I'll pick up some food for us. Does she like pizza?"

"Jackson, I don't know what relationship you had with my grandmother, but I don't need your help. We will be fine. Please, it's okay, you can leave." She rests her head on the wall, closing her eyes, the defeat of the day leaving her body.

21

"I'm going outside to finish mowing the lawn so Lilah doesn't have to go outside anymore today. Then I'm going to pick up pizza for myself. You won't have time to cook, so I'm going to pick one up for you. I want to eat with you guys, but I'm not pushing myself on you either after today. Now I don't want to fight with you or even discuss this, so just nod you understand."

She looks into my eyes, but nods yes.

"I can pay you for the pizza. I have money. I don't need a handout," she says while trying to push herself up to go get fucking money.

If she weren't so scared of things, I would punch the fuck out of something right now. "I don't want your money, now or ever. I have no doubt you can take care of yourself. Consider this a housewarming present." I get up, going to the door, not even giving her a chance to say anything else.

Right before closing the door, I hear a soft voice, "She's never had pizza before, so can you just get us plain cheese?"

I don't say anything, afraid of what will come out of my mouth. I nod, turning to walk out the door, closing it quietly so as not to wake Lilah.

I close my eyes, exhaling the breath I didn't even realize I was holding.

I don't even have my thoughts all in order when I hear another voice beside me, "She's barely holding on while fighting for her life. She has demons. They both do. Whatever happened to them, it's in there deep. Both of them are so scared, you can practically feel the fear coming off of them."

I look over at Brenda, who is on her porch watering her plants.

"Tread lightly, Jackson, or better yet walk away if you aren't going to do anything about it."

I don't have a chance to respond as Brenda walks into her house, closing her front door softly, leaving me fighting my own demons.

5

I sit in that spot Jackson left us in long after I hear the lawnmower stop.

My thoughts drift over the great day this started out to be.

Brenda brought us to a big Wal-Mart Super Store. It was a 'one shop stop.'

Lilah's eyes grew so big once we got to the toy aisle. I couldn't say no when I saw something I knew she loved. Case in point the plastic table and chairs that are now on the porch. Along with five coloring books, crayons, colored pencils, markers, Play-Doh, and one beautiful cabbage patch doll. Yup, to say I went overboard is the understatement of the year, but fuck did it feel good to be able to give her that.

Next was the food. We filled two carts. It almost looked like we were getting ready for the apocalypse, and maybe we were, but for the first time in a long time, I had a kitchen, I had money for food, and I actually had food to cook in it. I was going to be cooking every day from now on.

Brenda was the one who did all the talking. She kept telling me stories about her and Nan. I felt somewhat closer to Nan listening to those stories.

McDonald's was its own adventure. Lilah couldn't believe they actually gave you a toy with the food. She was so afraid to love it for fear of it being taken away. So when Brenda gave it to her with a loving smile, she took it and hid it beside her.

She's learned never to get attached to things because they were always taken away from her at one point or another. One year, I saved to get her one of those dolls with the stroller. She had it for a week before one of Adam's friends fell on it while he was high and then they set the doll on fire.

When we made it home, I quickly put away all the food. We had abundance, and it felt so good. I also found Nan's recipe box with all her recipes from when I grew up. Chocolate chip cookies, oatmeal cookies, sugar cookies, banana bread, lemon loaf, all the recipes that she made during my childhood. It was something that I would now give to Lilah.

"Look at this, baby girl, Nan's recipes for cookies. How about we go outside, you can color, and Mommy can mow the lawn? Then maybe we could make us some of those cookies?"

She smiled up at me, giving me her answer without saying anything.

Making our way outside, I knew it would be hard since I still had bruises on me so going out in shorts was not even an option. So I put on my long pants with a long-sleeved shirt. I grabbed a hat to help cover me from the sun.

It took me nearly forty-five minutes to figure out how the fuck this lawnmower machine worked. I read and reread the directions.

I mean, how hard could it possibly be to pull the string to get it started? When it finally did start, I let out a squeal of joy at the same time that Lilah clapped for me and said, "Good job, Momma, you did it!"

"I so did it, baby girl. Why don't you color me a picture we can put on the fridge inside and also one for Ms. Brenda that we can bring over to her later?"

She nodded, her pigtails bouncing with the movement.

I was mowing the lawn for maybe ten minutes before a shadow

came over me. I turned to look up—way up—into furious, blue eyes. We maybe exchanged a couple of words till the great day ended.

I'm not even sure what happened when I heard the screeching sounds from Lilah next to me. Her hands on her ears, I did the only thing I know to do. I grabbed her and searched for a hiding place.

I know I can't outrun anyone, but I'm still going to try my hardest to do it.

I made it to the corner right behind the couch and huddled myself over her until I felt heat by my legs. I knew Jackson had followed me in.

I've known him for a day, but just having him here brings me a disconcerting bit of peace, which is stupid since I know better.

Which brings me to now, two hours later, and I'm pulling myself up to put Lilah in her bed. I don't think she'll wake up for pizza. I tuck her in and go downstairs to wash up. I still smell like grass and gasoline.

I'm drying my hands when I hear a soft knock at the door.

"Who is it?"

"It's Jackson and a large pie."

I unlock the door. He steps in, filling the whole doorway. I haven't turned on any lights in the house, so just a small light is shining from the kitchen stove.

"Were you sleeping?" he asks, looking around. "Where is Lilah?" He moves around me to the kitchen to put the pizza down on the table.

"She's in bed. She's probably exhausted after such a busy day."

"Did she eat?" He places his hands on his hips, which makes the tight shirt he's wearing pull across his chest.

"She ate McDonald's at three. She might be up early. I don't want to wake her to eat."

I don't know what the protocol is. I've never been in a room with a man before without trying to shield myself.

"Is that pizza for all of us or just for Lilah and me?" I look from the pizza to him.

"It's for you two. I got my own waiting for me at my house."

I don't know why a sense of disappointment washes over me thinking he got two pizzas, but I pack it away.

"Well, thank you for cutting the grass and for dinner," I say while wringing my hands.

He nods. "See you soon." He turns around and leaves me in the middle of my kitchen with the delicious smell of pizza.

Making my way over to the table, I open the box and the aroma makes my mouth water.

I grab a slice, the cheese stringing to break apart. I eat it faster than I should have, causing my stomach to hurt from over filling it so fast.

I pack up the rest of the pizza, thinking about warming it up for lunch tomorrow.

Right before I go to turn off the light, I pick up Nan's recipe box and decide tomorrow Lilah and I are going to bake some cookies as a thank you to Brenda and Jackson.

I've made two friends in one day. Almost like they were gifts from an angel.

I make my way upstairs right after I lock all the doors, placing chairs under the handles of the front and back doors. If someone breaks in, I'm damn well going to hear them.

I take a nice hot shower, shampooing my hair twice.

When I make it to bed I close my eyes, but I'm haunted by the piercing blue eyes all night. Only in my dream, I'm not running away from them. No, even scarier is the fact that I'm running toward them.

6

"Momma." Little butterfly kisses touch my cheeks, making my eyes flutter open. "Momma, I'm so hubgry."

I pull my girl onto the bed and cuddle her close to my chest to give me an extra few moments to wake up. I know she went to bed without dinner, so she must be really hungry. As if on cue, her stomach lets out a grumble.

"Oh, boy, you must be really, really hungry. What about having pancakes today? Would you like that?" I kiss her before finally climbing off the bed and going to the washroom.

Once we get downstairs, I start the coffeemaker and open the blinds in the kitchen. It's the first time I've done this. One step at a time. I also put the chairs back to where they belong.

Grabbing the ingredients to make pancakes, I place them on the counter. "Come on, love bug, come up here so you can help me mix."

Her excitement shows as she starts flailing her arms, jumping up and down.

I pick her up, placing her safely on the counter. I pour the mix into a bowl while we both add in the water, milk, and oil. I make her break the egg, which of course ends in shells in the batter since she basically crushed it with her hand.

She immediately looks down at her hand, saying, "I sorry, Momma," her brown eyes filling with tears.

"Baby, it was an accident. Look, I'm going to make it all better." Taking a spoon, I scoop out the broken eggshells. "See? All better now, but how about Mommy breaks this one to show you how it's done?"

I break the egg and then give her a spoon. "Okay, let's mix this up so I can make us some big pancakes and we can eat them with extra syrup."

We mix it together, then she plays with the Play-Doh on the floor right next to the table while I continue to make us breakfast.

From my spot in the kitchen, I can see shapes outside the window shades. I really need to get some thicker shades.

I see Jackson's truck is already gone. I don't even let my mind wander there. He doesn't need me. I'm the last thing he needs in his life.

"Okay, ready to eat some yummy pancakes?" I serve up two pancakes on each plate. Getting her into her booster seat, another purchase from yesterday, I get her all settled and served.

The minute she tastes the pancake, or more accurately, the syrup, she hums in appreciation. "This so good!" she says as syrup dribbles down her chin and onto her shirt and her hair. She finishes nearly everything on her plate.

"Someone needs to take a bath or else you'll get eaten by bugs when we go outside to the backyard."

"No outside, Momma." She shakes her head left to right, her hair sticking to her chin.

"Love bug, we're going to go outside to see how Mr. Jackson cut the grass and then we'll come back in and bake some cookies as a thank you for doing all this for us."

"Scarby outside, Momma."

I pluck her out of her booster seat and head upstairs to start the bath. "It is scary outside, but how about we hold hands? We can do it if we do it together."

28

She looks up at me, her brown eyes so fearful and confused, I don't know what else to say to reassure her.

As she plays with her ducks in the tub, another new thing we bought, I tidy up the bathroom while mentally making a to-do list.

Once she is dry and dressed, I sit her on my bed with a couple of picture books while I get started on dusting the house.

People live here now. We live here now. We will thrive in this house now.

I tie the bed sheet curtains to the side, letting the sunlight shine in. I run downstairs to get the cleaning products and bring them all upstairs. Maybe forcing her outside today will be too much.

One step at a time. I start to work first on the room Lilah sleeps in. The closets are almost bare since most of Nan's stuff was given away to goodwill.

There are a couple of boxes shoved on the shelves. Reaching up, I pull a box down. The dust floating off the top just about chokes me. Placing it on the floor, I open the box. A gasp immediately escapes my mouth.

I'm assaulted with every single one of my childhood accomplishments. Every picture, every letter, every report card, every single award. It's a much-welcomed reminder of a happier time in my life.

I grab the other box and opening this one knocks me on my ass. There are hundreds of pictures of me. Well, not just me, but Nan and me, my friends and me. My childhood memories come flooding back to me. The teenage years and horrible hair choices make me laugh. Then, finally, the last picture taken right before I left for college.

I can barely recognize the girl in the picture. Carefree, the only thing on my mind was to get out from under Nan and be my own person.

I wish I could say I would go back, but if I did I wouldn't have Lilah, and I wouldn't trade her for anything.

"Lilah, come and look at these pictures of when I was a little girl."
I hear her plop off the bed, her feet padding softly against the floor as
she runs into the room.

She plants herself right on my lap, fitting herself in between my
crossed legs. "You small?" She looks up at me.

"Yup, I was small just like you." I rub my nose on hers. "This is
me and my Nan." I show her the last picture we took. "She would have
loved you. She would have braided your hair and made cookies with
you, and she would have protected you." A tear escapes at the thought
she will never sit and do those things with her.

"Momma, you sad? You have ouchies?" She carefully gets off of
me, looking for my ouchies.

"No, honey, no more ouchies. Ouchies all gone," I tell her. "You
want to go downstairs and eat some pizza?" I remember Jackson
dropping it on the table and leaving quietly so as not to wake Lilah.

"Pee-sah?" she asks, confused.

"You'll love it, I promise. After that, we can make cookies. Would
you like to do that?"

"I wan pissa and cookees."

The afternoon flew by after heating up pizza for Lilah, which she
now says is her favorite food ever. We carefully got Nan's recipe box
out of the cupboard and made her famous chocolate chip cookies.

The house smelled like so many memories of arriving home after
school and her having them waiting for me. Of sitting at the table with
cookies and a glass of milk while telling Nan all about my day at
school. It never got old no matter how old I got.

Lilah finally went down for a nap long enough for me to start on
dinner.

She ate the chicken I made with mashed potatoes but made sure to
let me know she liked the pizza better. I sat at the table, my eyes
always finding a way to look at the house in front.

After I washed all the dishes, I set a plate down and filled them with the cookies we made today.

"Okay, baby girl, let's go see Mr. Jackson so we can thank him. Okay?"

"Shoes?"

"Yes, baby, get your shoes."

I assess myself in the mirror to make sure I look somewhat decent. My stomach flutters, and my heart is beating erratically, not knowing how he will take this.

Making our way over to his house, I notice there are two cars now parked in his driveway. It never even occurred to me he might be with someone. He could be someone's husband. He could be someone's something.

I'm all of a sudden regretting my decision once we get to the door and Lilah reaches up to ring the doorbell.

Fuck me. I think I'm sweating.

The door opens and the most beautiful woman I have ever seen smiles at us. "Well, hello there. Can I help you guys?"

"Um...umm...Lilah and I were coming by to thank Jackson for cutting our grass yesterday."

"Oh my gosh, aren't you the cutest little girl I have ever seen." She gets down to her level, and Lilah becomes shy and hides behind my leg.

"I'm so sorry. I didn't mean to interrupt your dinner. I just wanted to thank him." It's almost like I'm stuttering, feeling I'm doing something wrong, hoping she doesn't know that last night I dreamed of her boyfriend, that he's been on my mind all day. "You can enjoy them for dessert." I try not to make eye contact in case she can somehow see the disappointment knowing he has someone he keeps safe.

She gets up and smiles at me. "Thank you so much. Jackson is on the phone, but I will give this to him the minute he comes back down."

I reach out to give her the plate, which she takes with a real genuine smile.

"They smell delicious. We will definitely be eating this tonight."

I nod and smile at her, picking Lilah up in my arms. "Let's say good night to Miss...?"

"Kendall. My name is Kendall."

"Bye, Miss Kendall." With those words I make my way across the road, trying not to let my head play tricks on me.

"How about we take a nice bubble bath together, and then we can have a sleepover in Mommy's bed? We can read stories."

"Yeah. Momma bed?"

"Yes, baby, Momma's bed." I make it to the front door and turn around to lock it, taking in the house across the street.

The shadow in the upstairs window draws my attention up.

I know it's him. I feel him watching me. I can't see his face or his eyes, but I know they are on me. I feel him looking, I feel his stare.

I close the door, not taking even a second to look toward the window to see the man with the blue eyes, who's been haunting my dreams from the first time I saw him.

Jackson

I hear the doorbell the minute I press accept on my phone.

"My wallet is on the counter. Take the money."

I was surprised to see Kendall's car in my driveway when I got home.

I was even more surprised when I came in and she was lying on the couch watching television.

Kendall and I met in high school. First crush, first kiss, first everything. Till the day everything changed and she took a backseat.

No matter how many times I tell her I can't give her what she wants, she still shows up.

Don't get me wrong, she dates. I know this because when she is with someone, she doesn't come around. I also know the minute it's over because she gives me a call.

I've never called her. I've never chased her. Doing that would give her the wrong idea, and I'm not that guy.

"What have you got?" I ask Mick.

"So the sixteen-year-old Lori? You were right. Turns out she was dating an eighteen-year-old Evan Franks. The same Evan Franks who was dating Sarah Nickles. The same Sarah Nickles who disappeared six months ago."

"Fuck. I knew that guy was bad news the minute we showed up at his house. Came outside pretending to be all worried. Did you check his last address? Has he moved?"

"Last address is unknown. He was living with his mother then got evicted. From there we've got nothing. I put word out on the street to a couple of informants to keep me posted." Mick breathes out. "This smells fucking bad, Jackson. Smells like raw fucking sewage."

I reach up, pinching my nose. My head is already starting to pound with the headache I know is coming. "Nothing we can do tonight. Go home, get some sleep. Tomorrow we hit the streets. See if anyone is willing to sing."

"All right, later then."

I turn to look outside, trying to get my thoughts together.

Looking at the house across from mine, I haven't seen them at all today. I'm just about to turn around when I see both of them walking across the street leaving from my house.

What the fuck was she doing? Did she come here? My mind is running with questions. I watch her make her way to the front door. She turns and looks up. The light in the room is not on, so I'm pretty sure she doesn't see me.

The look on her face answers my question. She sees me, but she's not giving me anything else. She steps through the door, closing it immediately behind her in a clear signal, letting me know she's keeping me outside with everyone else.

I make my way downstairs just as Kendall places a plate of cookies on my counter in the kitchen.

"Your neighbor and her daughter just dropped off cookies for you." She turns around, heading right to me.

On her tippy toes, she wraps her arms around my neck and leans up to place a kiss on my lips.

"I really missed you today." She trails kisses along my jaw and down my neck.

She must feel I haven't wrapped my arms around her.

"Are you okay? Was it a bad phone call?" That's the Kendall I know. The one who thinks about me before herself. She's perfect; she just isn't perfect for me.

"Yeah, sorry, my head isn't really here tonight. I didn't know you were coming over. You usually send me a message first."

She doesn't have a chance to say anything before the doorbell rings again.

"I'll get it. Probably the Chinese I ordered. Get the plates, yeah?"

I move to the front door, paying for the food and sneaking a look over at that house whose occupants keep calling to me.

It's pitch-black. No lights coming from it. Nothing.

Turning back inside, I see Kendall has set the table for the two of us.

Sitting at the table, we open the containers, filling our plates up. My head isn't here. I don't know if I'm thinking about the girls who have disappeared or if my head is across the street in the house that's now pitch-black.

The silence goes on for practically the whole meal. Kendall has asked some questions but since I only give her grunts in reply, it's not a surprise when she stops asking.

"Will we ever be anything more?" She looks down at her plate and then up at me.

"Kendall, I nev—"

"I know, Jackson. Trust me, I know. You've never promised me. You've never given me anything. You've never even tried. Why, Jackson?"

"Kendall, don't pretend you have been waiting for me this whole time. Don't sit there making this more than it is. Do I love you? Yes. I do, but I'm not in love with you. We have fun. It's easy." I'm trying really hard not to be an asshole.

"We have fun? Do you know how hard it is to do this with you? Do you think I haven't tried to move on? But I can't because I am in love with you. I've always been in love with you. It's been seven years, Jackson. It's time to move on. It's time to let it go." She tries to reach out to touch me, but I pull back.

"Kendall, it's never going to be more than this for me. It wasn't before, and it isn't now. This went on for far longer than it should have. You need to meet someone who will sweep you off your feet. Someone who wants to hang the moon for you. Someone who will put you before anything and anyone. Someone who will cherish you. I'm not that person."

"I think I'm going to go." She gets up from the table, leaving her plate there.

I push up from the table at the same time. "Kendall, at least finish your dinner."

She grabs her purse on her way to the front door. I follow her, not sure what else there is to say.

Once the front door opens, she turns around and reaches up to kiss my cheek before turning to walk to her car. I watch her drive away.

I exhale long and hard, rubbing my face, pulling my hair. "FUCK!"

I close the door as I walk back inside. I move to the table to clear it, and I wind up throwing everything out.

The plate of cookies catches my eye, but more importantly, I see the white folded note with my name scrolled across it on top of the plate.

I grab the paper, unfolding it.

Thank you for cutting the grass and buying the pizza. Lilah says it's her favorite thing ever.

Thank you for making her smile. Perhaps one day we can grab pizza together?

Bella

Her name, I finally have a name. It's a name I call out later that night as my hand fists my cock in the shower. It's also the name I'm yelling in my dreams as I chase after a disappearing woman and child. Bella…

8

Bella

I sit on the couch, looking outside at the street, wondering things I have no business wondering.

It's been two hours since we came home. Two hours since I dropped off the cookies to his wife or girlfriend.

After bath and stories, it took Lilah ten seconds to fall asleep. I tossed and turned. I was so restless, I thought I'd make some warm milk with vanilla and a touch of cinnamon just like Nan used to make, to settle myself.

An hour later, I'm still restless. My thoughts go back to how I got here.

People will wonder why I didn't leave earlier. It happened gradually. Adam was so good at hiding things. Till I found the plastic little packet of cocaine. "It's just this one time. It's a pick-me-up." God, I was such a fool.

Next were the needles. Those fucking needles were everywhere. Not to mention the bent, burnt spoons, the lighters, and the rubber bands. It was a junkie's house in the end.

The first time he hit me, he was sorry, so sorry he didn't get high for a week. To him that was seven years.

After the first time, he didn't hit me again for a long time. He would push me, he'd yell and scream, his cutting, cruel words berating me. I would endure that as I waited for him to leave to go on a bender. He'd be gone, the fighting and yelling would stop, but unfortunately, we would have no money and sometimes little food. I should have left then. I know it now, but how could I call Nan and show her how far I had fallen?

I couldn't get a job because of Lilah. Daycare just wasn't an option. I was stuck.

Then it started getting worse. He was high more often than he wasn't, and he became angrier and more aggressive. The hitting started and quickly escalated to almost a daily occurrence. That's when he stopped leaving for his benders, and instead his 'friends' would come over, taking over the tiny, one-bedroom apartment we had, to go on their bender there. I was never let out of his sight, so leaving him was almost impossible at that point, since he was always there.

Then that night happened... He had two friends over. They had been getting high for a good twenty-four hours. Almost out of drugs they went around the apartment, turning everything over, trying to find anything to keep the high going.

I tried to stay out of his way, out of sight, out of mind, but Lilah had to go to the bathroom. I tried to pass them, till one of his friends grabbed us and pulled us into his lap.

Lilah started crying. I looked over at Adam with fear in my eyes, silently begging him to help me. His hands had started on my thighs and traveled up to my breasts.

"Adam, HELP!"

"We can get some good money for this bitch right here," his friend said with a leering smile, showing me his rotten, yellowed, decayed teeth.

Adam turned to us finally and said, "How much do you think?"

I fought to get away from him, pushing Lilah to the floor. He must have mistook my squirming to get away from him as me playing hard to get because I felt his dick get hard under me.

I finally managed to break free from him and crawl away, hoping they'd forget about me. But Adam grabbed my arm and roughly yanked me up from the floor, twisting it and causing me to cry out in pain.

"Shut up, Bella. You are going to do what I say, understand? Or else..." The threat hung in the air, but he turned to look at Lilah crying on the floor by my feet.

"Adam, she's scared, let me take her back into the room, and we won't bother you." The need to get her away from him was what was keeping me from losing my shit right then.

"You go shut that kid up and be ready for me when I come and get you." The pupils in his bloodshot eyes were big and dilated. I turned my head away from him, the bile rising in my throat.

A car door breaks me from my memories. She pulls out of the driveway, Jackson watching it drive away. He watches until she disappears and then he looks right over at my house. The shades are open, but the house is dark, so I know he can't see in. But I can feel him looking into the house.

I wonder why she left and who she is to him. I don't know who he is or what he does, but I somehow knew after he followed Lilah and me into the house, almost shielding and protecting us, I could trust him.

It could be that Nan trusted him. It could be that Brenda said he was the most loyal person she has ever known.

I get up to put my cup in the sink and rinse it with water. Walking back to the living room window, I pull down the shades. Jackson isn't there anymore, but I do see his shadow in his house.

I make the rounds, checking to make sure all the doors and windows are locked. Thankfully, Nan had upgraded the furnace and added an air conditioner in here so I didn't have to sleep with the windows open.

Making my way back to my bed, I cuddle up to my baby girl, who is stretched out in her sleep like a starfish, right in the middle of the bed. My mind is exhausted, my body is exhausted. This time, it takes me just a few moments to fall into a slumber.

***

I'm washing the breakfast plates the next day when there is a knock at the door. Lilah and I both stop moving, not saying a word.

I put my hand to my lips to tell her to be quiet, while I tiptoe to the door, looking to see who it is. I let out a breath of relief when I notice it's just Brenda.

Unlocking the door, I smile at her. My smile goes away when I see her talking to Jackson, who is across the street. His dress attire is the same as the last couple of days.

Nice, but faded blue jeans, hugging him in all the right places. His blond hair is wet like he just got out of the shower. Today his T-shirt is a navy blue, and it also fits him like a glove, tight across his wide chest. The sleeves wrap around the tops of his tatted biceps. The blue of his shirt makes his Caribbean Sea blue eyes stand out.

I look down at my shorts and a matching blue tank top without a bra. Even though my breasts are small enough to pull this off, I still cross my hands over my chest so he doesn't see me.

He looks me up and down and gives me a chin up. I nod at him and then turn back to Brenda.

"Good morning. You're up early," I say while two hands wrap around my thigh.

"Good morning, sunshine, how are you this morning?" Brenda ignores me, going straight for Lilah.

She hides her face in my thigh, fighting her smile at Brenda.

A honk makes us all look up to see Jackson drive away, waving.

"What a boy that one is." She sighs while waving. "What I wouldn't do to be twenty years younger." This makes me laugh because I'm thinking Brenda is close to seventy. Even if she were twenty years younger, I doubt she'd have a chance with him, but more power to her.

"So I was thinking today we hit up the hardware store, maybe go get some new drapes. I know your Nan was looking at replacing them right before she passed. So what do you say we go shop a little?"

I look around the house. It is in dire need of new shades, a new sofa, a television. It needs a makeover, and let's face it, I have the money to do it.

I will worry about how to replace the money soon enough.

"I think you are right. This house needs a little bit of a makeover. Is there a second-hand store we could maybe pass by to perhaps pick up a couch?"

"I think we could see what we can do. You don't know this, but your Nan, she saved me. She helped me when I moved in next door. I had just lost my Harold. I was lost. I begged death to come and take me. I begged to just go and be with him. I even tried to go with him. She found me. She saved me. Every day she would show up at my door. Knocking, irritating me. That woman"—she laughs while recalling the memory—"she didn't take no for an answer. So every day she got me out. Took me shopping, took me to the mall, took me to the zoo, took me to Bingo. Jesus, I was sixty, and we were already eating dinner at four-thirty. She never left me, though. Day in, day out, she would be there for me." She wipes a tear from the corner of her eye with the back of her hand.

"She was amazing, right?" I ask her.

"She was more than that. She turned out to be the best friend I ever had. Now it's my turn to return the favor. I'm going to do my all to save you. Because you were all she talked about. You were all she ever wanted to talk about. So, for that, I will be here for you. And you will let me, not for you, not for me, but for her." She points to Lilah. "And for Nan."

"I don't need you—"

"You do need me. I know, I said the same thing. We might not be running from the same thing, but I know when someone is drowning and is a second away from letting go. I'm your lifeline. Take it. Go upstairs and dress your little angel. Then you will let me buy you a new couch, a TV, some throw pillows, because God knows your grandmother hated them"—she giggles once again—"and then we are going to buy some beautiful drapes with color. It's time this house started living again." She turns around, walking away. "I'll meet you in the car in thirty minutes."

"I guess we are going shopping today with Brenda. Would you like that?" I pick Lilah up, closing the door and heading upstairs to dress us.

I have a shopping date with a sixty-five-year-old woman, and in that minute, I feel a draft move over me, almost like I'm being hugged. If I didn't know better, I'd think someone was trying to talk to me. It's the sign I needed.

9

Jackson

It's so fucking hot outside. The humidity is thick in the air. We've been up and down these streets, trying to talk with anyone who might give us any information.

The people in this neighborhood can smell a badge a mile away. They walk on the opposite side of the street to get away from us.

I wipe my brow. "No one is fucking talking, Mick. Plus, all the people we want to talk to are probably sleeping it off."

"We should come back down tonight, catch them in action. You up for it tonight? Or are you still nursing your sour mood?"

I can't hide anything from him. "Kendall and I have run its course. It's over. Been a long time coming." I place my hands on my hips, waiting for his snarky comments.

"It's about time you set her—and yourself—free. I've been waiting for this. No one could have said anything to make her turn around and walk away. It had to be you to pull the plug. She's a good girl. She'll be just fine." He turns to walk to the car. "What was the last straw?"

"I can't really pinpoint it," I say, getting into the car. "When I got home, she was on my couch watching television, and it just felt wrong. Then my neighbor dropped off cookies, and my head wasn't there. She sensed it, we had a conversation, and now we're just friends, without benefits." I pull out into the street, making my way back to the precinct.

"Your neighbor brought you cookies? That threw you off?" He turns around in his seat and takes off his sunglasses to look at me.

"Leave it be." I don't say anything else. He knows when I'm ready, I'll talk. "What time do you want to head out tonight? I think around ten should be good."

We make it to the precinct, and he nods his head. "I'll pick you up tonight. I'll get an unmarked car."

"Sounds good. I'll be at home if you need anything."

"Hey." He leans in the car. "Bring me a cookie tonight." He closes the door before I can reach over and smack his head.

"Bastard," I say to myself, pulling away from him and flipping him off as I make my way home.

My mind is all over the place, making lists in my head of things to do. Maybe I should write all of this down, make a plan I can stick with. One with boxes I can check and all. Who am I kidding? It'll just be ignored and then wind up as another thing lying around collecting dust.

Pulling into my driveway, I look across the street to see Brenda, Lilah, and Bella unloading a ton of shit from Brenda's car.

Walking over, I smile at Lilah, who gives me a shy smile while she looks down.

"Hey, what do we have here? Did you guys leave anything in the store?" I try to make the conversation light.

"Hey there, Mr. Muscle guy, you going to show us how big and strong you are by bringing in some bags?" Brenda jokes with me while Bella just looks toward the rest of the bags in the trunk.

"I have no choice now. My man card has been questioned." I pick out about five bags filled with more throw pillows than any house needs.

"You really don't have to. I'm sure you have other things to do,"

Bella finally speaks to me in a soft voice.

"Nope, I'm not busy at all. I have the whole afternoon and some of the evening free. Besides, my mother would skin my butt if she knew I didn't help." I'm walking behind her while she makes her way into the living room.

When I finally take in the bags scattered all over the place, I'm really wondering if there is anything left at Bed Bath and Beyond.

"You guys were not kidding with this shopping thing. Lilah, how many of these bags are yours, huh?" I look over at Lilah, who is trying to walk around the minefield that is now the living room.

"I got a pink pillow for my room, but I can't find it," she says sadly while she walks around looking for the pillow.

"Baby, I will find the pillow as soon as I finish helping Ms. Brenda unload the car. How about you sit on the couch and wait," Bella says while dropping her load of bags.

"I can finish outside with Brenda. Why don't you find her pillow so she can have it?" I'm standing in the middle of the room and finally take her in. Today she is wearing some sort of black pants, tights that mold her legs. A long-sleeved jean shirt that's one size too big on her, but she has the two buttons at the top open, showing just a touch of skin. The cuffs to the sleeves are tied tight so as to not ride up.

I'm standing here looking at her, trying to see what she's fighting with. I know she wants to send me to hell. I know she wants to tell me to just go home. Heck, she might want to scream at the top of her lungs and tell me to fuck off. But she doesn't do it.

"Sure." One word. One word and I know it's the end of the conversation, because she turns around and starts opening the bags, looking for the pillow in question.

Turning around, I follow Brenda back to the car. "Give her time, Jackson," she says as she leans in to grab more bags. "She's been through more than we think. I don't know what it is yet, but I do know she's scared. We went out, and she didn't look one person in the eye."

"I can protect her." I'm talking to Brenda, but I want Bella to somehow hear me.

"I have no doubt you can protect her. But that isn't what she sees. She sees one more thing to be scared of. Be patient, try to be her friend."

"I just want to be her friend. I want her to know she can ask me for anything. That she and Lilah will be safe with me."

"I've seen the way you look at her. She might not know that look. But I know that look. You want to protect her and Lilah. You want to be there for them. But you also want to be the one holding her hand. The one tucking Lilah into bed."

"Tha—"

"That is exactly what you want, and I know you, Jackson. Tread lightly. Not for you, not for Bella, but for Lilah." And with that parting comment, Brenda turns and walks toward the door where I hear squealing coming from inside.

"Look, Ms. Brenda, Momma found my pink flower pillow!" Lilah squeals while jumping on the couch.

"Be careful jumping on that thing, little heart. We wouldn't want one monkey falling off the bed," Brenda says to her while dumping the bags beside the couch she is jumping on. "Where is your momma?"

"I'm in the kitchen getting you something to drink," Bella says, coming back into the living room with two glasses of lemonade. "It's the least I could do after you did all this today."

"Oh please, honey, it was so much fun. A long time since I've been shopping like this. Makes me feel young again," Brenda says while sitting on the couch right next to Lilah, who holds a flower-shaped pillow in her small hands. "I can't wait to throw this couch out. I've always hated this flower print so much. I think I tried to spill bleach on it once, but Nan caught me." She laughs out loud, from the memory of that day.

"Where is this couch going?" I sit down on the other love seat with the same flower print.

"We bought a new living room set today and get this, Jackson, a television. Nan must be turning in her grave laughing at us."

I look over at Bella, who blinks away tears at the memories of Nan that are probably filling her mind.

"Nan would be laughing with us if she were here right now. You know, she once came to give me cookies for one reason or another. When I invited her in, she saw my seventy-inch television. She almost fell over her feet. She complained there was nothing so great on television to need one. She also spent four hours over that day watching a couple of movies with me." I share my memory with her while Brenda laughs.

"Momma, I'm hubry." Lilah stares at her mom. At the same time, Bella's stomach groans loudly, making us all laugh. The sound of Bella laughing is the sweetest sound God has ever made. It must even be better than angels singing.

"Me, too. Why don't we order some pizza?" I know she is going to argue, but Lilah speaks up first.

"Pissa like the last time?" She widens her eyes at me, waiting for my answer.

"Yup, just like last time. Would you like that?"

She nods enthusiastically.

"Perfect, I'll order. Would you like to come with me to pick it up? Leave your mommy and Brenda to put away all this mess?"

"No," Bella snaps at me, making Lilah retreat into Brenda. "I mean, it's okay. She doesn't get in the way here." She tries to calm herself down. I see the way her chest is heaving like she just ran around the block on a hot blistering day at top speed. "You don't have a car seat."

Looking straight into her eyes, I see the battle she is fighting. I nod my head. "I didn't really want to go pick it up anyway. I'll just have it delivered." I get up, making my way to the front door, taking my cell phone out while I call in the order.

My body is rattling with anger, shaking with the need to go in there and take her in my arms and promise her nothing will ever touch her again. I know it will only send her running in the other direction.

I place the order, putting it on my account, and turn around to go back inside where I see Brenda holding Lilah in her lap while Bella is organizing the bags.

"Okay, so the pizza should be here soon. You girls have fun with all these bags." I nod my head down toward Lilah. "I ordered cheese just for you, princess." I turn to walk toward the door.

"Where are you going, Jackson?" Brenda asks, making the noise of the bags rustling stop.

"I'm going to go. I have some things to do. You three enjoy the pizza." And with those words, I walk out the door and don't stop until I slam my door shut. I turn and punch the wall next to the door, leaving a huge hole in the sheetrock.

I make my way to the kitchen to wash off the blood that has started to trickle out. Flexing my hand into a fist under the water, I watch the blood and water swirl together on their way down the drain. The look of fear on her face when she thought I would be taking her daughter is more than my stomach can take.

I don't know who did this to her, but if I ever find him, I'll bury him ten feet deep. She has to trust me. She has to give me a chance. I have to show her she can be safe here. I have to show her not every man is evil like the devil. The only thing is how the fuck am I going to convince her or make her let me?

10

Bella

I just watch his retreating back, wanting nothing more than to call out to him to come back. But I know I can't call him back. It's better for him if he never sets eyes on us.

"Well, that was quite a show," Brenda says to me while rocking Lilah side to side.

"I just, I can't let him take her. I don't even know him. What if something happened? What if she got scared, what if she got lost?" I'm almost hyperventilating.

"I don't know who you're trying to convince here, me or yourself?"

"I can't do this. I promised her no more sadness. I promised her no more scared nights. I promised her only smiles from now on." I pull four bags with me to the kitchen.

When we stepped into Bed Bath and Beyond, Brenda clapped her hands together like she had just arrived at Disney World for the first time. She picked Lilah up, placing her in the shopping cart, and was on her way.

We started in the bath department. Jesus, I've never seen so many different colored towels. She picked up bath towels, bath sheets, hand towels, and finger towels. She didn't just pick up one color, either. Nope, she couldn't do that, she got us four purple, four pink, and four white. I had no idea where I was going to put all these towels, but I'd figure it out since it made her so happy.

Then she started in on the bathroom accessories. Toothbrush holders, decorative soap dishes, pumping soap dispensers, towel holders, trash cans. I had no idea why I needed all of this, but she was too excited for me to stop her.

The next aisle was the bedding department. I think we spent at least two hours in that department. She picked out everything from the down comforter, which felt like you were wrapped up in a cloud, to the matching sheets that appeared to be from Egypt. A bed skirt, pillow cases, and pillow shams were next. Then, most importantly, according to Brenda, were the actual pillows. She got us six pillows each. Fluffy, like big puffs of cotton, I was actually looking forward to laying my head down on these pillows.

The final stop was the kitchen part. She picked out a blender, a slow cooker, a new toaster, a new microwave, a new coffee machine, tea kettle, forks, knives, spoons, cheese knives, mixing bowls, measuring bowls, a can opener. It just went on and on. I couldn't even keep up with her, and I even ran off to fetch another cart—twice—since she just kept adding more stuff.

When we finally started to the head to the cashier, I quickly tried doing the math in my head. Let's just say it was nothing I thought it would be. When the cashier told us how much it was, I just stood there with my mouth hanging open, not sure what to do or if I could even cover that right now.

I didn't have time to contemplate what to do before Brenda pulled out her platinum American Express card and said, "This is going to get me so many points! Bed Bath and Beyond is a double point retailer! I can't wait to see what I'll be getting for free next!"

I looked over at her. "Have you lost your mind? Are you having a stroke?"

She just waved me off, turning around to speak to Lilah, "What do you say we go get you your very own bedroom set? I'm thinking a princess canopy bed. I've always wanted to buy someone that."

"No, absolutely not. We can't take it, you can't buy her that!" I started packing the bags into the basket. "It's insane the amount of money you just spent on us. I have…I'm just," I mumbled. Shaking my head, I tried to find words to tell her how crazy she was.

"Oh, please, I have all this money and nothing to do with it. I have no kids, no grandchildren, no one. I can't take it with me, so why not do something fun with it, right, Lilah?" She leaned down to kiss her on the nose.

"Right, Ms. Brenda," she agreed with her with a smile. "I'm going to get a princess bed?" She threw her hands up in the air like she just scored a touchdown.

"Lilah, I don't know what you are getting. We have to see how much money it is, okay, baby?"

She looked down at her doll in defeat.

I turned and glared at Brenda. "See what you did?"

I was waiting for her to answer when she threw her head back and let out a huge belly laugh. "Well, I guess it's too late, since I ordered it this morning online. Did you know you can just sit down, right in your own kitchen, drink your coffee, and order whatever you want?" She looked at the cashier, right after she signed her receipt. "It's magic, and then in three to five business days. BOOM. Stuff just gets delivered."

I turned to her. "You ordered her bed already?"

"Yay! I'm getting a princess bed, Momma!" Lilah started her celebration again.

I shook my head, thinking of ways to get her to let me pay her back.

"The good news is I've already ordered all the bedding, too. Oh, and I got some princess lamps."

Lilah let out a gasp and looked at her like she was her own personal fairy godmother.

"Momma, I gonna have my own bed with princess lamps!"

Then I broke, the tear escaped my eye, and I used the back of my hand to wipe it away, looking up at the ceiling to blink away the rest that wanted to escape. Then a cool hand slid into mine—Brenda's.

"Please, do this for me."

I couldn't answer because I felt like if I did I'd turn into a sobbing mess right there in the middle of Bed Bath and Beyond.

"Come on, we still need a new couch and a television. Boy, do I feel great today," she said, pushing out her basket with Lilah, chattering away about how she wanted everything pink.

I'm brought back into the present when the doorbell rings. Brenda sees the struggle in me and jumps right up. "I'll get it."

She answers the door, bringing in the biggest pizza I think the restaurant makes. "How much was it?" I start to head for my purse to get my wallet.

"No idea. The delivery guy said it was paid for." She places the pie on the counter, going to get some plates. "Darn it! We forget to get plates! That's because you rushed me out of the store," she says almost accusingly.

"Rushed you out of the store? We were there for four hours!" I open up the box, breaking the slices apart. "Do you think we should take a couple of slices over to Jackson?" I ask, looking down at the eight slices of pizza in front of me.

"If you want to bring him a couple of slices, go ahead. I'll stay here and have a picnic with Lilah."

I shake my head no. I'm not going over there. He makes me feel things I shouldn't. He makes me feel like there is hope. He makes me wish for things I can't have.

"Lilah, you want to go sit in the yard and have a picnic?" I squat down just in time to see her eyes light up and her head nod. My baby girl has been having lots of firsts these days.

"Wif Ms. Brenda? I don't wanna use my pink cover." She shakes her head side to side.

"Oh no, honey, we are going to get the big cover from your Nan's bed and throw that one outside," Brenda says from behind me. "And let's hope birds fly over us and poop all over it so your momma will let me throw it out," she whispers, making us both laugh.

"We are not using that cover. It was my Nan's." I look at her with my hands on my hips. "Don't even think about it."

She throws her hands up. "Okay, fine, let me go home and bring out one I have. You guys bring out the pizza." She heads out the front door toward her house.

"Okay, Lilah, I'll bring the pizza, you go get some pillows."

"I rwelly like Ms. Brenda. She said she wants to play Barbie wif me after pissa," Lilah says as she climbs down off her chair and walks over to the couch, grabbing an old cushion and dragging it behind her while she makes her way to the door. "I rwelly like it here, Momma. Can we stay forever?"

In that moment, tears well in my eyes, making them burn. "We aren't going anywhere, baby. This is our home now."

"I no want Daddy." She looks at me, the fear in her eyes coming to the surface.

I drop down and pull her to me.

"Never ever again. Momma promises you. Never again will we go back there." I smooth her hair, her tiny hands letting the cushions go so she can wrap her arms around my neck.

We stay like that for a while, the two of us holding each other in the middle of the kitchen, a box of pizza on the floor to one side of us and an old sofa cushion on the other side.

The knocking on the back door has us jumping up, but we hear Brenda shouting, "I hope you two didn't eat all the pizza in there."

I pick us up from the floor and head to the back door to unlock it.

Brenda must see the look on our faces but doesn't question it. "What can I help carry outside?"

"I get a cushion," Lilah says, pushing off me to grab the cushion.

"I'll carry the pizza out. How about you bring some napkins, maybe some water for us to drink?"

She just nods, going to collect the things, and we make our way into the back, where the cover is already set up on the lawn. A lawn without weeds thanks to Jackson and his inability to listen to anything I say. Turning my head over to the street, I notice his car is still in the driveway.

I shake my head from the thoughts that want to run through it. The what-ifs are a scary game to play, and I'm not sure the gamble is worth it.

"Now this is what I call a picnic!" Brenda says from her spot on the blanket as she dishes out pizza to us. "Best picnic ever, right, little heart?"

"Hmmm pee-sah," is all she says, and once again I'm laughing.

I take in my surroundings. I'm sitting on a blanket in the middle of my Nan's beautiful yard, eating delicious pizza with my girl and a woman who barely knows me, but who I know for certain has my back.

This, to me, is heaven. It might seem normal to most people, but to me and my daughter, this right here is cloud nine.

11

Jackson

I slam the door harder than I intended, making the picture frames on the walls shake twice.

The anger inside me is almost unexplainable. I want to tear someone to shreds. I want to cause injury and pain to someone whose name I don't even know.

Someone who had beauty the likes of those two women in his hands, and instead of cherishing them, he terrorized them. I throw myself on the couch and drag my hands through my hair as I look through the window at her house.

I need to let this frustration out of me before I go over there and force her to tell me what happened. I know it will only push her back inside herself.

Seeing her finally smile at Brenda was like the sun breaking out of the clouds after a rainstorm. Hearing that little girl giggle was like listening to money fall out of a slot machine in Vegas.

Making my way upstairs, stripping out of my clothes, I look down at my hard cock. He wants to let out his frustration in other ways. I fist it tight, urging it to go away, but the minute I close my eyes, ready to have my happy ending, I hear my phone ringing from my pocket.

Seeing Mick's name flash on the screen makes me stop in my

tracks.

"Yo."

"We just got a call from Lori's mother. She got a phone call from her today. She is freaking out. Called the precinct looking for you, but they called me first."

"I can be ready in ten. Where should I pick you up?" I'm already rushing around my room, changing into my jeans and T-shirt.

"Um, how about I just meet you at the station in about thirty minutes?" I hear rustling in the background.

"Station, eh? Should I even ask where you are or are we not getting into it now?"

"I'll see you in thirty." He hangs up without acknowledging my question.

By the time I make it outside, I'm already running through the details of the case. Lori, age sixteen, started hanging with the wrong crowd, and then one day she just didn't come home. Her mother hasn't seen or heard from her since. Until today.

Friends say she's been in touch with them. But her mother still filed a missing child's report. The thing is, she's seventeen, so it's hard not to consider this might be a case of a teenager just wanting to be out in the world on her own. Her mother said lately she'd become more distant than usual, and her grades began slipping. When she confronted her, they had a big argument that ended in Lori storming out of the house and not coming back.

I throw my truck into reverse and start to back out. I try not to look over at her house, but I fail. I see no movement, nothing. I do notice the blinds are up now.

The place looks so different now than it did a week ago. It went from deserted to looking like it's coming back to life.

I smile and take my usual route to work, stopping at Starbucks to get my coffee. Yes, I like lattes, sue me.

I make it to work at the same time Mick pulls up. I wait for him to get out of his car before I get out.

He looks like he spent all of three seconds getting dressed.

"Your shirt is buttoned wrong."

He looks down at his shirt and sees it's longer on one side than the other.

"Fuck." He goes about righting his shirt. "I wasn't expecting to be called in. I was…"

"You don't have to explain yourself to me. I just hope you know what you're doing." I make my way over to our unmarked car. I know he's pissed, which means he is going to want to be the one who does the driving, so I head to the passenger side.

"I know what you're going to say, so can we just skip this whole bullshit conversation right now?" He pulls into traffic, heading toward the center of town.

"I wasn't going to say anything. You're a grown ass man. You know what you're doing." I stare straight ahead.

"She says she's leaving him. I have to believe her."

"She said that last time, too, didn't she? Strung you on for four months before she told you she couldn't do it right then. Then there was your birthday, when she showed up and spent the whole weekend telling you she left him, only to go back home on Monday. Trust me, I remember. It was me who found you after you lost yourself in the bottom of a bottle of Jack. It wasn't pretty."

"She said it's finally time. She loves me."

I shake my head, knowing this is a game Sandie is playing with him. She's a fucking bitch if I ever met one. They met in high school, and she latched herself right onto his dick. The problem was that she latched herself onto some rich kid's dick, too. Played them both until she got knocked up. Thank fuck it turned out to be the other guy's kid. She's been stringing him along for the last fucking seven years now.

"I want nothing more than for that to be true. You know this. But it shouldn't be this hard, Mick." I want to continue, but knowing that

I'm starting to sound a bit too much like Dr. Phil, I back off and keep staring out the window.

When we pull up to the address on the sheet, Lori's mother's house, I'm instantly on alert because we're now in the projects. The five matching apartment buildings are known as Welfare Avenue.

A couple teenagers in the corner are trying to be intimidating and letting us know we're on their turf, puffing out their chests and taking us in. Right in the middle of the group is the leader of the pack. The two I suspect to be his seconds in charge are right beside him, chewing on toothpicks, sizing us up with their cell phones in their hands.

We open the door, unsurprised the lock is broken, allowing anyone to just walk in. The hallway is dark, with just a few lights working, while most are broken and a few are flickering. The smell of urine burns my nose. We get to the third floor and make our way to the door with the number five on it.

I knock on the door twice, taking a step back while Mick looks over his shoulder, making sure we aren't going to be ambushed.

We hear the locks clicking open, but neither of us is prepared for the sight we are met with.

A tiny girl, maybe all of five foot one, opens the door, wearing tight booty shorts and a tank top that has seen cleaner days. Brown hair that is at least clean sits in a messy bun on the top of her head.

"Are you the cops?"

"Yes, ma'am. Are you Marissa, Lori's mom?" I say, flashing her my badge. "May we come in?"

She stands away, holding on to the open door, ushering us in. I'm shocked. Inside it's completely neat and clean. The furniture looks almost new, and a television sits in the corner. There is a small kitchen with no table, just two stools.

Two bedrooms open to the living room, both rooms looking clean with beds and little furniture. I can tell one is obviously a teenager's from the posters hanging on the wall.

"Please have a seat. Can I get you anything?"

She's nervous. I know this because she is wringing her hands.

"We're good, thanks." I go to sit down while Mick stands by the kitchen, leaning against the wall.

"So you called in and said Lori got in touch with you?"

"Yes, I got a call on my cell phone sometime after ten a.m. I was asleep, but the minute I heard her ringtone I flew out of bed."

"What did she say?"

"She said she was fine and to call off the dogs." She looks between me and Mick.

"You weren't here when she went missing, right?" Mick asks from his side of the room.

"I was here when she left, but when I got home from work at three a.m. I noticed she hadn't returned." She looks down at her hands. "I was working. She usually just texts me, but since we got into a fight the night before I just thought she was pissed off."

"You're a stripper, right? Is there any way she got ahold of your drugs or saw something she shouldn't have?"

I whip my head around to glare at Mick with a clear 'what the fuck' expression on my face.

Marissa's shoulders go back like she's gearing up for a fight. "Yes, I'm a stripper, but no, I'm not on drugs. You want, we can take a piss test right now and ease your mind, Officer."

"Won't be necessary." I look over at her, then return my glare to Mick, hoping he takes the hint and shuts the fuck up.

"A seventeen-year-old sees her mother as a stripper. You don't think she'll follow in your footsteps?" He doesn't shut up.

"I don't know, I think her knowing you have to work for things isn't such a bad lesson. Considering her father left me with his bookie debt of eighty grand and the only way he wouldn't take it out on us was if I agreed to work for him. I think it's good showing her you don't run from your obligations, like her weasel father did, but instead you keep fighting and working to earn the things you want. So, if you came here just to pass judgment on me and my job while not taking my daughter's disappearance seriously, I think we've both wasted our time." Marissa goes to stand up, her hands shaking.

I grab her wrist, stopping her.

"I'm going to apologize for my partner and his mood today. Please know finding your daughter is very important to us."

She looks, or rather glares, at Mick, waiting for him to say something, but he just shrugs his shoulders.

"I asked around at work and there's a new guy who has been coming in. I don't have his name yet, but he's been in a couple of times. He is also in scumbag, Bentley's, crew. Owns a pawn shop, isn't fair, and sells whatever you bring to him to the first person who wants to buy it before you even get a chance to get it back yourself. He also doesn't care how you get his money just as long as you do."

"I need you to not try to do anything on your own and let us handle things."

"Oh yeah, it looks like you guys are really handling things. She's been missing for a week," she whispers and a tear escapes her eye, rolling down her cheek.

"We are working on it, Marissa, but if you're interfering, it's just going to create extra work for us. So, please, if you hear anything or see anything, call us first. Don't just go charging in, call me first." I take out a card and hand it to her. "My cell number is on there, so you can call me whenever you think you need to."

She wipes her face with the back of her hand. "I'm doing all of this for her. So I didn't uproot her and take her away from everyone and everything she knew."

I stand up, making notes in my head about this fresh new face out there, thinking we need to pay Bentley another visit. It'll be the fourth time this week.

"Thank you for calling us with this update."

I walk out the door with Mick following right behind me. He's barely in the hallway before the door is shut right behind him, almost bouncing against his head.

"What the fuck was that bullshit in there? Since when did you become such a judgmental asshole? Spewing bullshit like that to a victim's mother, what the fuck, man?"

He doesn't even answer, just walks away.

He makes his way to the car without saying anything. The door isn't even closed before he peels off from the curb and slaps his hand down on the steering wheel twice.

"FUCCCKKKK!" He pulls over one block down. He whips the door open and jumps out, slamming it shut before he kicks it.

"I'm going to go out on a limb here and say your head isn't in the fucking game today."

"That was fucked up. I'm on edge about Sandie, and I totally let that poor woman have it. Jesus, I'm surprised she didn't try to have me killed by the time I got to the car."

"We have a whole night ahead of us. Why don't we head over to see Bentley? Let's hear what he has to say about this new player in town. But you pull that shit again"—I point back in the direction we came from—"I'll fucking kill you for her."

He doesn't say anything and just nods as he gets into the car. I follow him. The rest of the night is a blur of us chasing a fucking ghost. From one side of town to the other, all empty leads, all leading back to this fucking new guy.

By the time I make it home, it's almost four a.m. I'm ready to face plant into my bed. Making my way up to my room, I manage to shed my clothes in record time before falling into bed. I'm asleep before my head hits the pillow, dreaming about running around town searching for a faceless guy.

Except every time I think I've got him in my reach, it's Bella and Lilah I see, and they disappear before I can grab them.

Bella

It's almost noon, and we have already baked muffins and cookies, and we're now working on banana bread. This is what happens when your nightmares just play on a constant loop in your mind, even in sleep.

The whole night I was being chased by some faceless guy. I knew when I saw Jackson, I was safe, but before I could get to him, he'd just disappear. After waking twice from the same dream, I decided to get up and start my day.

By the time Lilah screamed my name in fear because I wasn't in my bedroom, it was almost eight a.m.

The minute she saw the mixing bowl, though, she got super excited. When Brenda knocked on the door ten minutes ago, I had already made up my mind I would bring over some muffins and cookies to Jackson as an apology and a thank you.

While I made a fresh cup of coffee, I told Brenda I was going to be right back.

Walking across the street, I'm a nervous wreck. My hands shaking, almost spilling coffee on myself, I finally ring the doorbell. When he doesn't answer after one ring, I ring again. I'm not ready for what I see when the door opens.

He answers the door in a pair of loose, athletic shorts hanging low on his hips. As if that wasn't enough, he's also shirtless. I cannot stop myself from taking in his broad shoulders and his wide, smooth chest. His abs are cut and defined. But it's the tattoo on one side of his chest, under his collarbone, that draws my attention. He also has some trailing down his shoulders with a red rose that is red. So vibrant, I want to grab them so I can get a better look at the artwork and maybe trace the images with my finger.

His hair is sticking up all over the place, and he has only one eye open. The other one must be sensitive to the sun since he is keeping it shut.

"I'm so sorry, were you sleeping?"

He grunts at me, not really answering.

"It's noon."

"I was working till four a.m. Is that coffee for me?" He points to the coffee cup in my hand.

"Yes," I say, handing it to him. "We also made muffins and cookies." I try to hand him the basket, but he just turns and heads for the kitchen.

"Come in, Bella," he shouts from inside. Turning to watch the house, I see Lilah is still at the counter mixing with Brenda.

"I really should go." I make my way to his kitchen, leaving the door open, in case I need to run out of here.

His kitchen is newly renovated with all stainless steel appliances. The chestnut color of the cabinets stands out against the light caramel slate countertops.

In the middle of the kitchen is a high, square brown table with eight chairs around it. He pulls out one, throwing himself into it, reaching for the basket I'm still holding in my hand.

"Oh, sorry, here it is. We baked. Well, actually I baked them this morning when I couldn't sleep, but Lilah did help with the cookies." I laugh nervously as I babble. "Although she ate more cookie dough than she actually got on the baking sheet." I shake my head, thinking of her face with her eyes practically popping out of her head at the sweetness of cookie dough batter.

"Why couldn't you sleep?" he asks me as he pulls a muffin out and eats half in one bite. He chews and sips on the coffee as he waits for my reply.

"I had a nightmare." I shrug. "I kept waking up, and when I'd fall back asleep, I'd go right back to it. So I just got up and baked instead."

"Sit down, Bella." He motions to the chair.

"I really shouldn't. Brenda is with Lilah, and she might need me."

"She knows you're here. If she needs you to come back, she'll just come and get you. Besides, you left the door open so she wouldn't even have to knock." He finishes one muffin and starts on another.

"How did you kno—"

"I'm a detective, Bella. It's my job to notice everything, but most especially the things other people don't notice. Like the fact you're scared." He leans back. "I won't hurt you or Lilah, not now, not ever. You have my word on that. So, since you woke me up, you can sit down and keep me company while I eat these muffins. Hopefully, that little girl of yours wants her mom and comes over, so you can relax and enjoy getting out of the house. Besides, I have a play set in the backyard, which by the way, you're welcome to use."

I look over his shoulder at the window behind him. I see a huge play set with a slide, a couple of swings, an obstacle course, a climbing wall, and a sand pit. I walk farther into the kitchen, stopping beside him to stare at this playground Lilah would love.

"You have children?" I ask him, not sure why this bothers me so much.

"Nope, not yet. It came with the house when I bought it. I never had the heart to tear it down."

"Heeelllllooooo, is anyone home?" The unfamiliar female voice has me jumping in response, and Jackson reaches for my hand to calm me down.

"It's just my mom." He pulls me close to him and whispers in my ear. With him sitting on the chair and me standing, we are almost the same height.

"Jackson, you left your front door wide-open." I hear the voice entering the room. "Oh, dear, I had no idea you had company! I'll go. I just came to drop off—"

"Mom, this is my neighbor Bella. She's Nan's granddaughter," he says while I eye this beautiful lady.

She has short, silver gray hair perfectly styled. Startling blue eyes just like her son, she stands at about five foot five and is wearing a pretty, white summery sundress with a royal blue, short-sleeved cardigan. Her sandals are low-heeled, strappy wedges. She looks like she stepped out of a catalogue.

"Oh my goodness, aren't you beautiful." She comes over and hugs me tightly. Jackson never lets my hand go. I don't know why, but I squeeze it just to make sure he's still there. He reassures me by squeezing my hand gently in return.

"I've heard so many stories about you. I feel like I know you already. You're all Nan spoke about!" She lets me go long enough to take in my appearance. I'm sure it isn't lost on her that her son's fingers are intertwined with mine.

"Um, thank you, ma'am," I answer her.

"Oh, none of that ma'am crap, you can call me Nancy."

"Is anyone home?" Brenda's voice echoes through the house.

"What is this? Let's visit Jackson day?" His frustration makes me giggle.

I finally let go of his hand when Lilah runs into the room yelling, "Momma."

"Hey, love bug, I see Ms. Brenda let you eat more cake batter," I say as I eye some of it dried up on her nose.

"No," she says while nodding yes.

"You little devil, I said secret," Brenda says from the kitchen entrance. "Oh, Nancy, I thought I saw you coming in here." She goes right to Nancy and greets her with a hug and a kiss on the cheek.

"Hey, baby girl, thank you for making me cookies." Jackson leans in and says to Lilah, who has her face buried in my chest. "Did you eat pizza yesterday? I ordered the biggest pizza for you and told them it was for a special girl."

"I hab two pieces," she says on a nod while she holds up her hand, showing five fingers.

"Did you? Wow, you eat more than me! We're going to have to call you dough girl." He tickles her belly while she squirms to get away from him.

"She is so adorable! Hello there, princess, what's your name?" Nancy asks her.

Jackson leans into her and whispers something in her ear I can't hear, but she nods her head yes. "Go ahead, tell her your name and then I'll take you out to play in the sand."

"Lilah," she says to Nancy then turns to Jackson. "Now we go sand? We go park?" She looks at me. "Momma, park, you come park? With Ackson?"

"I don't—" I start to talk and then Nancy cuts me off.

"Oh, you have to! She is going to love it. Go ahead and take them outside, Jackson. Brenda and I can start on the lunch I brought over, and we can all have a late lunch or early dinner together. Do you like meatballs, Lilah? I made my special kind, and we can have it with spaghetti."

"Pizza?" Lilah asks her.

Jackson grabs her from me, stunning me with how easily she went to him. Her eyes never leaving mine, I nod okay. "My mom's meatballs are better than pizza." He kisses her forehead and turns to walk outside.

"Aren't you going to go put on a T-shirt or something?" I say to his tanned, muscular back, which is also covered in some ink designs.

"Are you uncomfortable with me being without a shirt? If you are, I'll go inside and put one on." He stops walking and looks at me. I'm being silly. He isn't like them. He isn't flaunting it, looking for a reaction. I shake my head no. He turns around, asking Lilah where she wants to go first, the sand pit or the slide.

It's no surprise she says the sand pit. Once he sits her at the edge of the box, he brings out a plastic bag with shovels and pails and animal-shaped forms.

What he does next stops me in my tracks, though. He sits down right next to her in the sand, his big body bending in half to get close to her as he fills the pails with sand for her to turn over as she follows his instructions to build the castle.

"We should make four castles and then put water all around so no one can come in and see you without swimming over." Jackson fills up a bucket while Lilah fills in another one.

"I want four castles. No monters in castles? Momma no ouchies in castles. We go castles, Ackson, come castles?"

"No, sweetheart, no one gets ouchies in castles," he says to her, not even making eye contact with me. His hands shake as he continues to fill the pail up with sand.

"You don't have to play with her. You can go rest or help your mom. I can take it from here." I walk slowly to them.

He looks up, his eyes shooting daggers at me.

"I'm making castles with Lilah, where there are no ouchies or monsters. Got it, Bella? I'm going to make it safe for her and for you. So why don't you go help my mother so I can make it safe?"

The determination in his eyes makes my breath catch. I have no idea what he's talking about, if it's the monsters or the ouchies, but I hear his message loud and clear. He is going to do his damnedest to make sure I'm safe and so is Lilah.

With that thought, I sit on the grass right next to the sand pit and listen to them talk about how they will build bridges and put alligators all around to eat the monsters.

13

Jackson

"What are you doing?" my mother whispers to me while I bring in the rest of the dirty dishes.

After playing in the sand box with Lilah, her telling me about monsters and fucking ouchies, it took everything I had not to go hulk over the whole situation. I sat in my corner, filling buckets and more buckets with sand, trying not to glance over at Bella, who was sitting with her knees up, her head resting on them.

My mother and Brenda finished preparing lunch and called us in, where we devoured everything. Not a single meatball left over. Lilah's face had tomato sauce from ear to ear. She slurped up the spaghetti faster than I cleaned my plate.

I knew Bella was nervous because she kept pushing her food around her plate. It also had to do with the fact my mother just didn't know when to stop asking fucking questions.

Finally I dropped my fork onto my plate, which made an echoing sound that had Lilah covering her ears. The look of fear in both girls' eyes finally got my mother to stop with the questions.

Brenda filled the awkward silence with the stories of their shopping trip. Once everyone finished eating, I told Lilah about my big television and my cartoon channel.

Her eyes were big like saucers, begging her mom for just one second of watching.

She tried to tell Lilah no. She also tried to help us clean up, but both my mother and I put our foot down. "Guests don't touch a thing. House rules."

She just nodded, trying to make an excuse to leave, but Lilah was too busy pulling her hand toward the living room.

Brenda quickly made her escape, claiming she was tired and needed a nap, leaving behind the two girls, who are now curled up on my couch, sleeping.

"I'm not doing anything, Mom. I'm helping my friend's granddaughter and her daughter feel safe." I put the dishes down next to her quietly.

"Jackson, I see the way you look at her. You want to save her. She isn't going to let you save her if she can't save herself." She just continues washing the dishes, not making eye contact with me.

"Mom, look at me!"

"Did you see Lilah when I dropped my fork? You know they are fighting something even bigger than I can save them from."

"Jackson, I do—"

I cut her off before she finishes her sentence. "She asked me to help her build a castle to keep the monsters away."

My mother gasps, bringing her hand to her mouth, water leaking everywhere.

"And that isn't the worst of it. She wants to make sure they don't get any ouchies, Mom, fucking ouchies."

The tear runs down my mother's cheek.

"I have no idea what they are running from, but I'm going to make fucking sure when they are here or when they are in that house"—I point to their house across the street—"nothing and no one will touch them."

"I just don't want you to get hurt. I've never seen you look at

71

someone like you look at them. Not even Kendall."

"That's over and done with."

"Jackson, Kendall will never move on no matter how much I tell her she is chasing empty promises."

"I told her it was over. It's over. She deserves better than to wait for me. It will never happen. I will never love her the way she should be loved."

We stop talking, and she continues washing the dishes with me drying them.

"You have a beautiful heart, Son. You just have to forget the past. We need to move on. You have been stuck there. Nothing you could have done would change what happened. You need to forgive yourself." She cups my face in both hands. "I love you more than words, so I'm going to be the bearer of bad news. That girl is so broken, I don't think even you can fix her. I don't think anyone can."

I try to shake my head out of her grip.

"But I know if you set your mind to something, you won't let it go. So, for the sake of you and for your heart, I hope you get through to her. If not for her, then for that little girl." She leans up and kisses me.

"Now I'm going to let myself out quietly so I don't wake them, but I expect you to call me and fill me in. Frequently." She grabs her purse. "Don't make me pull out the poor old mom card, because I will." She walks out of the house, shutting the door with a quiet click.

I laugh at the thought she is an old mom when I make my way into the living room. Bella is lying down with Lilah in front of her. The television is playing some kids TV show.

They are so small they don't even take up half the couch. I sit next to them and switch the channels, trying to decide what to watch. I finally land on *Die Hard*.

Throwing the remote next to me, I put my head back and think of the day. It takes me four seconds to close my eyes.

When I feel my hand being tapped, I wake up confused for a

second. The television is on a blue screen. The lights from outside bring some light inside.

"Your hand is blocking me from getting up," Bella whispers.

I look down. Her feet are in my lap, and my arm is draped across them.

"What time is it?" My eyes get used to the darkness.

"I have no idea. I think I've been up for about an hour now, hoping you would move. I didn't want to wake you, but...ummm, I have to pee."

I move my hand from her leg, leaning over to grab Lilah from her so she can move. Placing her in my lap, I cradle her while Bella goes to the bathroom.

"Let me take her. I'm going to go. I'm so sorry we fell asleep. Must have been all the fresh air." She goes to take Lilah out of my arms, but I stand up before she can reach her.

"I'll carry her over. Go ahead."

"Jackson, you don't need to do that. I think I can walk across the street." She places her hands on her hips.

"Good to know, now walk across it. I'll bring Lilah."

"Fine, ass," she says under her breath. Once she opens up, you can see she's feisty. Coming into her own.

When we make it to the door, she opens it, trying to grab Lilah again. Walking right past her to the stairs, I ask her, "What room does she sleep in? Or does she sleep with you?"

"Umm, she has her room, but she likes to sleep in bed with me. She's growing out of it." She walks past me up the stairs, so I follow.

"I slept with my mother and father until I was eight, maybe nine." I laugh, thinking about my father complaining every single night when he couldn't get comfortable.

Making my way into her room, I see she has already changed the covers to the new ones she bought yesterday. Little touches here and there show me she is making it her home.

She takes off the million throw pillows she has on the bed, turning down the cover. I place Lilah in the middle of the bed, then pick up a couple of throw pillows, placing them on the sides of the bed just to make sure she can't fall off.

Once I see she is safe and secure, I make my way out of the room. I hear Bella following behind me.

"Thank you for today. She had a great time. It was her first time playing in sand."

I turn to look at her. I'm two steps below her, which makes me even in height with her.

"Anytime she wants to play in the sand box, you can bring her over."

"I don't want to intrude. I'm going to see if there is a park around here, maybe take her there."

I grab her hips in my hands. Her body starts to shake. "I will never, ever hurt you." I don't move my hands off her. "I will never, ever hurt her. I would die before I let anything happen."

"You don't know anything about us." She pushes my hands off her hips.

"I don't need to know anything about you to make that promise. I'd do anything to make sure you two were safe. Now I'm going to leave before we say things out of anger."

I turn to walk away, knowing if I stay, shit will fly out of my mouth.

"I'm broken. Your mother is right. You can't save me, and you can't heal me. I have one goal in my life now, and it's to make sure Lilah knows what love is. Unconditional love. The kind of love that fills her heart and she feels in her soul. The kind of love where she feels cherished and protected and never, ever on guard. The kind of love where they accept her just as she is so she never has to be someone she isn't. That is my goal." She starts to walk past me, but I grab her arm, turning her toward me.

"I'm not going anywhere. I'm not saying anything will happen between us, but from now on, my goal is to make sure that you both have that." She opens her mouth to say something, but I place my finger on her lips before she can say anything. "Good night, Bella. Sweet dreams, see you tomorrow." I walk out the door.

I'm halfway across the street before I hear the telltale signs of the lock clicking. She's letting me know she is locking me out. Little does she know, though, I've just accepted the challenge she dished out.

14

Bella

Turning off the shower, I take a second to listen to see if Lilah is up. I finally dozed off at around five when the sun was coming up, but my dreams were so vivid again. I didn't want a repeat.

Drying myself off with the big, cushiony white towel, I run my hand through the fog coating the mirror.

It's the first time I really look at myself. My cheeks are still a bit hollow, but my skin has some color to it again. My hair is clean and shiny, but the biggest change is my eyes. It's no wonder what a month of healing can do.

They are the eyes of my past. The eyes I had before the nightmare began. My blue eyes aren't shinning with light. You can still see the sorrow, the pain. But I also see determination in them.

I didn't recognize the girl who stared back at me the last few years, but little by little, I'm starting to see an older, wiser version of the girl I once was. Too bad it took losing myself in order to fight for myself.

"Mommmmmmmmmaaaaaa, Mommmmmmmmmaaaa," Lilah screams, making me bolt into the room. I see her sitting in the middle of the bed surrounded by the throw pillows Jackson put all around her last night.

"Hey there, pretty girl. What's with all this noise this morning?" I gather her up in my arms.

"I fink you leabe me."

"Never. I will never leave you. You know that, stinky face." I kiss her nose. "Now let's go brush your teeth and then see what we can make for breakfast."

I quickly drop her on the stool, putting toothpaste on her toothbrush, and go to get myself dressed.

The bruises are finally gone, so I'm going to wear shorts and a tank top. At least I won't melt today. The last couple of days with the long pants and the long sleeves, I thought I was going to faint a couple times a day.

The day runs smoothly with just the two of us. Brenda has passed by earlier to let us know she's going to visit a friend a couple of towns over and will be back late tonight or maybe tomorrow, she hasn't decided yet.

Lilah and I are starting our very own routine. Except for the fact she asks for Jackson sand castles a million times an hour.

I start dinner in the crock pot. Thank you to Google for those recipes. Let's hope they actually turn out okay, or we will need to order pizza that Lilah keeps asking for.

"Momma sand castles?" She looks up from her coloring book.

"No sand castles, love bug, but how about we go blow bubbles outside?" I'm bringing out the big guns.

She scoots her chair back and runs to the front door, picking up the bag that holds all the bubble stuff in it.

Another present from Brenda. She even bought a bubble machine. You plug it in, and it blows out a constant stream of bubbles. I make a mental note to hide it in the closet, deep, deep in the closet.

We've been blowing bubbles for about five minutes when I hear a truck slow down and turn into Jackson's driveway.

"Momma, look, Ackson." She points across the street just as he gets out of his truck, smiling at us.

He makes his way over with Lilah yelling, "Ackson, we make bubbles, no sand castles."

He scoops her up in his arms kissing her cheeks, making her giggle.

"What do you mean no sand castles?" he asks her.

"Momma said no."

I look at her and think traitor in my mind.

"Is that right, princess? Would you like to order pizza and then make some sand castles?" he asks her like she really has the power to make these decisions.

"Actually I've got the crock pot on with some chili. It has been going all day. So pizza is a no-go." My hands are itching to grab Lilah away from him.

"Okay, princess, no pizza, but maybe Mommy will let you come play in the sand while I take a shower before we eat chili."

Did he just invite himself over for dinner? I'm thinking about how to play this off and how to uninvite him.

I hear a gasp, which knocks me back to the present conversation.

"Momma, Ackson say we go sand." She wiggles herself out of his arms to grab my hand, dragging me across the street, while she follows Jackson to the side gate.

"Okay, princess, you can go play while Mommy watches, and I take a shower. Then we can have some chili and maybe some ice cream." He stoops down to her right before she runs into the backyard, diving for the sand box.

"Now you will have to break a promise to her, because one, you aren't coming for dinner, and two, I have no ice cream." I fold my hands over my chest, making my small breasts seem fuller.

I see Jackson's eyes travel down.

"Why can't I come for dinner? You were here yesterday. I was thinking we could walk to the ice cream parlor in town. She has a stroller or you think she'll be okay walking there?"

"I don't know if you will even like it. I made it with ground turkey meat because it's healthier. You don't look like you eat healthy." I try to look past him toward the sand box where Lilah is playing.

His laughing makes me look back at him. "How does someone who eats healthy look, Bella?" he says, teasing me.

I wave my hand up and down in front of him. "Not like that. I think they look smaller than you."

He continues to belly laugh. "I like when you keep looking at me like that, Bella."

"I don't look at you." I stumble, walking past him now to get Lilah. "Come on, baby, I have to go check the chili."

"Momma, you play castle with me?" She fills up another pail with sand.

"No, baby, not today, maybe tomorrow. Come on, we need to go." I pick her up and dust the sand off of her while she starts to cry. Turning to look at him, I glare.

"Now look at what you did!" I accuse him.

"I didn't do that, you did that." He points at me. "Why don't you leave her with me, go check the chili, and then come back?"

"I don't want her to get in your way," I say while Lilah uses the back of her hand to brush away the tears that fell. "What if she needs me?"

"Bella, you're going to be like twenty feet away. If she really wants you, I'll bring her to you. Give me your phone." He holds out his hand for me to hand him my phone.

"I don't have it on me. I don't need it. It's somewhere in the house. I think the kitchen," I say while thinking of where I left it. I've got no one to call or anyone calling me, so I never carry it with me.

"From now on, you keep it in your pocket. What if you fall and you need help? What if something happens to Lilah and you can't move? You need to always have it just in case."

I don't even want to think of how right he is. I can't even let my mind wander to the possibility of someone getting me or Lilah and not being able to call for help.

"I'll get my phone, check the chili, and come right back." I look down at Lilah while I feel his hands gently cup under my chin to lift my face up.

"I've got her, babe."

I throw his hands off me as the memories of the past come roaring back.

Memories of when Adam wasn't high and was trying to be nice. It was always, *Babe, I love you. Babe, I need you. Babe, babe, babe, babe.*

"Don't call me that." I don't make eye contact as I rush past him before I have a meltdown in front of him.

By the time I make it to the house, my heart has started to beat at a normal pace. My breathing is almost catching up, and my shaking hands are now calm.

I grab the phone, check the chili, and rush back out to get Lilah.

By the time I make it into his yard, I'm stopped in my tracks. There in the middle of this square box sits this almost stranger with my daughter in his lap while he helps her put sand in the pail. But that's not what stops me.

It's the smile on her face, it's her voice talking to him, it's the sound of her giggles and laughs as he tickles her sides and she spills the sand.

It's almost too perfect. I have to stop myself from dreaming, from thinking this is what I'm supposed to have. I made my deal with the devil, and I got out. I don't deserve anything more.

15

Jackson

The minute I hear the gate door click shut, I look up. She's beautiful, she's absolutely fucking beautiful. The way the sun is hitting her from behind, she looks like an angel.

In the weeks since she has moved in, she's gotten fuller. She's starting to look healthy again. When she folded her arms across her chest defiantly, I noticed she has definitely filled out in that area.

What gets me every single time, though, is the life I see coming back into her eyes. The way she smiles more without even realizing she is doing it. The way her voice sounds when she is happy or the feisty attitude that is buried in there.

The way she reacts when I push her buttons. I know if I get in there, she is going to light up my dark world. She is going to bring light back into my life, too. Can't say I can walk away from that.

"Did you get the phone?" I ask her as she makes her way closer to us. She replies by just giving me her phone. I don't even have to use a code to unlock it.

I shake my head. "Do you know anyone can access your phone and information like this?" It's safety 101.

"I have no idea. I've never had this type of cell phone before, so I have no idea what it does or doesn't do. The last phone I had was a flip phone."

"Imagine you lose this phone and someone finds it. They have access to whatever data you've got stored in there. Pictures, web browsing history, location data from the GPS. You have to have a lock on it to protect your information. It's a scary place out there. Trust me, I know. I've seen it."

"Okay, Jackson. You're right. I'll read the instruction manual tonight. Learn to lock it."

I look down at the phone, entering my contact information. She isn't lying when she says she has nothing else on it. She has one other contact, someone named Brad. Who the fuck is Brad? "I'm in there under Jackson, right after Brad."

"Thank you," she says softly, taking the phone from me. Not even setting my mind at ease about this Brad guy.

"Chili still cooking?" I see her playing on the phone, trying to figure stuff out.

"Um yeah, I have to put the corn bread in, but it takes forty minutes, so, Lilah, we have to go, honey, and leave Mr. Jackson to take his shower."

"Ice ceam?" Lilah looks at me and asks. Her little ponytail loops more to one side since she was leaning against my chest.

"We can try and convince your mommy while we eat, how about it?"

I look over at her, waiting for her to chime in. But she just glares at me. Fuck, that mouth. What I want to do to it, what I want it to do to me.

"Come on, Lilah. Let's go set up the dinner table with the special napkins Ms. Brenda got us while Mr. Jackson showers."

"Okay, Momma. Ackson come our house?"

I set her down next to Bella. "Wouldn't miss it for anything." I smile at Bella. "I'm really hungry. Can't wait for that turkey chili."

"You can stay home if you like. Or better yet, I can prepare you a

Tupperware and bring it over to you."

There's the firecracker. "Nope, I'm so happy I get to have dinner with two of my favorite girls."

Lilah giggles while Bella reaches down, picking her up. "We eat in forty minutes. If you aren't there, I'll bring something over," she says as she saunters away.

Fuck, I'd love to have her under me as I dared her to use her sassy mouth. My cock doesn't know this isn't the time or the place, because he's ready for action.

I laugh to myself while I make my way upstairs to undress and shower.

My hand is very well acquainted with my cock. I feel like I'm twelve-year-old again with how easily and frequently I'm getting hard.

I shower in record time, even with squeezing one off. I put on shorts and a shirt, not bothering with my hair.

Once I make it to their door, I smell the corn bread. Knocking, I wait for her to answer. I would just walk in, but I don't think we are there yet.

When she opens the door, I see she has tied her hair up on top of her head, making her look even younger than she is.

"Ackson, look, I set table." Lilah runs around the table so she can show me what she did.

The table is set with a white tablecloth and pink napkins. "Is that your favorite color, princess?" I ask her.

She nods yes while she runs back in the kitchen, returning with two pink plastic cups. "You get one, I get one. Momma can have a glass."

"Please come in." She walks away from the door, and my eyes automatically make their way to her ass. It would fit perfectly in my hand.

A groan escapes me before I can take it back. She turns around and looks in my eyes. The need is there, the lust is there. Her cheeks turn a bit pink while she goes to the oven and bends down to check the corn bread.

JESUS FUCK. I tilt my head up, trying to picture Freddie Krueger and his knives getting close to me in order to get my dick to calm down.

"Oh, it's ready," she says as she places it on the stove. I make my way into the kitchen to see if I can help her.

"What can I do to help?" I expect her to say nothing, but she surprises me when she tells me to bring the pitcher of lemonade to the table and the crock pot.

When everything is set, she comes out with the piping hot corn bread.

"It smells so good, Bella. Thank you for inviting me." I wink at her when her head whips back at me.

"Lilah, you have to be very, very careful. This is really, really hot. Okay, love bug? So don't forget to blow on it before you put it in your mouth." She gives her a small pink bowl matching her cup.

I look over at Lilah, who has climbed into her booster seat and is tucking her napkin in her shirt.

"Ackson, you habe to bow." Lilah looks at me.

Bella serves me a big, heaping bowl. The mixture of spices hits my nose right away. My stomach grumbles loudly.

"Well then, I guess I'm hungry," I say and watch as both girls giggle a bit before Bella finally sits down.

I look over at her when she grabs Lilah's hand, and they both lower their heads. I grab Lilah's hand and then Bella's while I also lower my head.

I haven't said grace in a long time. I think it's time I start giving someone thanks these two came into my life.

"Amen," Bella says while Lilah picks up her spoon, blowing so hard some chili flies off the spoon.

"Bow, Ackson," she tells me with all the seriousness that a three-year-old can muster.

I watch as Bella reaches over to wipe her face and then helps her get the chili in her mouth. I really do have to thank someone I get to sit here with them.

16

Bella

The minute I feel his fingers hold mine, shivers run through my body. I'm nearly overcome with the need to snatch my hand back so he doesn't feel my sweaty palms. But his grip is like a wrench holding tight to a pipe.

"Amen," I say quietly. I don't even think I said grace. I just wanted to snatch my hand away from him.

"This smells delicious, Bella. Doesn't it, Lilah?" He scoops up a spoonful of chili, blowing on it first before he puts it in his mouth.

"Hmmm is good." Comes from Lilah, who is blowing and scooping.

"So let's get to know each other. Lilah, how old are you?" Jackson asks Lilah, who drops her spoon into her bowl and says three while showing him five fingers, several of which are covered with chili.

"You mean three." He tries to show her how to hold down her thumb with her pinky. After ten tries, he gives up and says, "Yeah, that's right, three. What about you, Bella?"

"I'm twenty-four going to be twenty-five," I tell him, not making eye contact with him. I don't want to see if he's judging me for having Lilah at twenty-one. I know I was an adult, but I was still young.

"I'm twenty-six, almost twenty-seven." He shares with us. Lilah is not even paying attention, though. She's dipping the corn bread in her chili now, trying to copy Jackson.

"Were you in school before you had Lilah?"

"I was in school for a bit. I dropped out."

"Why did you drop out? Surely, you could have done night courses while you were pregnant?"

I get an uneasy feeling in my stomach. I don't want to give out too much information. The mere thought of him finding out what I'm running from is too much.

"I couldn't manage the two because I couldn't find childcare for Lilah," I say, pushing around my chili as my stomach starts to form knots.

"So, what were you studying in school?"

"I wanted to be a social worker," I murmur. I always wanted to work with kids. When I lost my parents, I was lucky enough to have Nan, but what if I didn't? I wanted to make sure kids were taken care of.

"You would have been awesome at that."

I look up at him, catching the softness in his eyes.

"You should take online courses. They do that now."

I think about the computer I have and know nothing about. Maybe I can do online courses. Lilah will be going to school soon.

"Maybe I'll look into it. What about you? I know you are a police officer. Do you like your job?"

"I'm a detective for the special victims unit. I love doing what I do, some days. I've seen lots of things I wish I didn't." The minute he says that, I feel like I'm going to vomit. What are the chances I get a hot ass neighbor and he's a detective? I swear someone hates me.

"Are you okay? You look really pale." His words have me shaking my head. Yes. I don't think I can answer without my voice giving me away.

I want to usher him out of the house and hide with Lilah under the bed and hope everything goes away.

He must sense my mood change because the questions stop. He turns to Lilah, asking her most of the questions now. What her favorite television show is. What her favorite ice cream flavor is. Her favorite color. She answers pink, of course, no surprise there. He asks her what her favorite things to do are. She says her favorite thing is playing with the sand at Jackson's house and blowing bubbles with Ms. Brenda.

"What don't you like to do, princess?"

"I don't like being in the closet in the dark," Lilah says in a quiet whisper.

I gasp out in shock at her response. But my thoughts are pushed aside when I hear a spoon clatter on the bowl and a chair scraping against the floor.

"I'll be right back." He throws his napkin on the table, turning to walk out the front door.

"Orry, Momma," she whispers to me. "Ackson mad?"

"No, baby, he's not mad. He just forgot he left his front door open," I lie to her as I see him sit down on the step outside the house.

"Why don't you finish up so we can get you in the bath? I'm thinking pink bubbles tonight." I try to get her back to her happy place.

"The pink big bubbles?" she asks.

I know those are her favorites.

"Yes, baby girl, those." I pick up his plate and mine and bring them to the kitchen sink. I put the leftovers into a storage container, freezing a good portion for us, but also preparing a portion for Jackson to bring home.

I look over and notice he is now pacing on the front lawn with his head down. He stops mid-strut when his phone rings.

"Baby, why don't you go and put your bowl on the counter and I'll be right back to give you a bath, okay?"

She nods at me while I walk to the door.

Opening it slowly so it doesn't make any noise, I hear his half of the conversation.

"Marissa, it's okay. Stop crying, it'll be okay. I don't know what is going to happen. I'm going to swing by. Would that help? I can be there in twenty minutes," he says quietly and softly to her.

He closes off the phone, turning around, and stopping when he sees me standing here.

"I have to go," he tells me, and I nod my head.

I don't say a word because I don't trust my voice to crack and give me away.

"I'm just going to say bye to Lilah."

Again, I just nod my head and watch him walk past me.

I take a second to blink away the tears threatening to fall. After that, I look up at the sky and ask for strength. I make my way into the kitchen and hear the conversation between Jackson and Lilah.

"You go bye bye?" Lilah asks while she sits on his lap, looking up at him.

"Yes, I have to go bye bye. But how about tomorrow we go back and play in the sand? We can ask Mommy if you could eat at my house." He leans in and whispers, "We could even ask her to order pizza."

She smiles and shakes her head yes. He kisses her cheek, placing her down, and turning around to look for me.

"Bella, I gotta take off. I'm really sorry. I didn't know I would—"

"You don't owe me anything," I say to him while I turn around and grab the bag of chili and corn bread I wrapped up. "Here, I know you didn't finish your dinner and you might be hungry later or maybe not. I don't really know." I have no idea what to say to him. I don't even want to look at him. To know he is probably judging me for putting my daughter through that. I can't see that, not from him.

"Bella, look at me," he asks, but I shake my head no.

I will not fall apart in front of him. He doesn't get to witness it.

"Lilah, come on, let's get you in the bath." I grab her and walk to the stairs. "Can you close the door when you leave? I'll come down and lock it."

"Bella, this isn't finished," he says with his teeth clenched.

"There isn't anything to finish since there isn't anything started. Please shut the door." I don't give him a chance to answer, instead jogging up the stairs.

The minute I set Lilah down on the toilet so I can start the bath, I hear the click of the front door closing. Turning off the water, I run back downstairs to lock the door.

Leaning my head on the door, I allow the tears to fall. I allow them because I'm allowing myself to feel hurt. Not because I'm hurt or I feel sorry for myself, but because my heart hurts for my baby, who is scared of dark closets. For not having enough faith in myself. For not getting away sooner.

"Momma, I naked." I hear Lilah yell and know if I don't go back up there, she'll empty the whole bottle of those damn pink bubbles.

"I'm coming, baby girl. I'm just getting some water." Drying the tears with the back of my hands, I walk back upstairs and give my girl and myself a pink bubble bath.

We sing songs, and I tell her stories about when I was little. We sit outside, watching the stars. I have one eye on the house across the street that remains pitch-black.

When she finally nods off to sleep, I take her inside and tuck her in. Grabbing a blanket and some throw pillows, I turn on the baby monitor and head downstairs to sit in the swing.

I sit in the swing, watching the stars, daydreaming and wishing things were different.

17

Jackson

When the phone rang and I saw Marissa's number, I knew I would have to leave. I wasn't wrong. She said Lori called her whispering, crying, and asking for help.

Fuck, I can't deal with this right now. Not after sitting at the table while the little girl who has woven herself into my heart tells me she hates dark closets. I'm supposed to enforce the law, but in that moment, I knew I would kill the person who forced her into a dark closet without thinking twice. I'd end his life, just like that, no hesitation.

I don't even feel bad about it. What I did feel bad about was running out on Bella before we had a conversation that was a long time coming.

Rubbing my face, I turn around and I'm shocked to see her on the porch waiting for me. I wish I could say things went smoothly after that, but it was like a tornado brewing picking up speed.

When I left there, I waited to see if she would come downstairs to lock the door and not two seconds later, I heard it click. It was her locking me out of her world. Little did she know I'd be busting down that fucking door tomorrow.

I called Mick as I put my car in drive. He made plans to meet me at

Marissa's, but not before mentioning we are wasting our time.

I make it to Marissa's club before Mick does. When I ask him for his ETA, he says he's ten minutes out.

I know I should wait for him. Rule number one, never go in alone, always wait for backup, but before I get a chance, I see Marissa running toward me.

I barely make it out of the car before she throws herself into my arms. I almost don't catch her.

"She's hurt, my baby is hurt. I can tell, I heard it in her voice," Marissa says before she starts sobbing.

"You need to calm down, Marissa, and tell me everything," I say as I try to pull her off my neck.

She finally releases me as Mick is walking up. He takes in Marissa in her work outfit. I didn't even get a chance to see it, but she's wearing a miniskirt. I mean, if that is what they are called since her ass cheeks are out. Her tube top is white and almost see-through. The outfit is completed by her sparkly, six-inch platform, clear acrylic heels.

Mick takes off his jacket and almost throws it at her. "Jesus, cover yourself up. You're almost naked."

I glare at him, sick of his attitude toward her. He doesn't even look at me. "So what happened now, Marissa, that you couldn't wait till tomorrow before calling us?"

"Lori…she, she called again. She called my cell." She hands him her cell phone, which he takes and starts to look through it.

"Unknown number. We can't do anything." He hands it back to her.

She turns to me. "She said she wants to come home. She just can't get here." She looks back and forth between us with panicked, teary eyes. "I have to get her home." The tears start to run down her face, taking her mascara with them. "Help me find her."

"Did she tell you anything? Where she was? Who she was with?" I ask her as she is rapidly shaking her head no.

"Nothing. The call lasted maybe twenty seconds, but I asked her. I told her to tell me where she was and I'd come get her. She just kept saying she wants to come home." She wraps her arms around her waist as she starts to shake.

I lean in and take her in my arms just as she starts to fall to the ground.

"How did you get to work? Did you drive?" I ask her right before a skinny black man approaches us.

"I don't pay you to come outside and turn tricks. I pay you to shake your ass and show off your tits. Now get back in there and do what I pay you for." He looks back and forth at us.

Mick goes toe-to-toe with him. He may be the same height as Mick, but Mick has a good sixty pounds of muscle on him.

"I would watch your fucking tone, man. Can't you see the lady is crying? Instead of making sure we aren't forcing ourselves on her, you tell her to get back to work. Disgusting."

"Ain't no one need to force her to do anything. She does that shit for free."

The minute he says that, Mick's fist flies faster than a lightning bolt, popping him right in the jaw. The man is knocked to the ground. He picks him up by his collar and gets right in his face. "Talk to her like that again, I'll have you eating through a fucking straw for a month," he growls out menacingly as he pushes him away. I grab his arm before he does something more.

"Marissa, you get your ass back in there now or you look for something else."

"She fucking quits, asshole," Mick says, then turns and looks at her. "Go get your shit. Now."

Marissa is either still in shock or just scared of the look in Mick's eyes, but she nods and hurries inside.

"We are giving her five minutes. If she is not back, then you go in and get her," Mick tells me, shaking his fist, which is starting to swell.

"Mind telling me what the fuck is going on there, partner? You talk to her like she's trash one minute, and then you step up like a knight in shining armor the next." I look at him with my hands on my hips.

He doesn't answer, and I know he won't answer since he just shakes his head. The look in his eyes is something I haven't seen before.

Before I have a chance to press him more, Marissa comes out dressed in jeans and a shirt. A huge bag of clothes is in her hands.

"I have no idea how I'll pay my next month's rent, but I guess I'm done with this shithole," she says quietly as she looks at us. Her face is cleaned of the black streaks that were running down her cheeks, and she looks much younger without all that makeup on her face.

"Did you see anyone out of the ordinary come in tonight?" I ask her.

"No one. It was really slow, which is why I had my phone on me. The minute I felt it ring, I jumped." The tears start to fill her eyes again. "I need to find her."

"We are doing everything we can right now. If she calls you back, you tell her to tell you anything. Preferably where she is, but if she doesn't know then ask what she sees, what she saw on her way there, anything that can get us to her."

"I'll take you home, see if maybe there is anything there you might have missed," Mick says to her.

"I have my own car. I don't want to come back here," she says to him while handing him his coat back.

"Fine, I'll follow you. Jackson, I'll send you a message if I find anything or if Lori calls again." He nods at me.

I have nothing to say to him, so I give him a silent nod. I'm hoping he sees the questions in my eyes and will call me anyway.

I stay here as Marissa gets in her car with Mick following closely behind her.

Getting myself back in my truck, I make my way home. I'm so wired. I don't know how I'll fall asleep any time soon.

By the time I make it onto my street, I notice all the houses are dark. Pulling into my driveway, I turn off the truck and take a deep breath.

Pulling myself out, I do what I have been doing for the last three weeks, looking over at the house whose residents have become very important to me.

I'm surprised to see blankets on the swing outside. I make my way over, and I'm even more shocked to see Bella curled up in the middle of the swing, sleeping, the baby monitor held tightly in her hand.

Squatting next to the swing, I run my thumb lightly across her cheek. I wonder how someone could put his hands on beauty like this in anger.

I brush the hair that has fallen on her face away. Her lips slightly part. "You're so beautiful," I whisper to her, knowing she can't hear me.

"I won't hurt you, Bella. I swear it on my life."

Her eyes flicker open. "Jackson?" she asks, confused and rising to sit.

"It's me." My hand falls into her lap.

"I must have fallen asleep watching the stars," she says, her eyes meeting mine before they drop to my neck.

"I didn't mean to wake you."

"What time is it?" she asks, trying to move so my hands fall off her lap.

"A little after midnight. I just got home. I'm sorry I left," I tell her.

"It's okay, your girlfriend probably misses you," she says while looking me in the eye.

"I don't have a girlfriend, Bella."

"You have lipstick on your collar." She touches the collar softly, her fingers grazing my neck also.

I turn my cheek so I can hold her hand closer to me before she draws her hand back.

"I had to go see a woman whose daughter is missing. A runaway.

She called her mother tonight, scared, crying, and begging for help to get home, but hung up before she told her mom where she was."

Her hand falls into her lap on top of mine.

"Is she okay?" she asks me, her face scrunched up with worry now.

"No, not even a little bit." I move my hand over so her palm is against mine and I can intertwine my fingers with hers.

"Bella, if I ever find him, I'm going to kill him." I don't wait for her to say anything more. "When I heard Lilah say what she said earlier, I knew right then and there, I would kill him with my bare hands and wouldn't think twice about it. I was just so angry, and I didn't want to scare her, so that's why I left the table."

"I thought you were thinking how I could let someone do that to her. You have to know—"

I place my finger on her lips, silencing her. I don't want her to talk. I can't take it.

Being next to her. Being in her space. Holding her hand. It's my breaking point. I'm not walking away from her without tasting her lips.

"I'm going to kiss you, Bella. In the next few seconds, I'm going to lean in and kiss you. This is me giving you a chance to tell me no." I hold my breath, hoping to fucking God she doesn't say no. Not knowing how I would walk away from her or if I even could. But she has to make this decision. She has to be the one to make the choice. She has to choose me.

"I look at you, I watch you, and it takes everything I have to not lean in and hold you. To pick you up and carry you to my bed. To hold back and not tell you what I'm feeling." This time, it's her placing her finger on my lips.

I kiss her finger. My heart is almost beating out of my chest. She removes her finger from my lips.

Three things happen.

First, my hands cup her face as my thumbs stroke her cheeks while I pull her toward me. Second, she looks me straight in the eyes, and third, I lean in and place my lips on hers.

The minute our lips touch, I hear her sharp intake of breath as my tongue seizes the opportunity to invade her mouth.

It's gentle, it's soft. I kiss her gently, softly, and it's exactly like I thought it would be. Her tongue tangles with mine, and I tilt her head to the side so I can deepen the kiss.

Her hands rest on my shoulders, anchoring her in place as she kisses me back.

I slowly pull back, trailing little kisses along her jaw. "Bella, promise me tomorrow things will change. Tomorrow, I'll ring the bell and we'll start this—me and you and Lilah."

"Jackson "

"No, Bella, no. There is no pushing me away now, angel. Just take my hand. We'll go slow and take baby steps. Please, Bella. I need you two as much as you two need me."

"Jackson...there is so much you don't know."

"And you'll tell me when you're ready. But I'm going to tell you right now, nothing you say will change how I feel. Bella, honey, I already know whatever happened wasn't good, but I don't give a shit about what happened. I do care about what happens from here on out, though."

I lean in to kiss her again before she can say anything else. I need to show her this thing between us is real. There is no fighting this force that is pulling us together. We'd be stronger together than we are apart.

"Promise me, Bella," I whisper as my forehead rests on hers.

"Okay, Jackson, I promise. But I don't know how this will work."

"That's the beauty of it, sweetheart, we can figure it out together. We can do this."

"Okay."

I kiss her once more. The taste of her on my lips is delicious, and it's something I know I'll never forget.

"Bella, you need to go inside before we get carried away and do something you aren't ready for." I pull her up with me.

She leans over to grab the blankets, pillows, and baby monitor.

"Good night, Bella." I lean in, kissing her lips lightly.

"Good night, Jackson."

She turns and walks inside, watching me as she closes the front door and locks it. Once I know she is upstairs, I make my way across the street to my own house.

Once I get to my own porch, I turn around and sit down on the top step, looking at the house across the street.

It's a house that holds two broken-hearted girls, but it's a home where I'm going to work on mending those two hearts. It's been seven years since I've felt the kind of peace I'm feeling right now, and I know it's a feeling I'm going to fight to give her.

18

Bella

I dump the blankets on the couch before I drop down on them.

If you had told me this morning my life would be changing by the time tomorrow came around, I would have laughed at you and rolled my eyes.

When I felt something rub my cheek, a sense of calmness engulfed me. It's hard to explain, but I didn't feel fear, like I have these last few months.

I knew I was safe. When I opened my eyes to see Jackson touching me, I thought I was dreaming. It had to be a dream.

But then I sat up and immediately saw the lipstick on his collar. My stomach rolled. I have felt many things lately, but that was a first. The thought of someone else touching him, seeking comfort in his arms, it was my breaking point.

Then he opened his mouth. The words were from his heart. The feelings he was feeling, I felt them all. Then he touched me, and I was a goner. There was no going back.

His hard hands on me, I felt like we could fight all my demons away together. He wanted to do that with me.

He wanted to do that for Lilah. I had to take this leap of faith. I had to be the one who made that step to him, and I knew I couldn't walk away. More importantly, I didn't want to.

Making my way into the bed, I gather Lilah in my arms. Her small frame fits perfectly, and I can't help thinking we would fit perfectly in Jackson's arms.

It doesn't take me long to fall asleep. For once, I sleep without dreaming or, at least, I don't remember dreaming.

Sitting at the table the next day at breakfast, I finally open the computer to check into those online courses Jackson was talking about. Lilah is perfectly content with coloring while eating pancakes with a ton of syrup.

The knock on the door doesn't scare me anymore. Instead, I smile. Opening the door, I smile wider as soon as I see him.

Jackson. In worn blue jeans that mold him perfectly. His blue Henley stretched tight along every curve and cut of his upper body. His hair glistening in the sun, still damp from the shower. The big black chunky watch on his left hand. He looks like my own personal badass.

"Good morning," I say as I move out of the way so he can come in. He leans down to kiss my cheek, but it is really the corner of my mouth.

While he walks past me, his fingers graze mine, his pinky wrapping around mine while he pulls me inside with him.

"Good morning, Princess Lilah." He greets her with a kiss on her head.

He releases my finger, and I still feel his heat on me. "Do you want coffee?" I ask him. "Brenda made me buy this machine that makes lattes. It's the bomb." I laugh at how his face lights up when I say latte.

"Anything is good, Bella," he says with a smile. My hands are itching to touch him. To just hold his hand would be enough.

I make his coffee while he discusses the day with Lilah. He doesn't have to work today since it's Saturday, but he is on call, so if anything happens he might have to leave.

I bring his coffee to him with the milk and sugar bowl.

Placing it in front of him, I stand next to him as he slides his hand around my legs so Lilah won't see him holding me.

I have no reason to move, so I just stay here next to him, enjoying the moment when there is another knock on the door. This time, I don't have to open it since the door opens on its own and Brenda comes in.

Her eyes take in the scene before her as she looks back and forth between Jackson and me. "Jesus, I go away for one day, and I miss the whole thing!" she says on a laugh as she makes her way to the table.

I don't say anything because Lilah is squealing Ms. Brenda is back. Clapping her syrupy hands together, you would think Santa just walked in the door with all the Christmas gifts.

"Jackson, this is a nice surprise. You're here early." She sits down with Lilah on her lap.

"Yup, I am," is all he says. Brenda doesn't push it. She just nods and goes back to asking Lilah about what she did while she was gone.

I sit down at the table, taking in the changes that have happened over the last five weeks. Five weeks ago, my daughter would have been hiding under the table. Now we don't even bat an eye when someone walks in our door.

"There she is, my little heart. Did you miss me? I missed you so much. I showed all my friends the pictures we took together," she says, kissing her head.

I walk away from Jackson to grab a wet cloth to clean Lilah's sticky face and hands. His hands move to the table, and it's a movement Brenda doesn't miss.

"Why don't we go upstairs and get dressed? I missed you so much I want to go doll shopping. Would you like that? Mommy can come with us or she can stay with Jackson."

"Momma doll shopping." Her eyes open like saucers.

"We will see." I can't even understand what doll shopping is.

"Sounds like fun. We should go," Jackson pipes in. Brenda turns and looks at him with her mouth hanging open.

"Jackson, you want to go doll shopping with us?" Brenda asks incredulously.

"Sure, why not?" He shrugs. "I have the day off. Let's try new things." Looking at me sideways, he smiles at my shocked look.

"Then it's settled, my little heart. Let's go get dressed and Jackson can convince Mommy to go doll shopping." Brenda takes her upstairs, leaving Jackson and me all alone.

"Bella, come here," he says softly.

"I am here, Jackson," I tease him. My heart beats faster, my stomach fluttering at the look he is giving me.

"I mean come here and kiss me." He pushes himself from the table, turns in the chair, and opens his legs so I can walk into them.

I look down into his blue eyes as I wrap my arms around his neck, my fingers tunneling into his hair.

"Morning," he says softly.

"Good morning, Jackson," I whisper as I lean down and kiss him. Our lips connect, and my mouth opens to him. Our tongues dance together. Tasting, sliding, learning.

His hands roam from the back of my thighs up my ass to rest on my hips. He groans into my mouth, and that sound coming from him makes my knees weak. I break the kiss, breathless.

"I need that kind of kiss every single morning," he teases me.

"Not sure about every morning, but I'm happy to participate when I can." I laugh when his eyebrows pinch together.

We hear running upstairs, and I know Lilah will be coming back down any second. I lean down and give his lips a peck before I walk away to put the dirty coffee cups in the sink along with Lilah's plate.

Two seconds later, Brenda is downstairs with Lilah at her side dressed in a cute pink sundress we picked up on one of the shopping excursions. Pink socks, pink shoes, and pink hairpins complete her outfit.

"So are we going? American Girl isn't going to wait for us forever," Brenda says.

"American girl?" I ask her, confused.

"Momma, they make Lilah dolls. Ook like Lilah."

"I have no idea what that means, but I guess I'll go change so we can go." I walk past them and head upstairs.

Ten minutes later, I'm standing in front of my dresser, looking at myself in the mirror. I've put on a flowy white skirt with a yellow fitted top. My ribs aren't visible anymore, and my skin is now glowing with a golden summer tan. I look healthy. I look like me or what used to be me.

I'm taking me back. I'm making me, well, me again. Tying my blonde hair into a ponytail, I smooth my shirt down before sliding my feet into my new white ballerina flats.

Yup, I'm ready for this.

I make my way downstairs to find them sitting on the couch. Lilah spots me first. "Momma ready. Let's go." She jumps up.

"Okay, let's go. Jackson already put the baby seat in his truck since it's bigger," Brenda says, grabbing Lilah's hand to head outside toward Jackson's house.

"Fuck me." I hear him hiss out.

"What's the matter? You don't have to come. You can stay home. We can catch up later." I look at him, hoping he still comes with us.

"You're so beautiful." He makes his way over to me and leans down to kiss my lips. My lip gloss shimmers on his lips when we break apart.

I reach up and wipe it off his mouth. "Thank you." It's all I say. It's all I can say without giggling like Lilah.

I grab my purse at the door, making sure my phone is inside it. Taking the keys from my hand, Jackson makes sure the door is locked before grabbing my hand and walking across the street.

Brenda and Lilah are already settled in the backseat. I'm surprised Jackson walks me to the passenger side of the car. He opens the door to help me in before closing it.

Brenda clears her throat in the back. I don't turn around. "Don't, just don't, not now," I say to her while she belly laughs.

Jackson makes it into the car. "Everyone buckled up? Let's go check out this American Girl place," he says while backing out of his driveway.

Lilah shoots her hands up in the air. "Yeah, we go."

With that, the three of us laugh. I look out the window, watching the houses zoom by when I feel his hand in my lap grasping at mine.

Looking down, I see both of my small hands wrapped in one of his. I take his hand into mine and hold it there. Nothing else is said. I just accept it while looking outside, listening to the music playing on the radio and finally relaxing enough that I'm enjoying myself.

Jackson

I'm in the middle of girl hell. I'm sitting down at a table, having lunch in a doll store with Lilah and her new hundred-dollar doll.

The minute we walked through the doors I groaned. This isn't what I thought it would be.

There are dolls everywhere. Shorthaired dolls, dolls with long hair, blonde hair, brown hair, blue eyes. You name combinations and they have the doll to fit it.

As if that weren't enough, then you have to clothe them. Every conceivable outfit is available here for you to buy for them. Let's not forget the matching outfits for the doll owner, because you know, it's apparently important they match.

I shake my head when I look down and see four big red American Girl bags filled with outfits, props, books.

Brenda didn't even give us a chance to see anything. She took off with Lilah, leaving Bella and me to just wander around the store awestruck and a little overwhelmed.

By the time we found Brenda and Lilah again, they were sitting at a table in the American Girl Bistro, having lunch with a new doll that looked eerily like Lilah.

"What is in all those bags?" Bella asks when she sits down with them.

"Doll stuff, Momma," Lilah says, grabbing her apple juice to take a sip. She looks up at her with a bright smile, complete with an apple juice mustache.

"Brenda, how much did you spend?" Bella looks over at the woman who is drinking a coffee with laughter in her eyes.

She doesn't answer, just shoos her away with her hand. "I don't know. Who cares? Look at the smile on my little heart."

"Momma, is doll stuff, Momma," Lilah says in a serious voice.

"Lilah, did you say thank you to Ms. Brenda?" She looks at her daughter.

"She did, she did," Brenda answers. "We have a hair appointment in twenty minutes."

I look at her, wondering if she is losing her mind.

"What do you mean, a hair appointment?" I ask her, crossing my arms across my chest.

"We are going to have the doll's hair done and styled. Isn't it exciting, little heart?"

"Hmmm," Lilah answers while nodding her head.

"You have lost your mind. Are you crazy? How much are you paying someone to style the doll's hair?" Bella looks over at her, asking her the question I'm dying to hear the answer to.

"I'm not sure. It's the first time I've ever heard about it, but I'm so excited to see what they can actually do with a doll's hair." She has officially lost her mind.

Four hours later, we are finally back in the car on our way home. The hairdressing salon showed them how to care for and style the doll's hair. Braids, ponytails, hairpins, curls, and everything else that can be done to hair.

"Ackson, pizza?" Lilah says from the backseat while looking out the window at a pizza billboard posted on the highway.

"You want pizza, baby girl?" I look sideways at her.

Her head nods yes.

"How about we swing by on the way home and pick up some? Would that be okay with you, Bella?"

"Sure, that would be great. I don't think anyone has the energy to cook after this afternoon." She cuts her eyes at Brenda, who has her head resting on the backseat with her eyes closed.

"I think we finally found something to slow her down." Bella laughs at her.

"I need a shower and my bed or just my bed," Brenda says to no one, her eyes still closed, making us all burst out laughing.

Two hours later, Lilah is passed out like a star fish on the couch, doll tucked into her arm, pizza sauce still on her face.

"Who knew shopping for dolls would make them so tired?" Bella says from beside me on the other couch. Her feet are in my lap where I put them, her head resting on the back of the couch.

I pull her legs more on me till she is sitting in my lap. "Jackson." She puts her hand on my chest.

"You're so beautiful," I say, kissing her cheek. "I look at you and I catch my breath at how beautiful you are." I kiss her under her chin on the side.

Her hand bunches my shirt. "I should really get home." She moves her hands up to my neck.

"Not yet," I tell her while I look into her eyes, leaning in, and kissing her lips. "Not yet." I lick her lip, waiting for her to open for me.

The minute she does, I invade her mouth with my tongue, sliding it in, waiting for her to tangle her tongue with mine.

Her one hand on my chest, the other on my cheek, I just can't fight the feeling in me.

The gentleness she has, the calmness she makes me feel, the feeling of complete and utter peace.

Pulling her closer to me, not giving her an inch, I tilt my head to the side, deepening the kiss. Her nails dig into my chest, causing me to groan out.

"I'm sorry," she says, biting her bottom lip. "I...I...I don't know." She shakes her head, trying to dislodge herself from me.

"Hey." I pick her chin up, making her look at me. "None of that. One step at a time, okay?"

She just nods her head yes.

"Now let's take sleeping beauty home and tuck her in."

"Okay," she whispers, rubbing her thumb across my jaw, feeling the stubble from yesterday.

Getting up, she collects all of Lilah's things, putting everything in her big American Girl bag. I pick up Lilah from the couch, her head resting on my shoulder, drool already pooling on me.

Once we make it upstairs into their room, Bella washes her face, changing her into her PJs while I watch from the doorway.

"She's out like a light," she says while she yawns.

I laugh at her. "She isn't the only one. Come lock the door, angel."

I turn around, making my way downstairs to the front door.

I've never wanted to stay someplace more in my life. I've never wanted to be asked to stay as much as I do in this one second.

"Will you come by tomorrow?" The only light on her face is from outside.

"Yes, I'll be over for breakfast." I lean in, kissing her lips before turning and leaving.

When I've made it down the steps, I hear her say, "I can't wait."

I turn around to see her wave once and then softly close the door.

I smile to myself, thinking, *I can't wait either, my Bella.*

20

Bella

It's been a whole month of breakfasts, some lunches, and every single dinner.

It was all moving in baby steps. I couldn't even begin to think of taking it to the next level. I mean, I want him, I'm attracted to him. But my body is still in the past. Whenever I start to think of maybe taking the next step, I just shut down. My mind immediately goes back to that night.

"Hello, angel." Jackson's voice brings me back to the present.

We are now standing in the middle of the grocery store aisle. Another thing we started doing together since we eat breakfast and dinner with each other.

Lilah sits in the carriage while she eats the goldfish crackers Jackson opened for her.

"I'm sorry. What did you say?" I look at him to see that his eyes are trying to ask me questions.

"I said do you need more mac and cheese or do you still have some from last week?" He points to the boxes of mac and cheese.

"Oh, no, she is out of that phase, it seems. She is now all about chicken soup with princess noodles," I say, laughing. Once Lilah tastes something new she likes, it's a week of her wanting that, and only that, to eat before she's on to the next new food.

"What did you want to make tonight?" he asks while he pushes the cart down the aisle, stopping to add the crackers, gummy bears, and jelly beans he knows Lilah loves.

"It's your turn to cook. I did it last night. You know you said we'd alternate days. So you tell me, what are you making us tonight?" I laugh at him as I lean into his side. One hand goes around my shoulder while the other pushes the cart with Lilah in it.

His thumb rubs down my arm, giving me goose bumps. I feel so comfortable with him now. Lilah actually caught us kissing a couple of times in the kitchen in the morning.

She giggled the whole time, so at least that was another easy transition for my girl.

"Lilah, how about we eat pizza and ice cream?" Jackson asks her, knowing full well what her answer will be.

"Why would we eat pizza when we are at a grocery store picking up food?" I ask while he leans down and kisses my lips.

"So I can spend more time cuddling with you. I have to work all day tomorrow, plus tomorrow night so I need my Bella fix." He kisses me one more time then leans down and kisses Lilah on her head while she shovels goldfish into her mouth.

Five hours later, we are at my house finally settling in on the couch. Lilah's sugar high finally brought her down with her falling asleep while cuddling with her doll while we washed up the dishes from dinner.

"What are we watching tonight?" I ask. He's lying down so I pick up his legs, placing them into my lap while he flips through the channels, settling on *The Big Bang Theory*.

He throws the remote on the table and flips to the side, holding out his arms. "Come lie with me, Bella," he asks softly. His eyes are blue like the sea, and all I want to do is get lost in them.

I go into his arms, lying chest to chest. His arms circle around me, caging me in. His scent is all around me. Jackson.

Taking one hand, I run it through his hair, rubbing his neck.

"You look like an angel," he says, kissing my cheekbone, moving down to my cheek, my jaw, and then back up to my lips.

The minute his lips touch mine, I sigh. Letting his tongue in, I let out a moan. His hand cups my ass now, pulling me closer so I can feel his erection.

My hand moves from his neck all the way down his back where I cup his ass in response. Fuck, it's hard just like the rest of him.

He assaults my mouth. It's almost like he's making love to me. My hands move up into his shirt, over his muscles and soft skin.

My fingertips try to trace the tattoo I have memorized from all the time he is without his shirt.

His hands are following my lead by going up my shirt, slowly coming to the front, cupping my breasts.

He pulls away. His eyes are now the color of a dark, stormy, blue sky.

"Is this okay, Bella?" he asks while I just nod. "I want to see you, Bella."

I know what he's asking. I'm not sure how my voice will come out, so I lean down, kissing his neck as I pull back and tug my shirt over my head.

I'm now lying with him in my white cotton bra. Nothing fancy, since I didn't think this moment would come now. At least it's filled out a little more.

His finger traces the top of my bra's cup. "So beautiful, even more than I could ever imagine." He is looking down at my breasts, and my chest heaves heavily.

Grabbing his shirt, I pull it over his head, getting his head caught in the process.

I'm finally able to touch the tattoos that have been taunting me since that first day I saw him.

I trace the one wing he has on the left side of his chest. One lone, broken wing. It's beautiful. The way the feathers are tattooed on it looks like I could actually feel them if I rub them enough.

"My father passing away was the roughest thing I had to face. But I knew, in the end, he was my anchor." I lean in, kissing it.

"You're a good man, Jackson." I hook one leg over his hip, trying to get closer to him. Any more closer and I'd be inside of him.

I kiss him, tilting my head to the side to deepen the kiss. Our tongues fight to control the other.

He snaps my bra open, using his hand to move the straps over my shoulder and down, letting my pink nipple free. The air makes it pebble.

He rolls it softly, the sensation going straight down to my core. My thoughts are that I've never felt this. Sex was never like this.

He pulls back. Bending his head, he takes it into his mouth, sucking it in slowly. My head falls back as I bask in the moment of bliss.

My hands rub his back down to his ass and up again. I'm not courageous enough to grab his cock. But I don't stop myself from rocking into it.

"So beautiful." He kisses me right next to my nipple before bringing his mouth back to mine. My chest flushes with the heat from his chest seeping through me.

He keeps kissing me. Keeps sending shivers up and down my body. His hand snakes lower now till he gets to the button on my pants.

He tries to open it, turning it right, trying to shake it left. The shaking of my pants brings me back to that fateful night.

The time I fought them not to touch me. The time I begged Adam to help me and not do that. The pulling of the button is too much. Before I know it I have slipped back in time, and I am shaking.

Jackson notices the mood shift. His hands rub up and down my arms, trying to talk to me, but my body has disconnected from here and now.

I jump up, looking for my shirt, my hands trembling as I hold it close to my chest to cover myself. My teeth chatter with the coldness I now feel.

Jackson comes to a sitting position. "Angel?" He tries to reach out to me, but I take a step back. The hurt in his eyes flashes before me.

"You should go." My voice cracks as the tears start to flow down my cheeks and silently drip off my chin.

"I'm not going anywhere." He stands up, putting his own shirt on. "Come here and sit with me. I promise not to touch you." He pats the couch next to him.

I turn around, attaching my bra and putting my shirt back on as the shaking finally subsides. "I'm sorry. You should go," I tell him while looking down at the floor, not sure what to say.

He doesn't give me another second until he is up and holding me in his arms. "You have nothing to be sorry about, but I'm not leaving. You promised me cuddling. You owe me cuddling," he says while picking up my chin and looking into my eyes.

"We are going to go sit on the couch," he says, pointing to my biggest nightmare now. "You are going to sit with me and cuddle while we watch a show I choose. Got it?"

I nod, a lone tear falling, stopped by his thumb. "One day you'll let me in completely, Bella. One day you'll learn you can trust me completely. One day you'll give me your heart, and I am going to cherish it." He kisses my nose, turning while grabbing my hand where he holds me all night long.

Both of us fall asleep within ten minutes of the show starting, him holding me close and keeping me safe the whole night.

21

Bella

The doorbell rings, and I run to it, wiping my hands on my jeans.

"Hey," I greet Jackson with a big smile. It's been over a month now since that disastrous night, and things between us have been progressing.

I mean, we haven't even tried to get to *that* point again. I can't tell you I don't think about it, because I do, but I'm just not ready yet for the next step.

We have had some pretty heavy make-out sessions, though, which have left us both breathless and strung up. I know he doesn't want to push me, but every single time I feel him touch me, I get tingles all over.

"Looking good, beautiful." He comes in and drags me to him. Picking me up by my waist so we are the same height, he kisses me on the lips with a big smack.

"Where is Lilah? Are you guys ready?" he asks, putting me down.

"She's coming. She was just putting her doll to bed." And before I continue, I hear her running down the stairs, one step at a time.

"Ackson, Ackson! We go to the phair?" she asks while Jackson picks her up, kissing her nose.

"Yup, come on, Bella, grab your bag and let's go." He turns to walk out, leaving me to grab my purse and close up the house.

By the time I make it to the driveway, Lilah is already in her seat and Jackson is buckling her in.

I climb in the front seat, shut the door, and buckle myself in. Jackson opens my door, startling me when he pops in, kisses my cheek, and closes the door.

Lilah must think this is the funniest thing ever since it set her off into a fit of giggles.

The county fair is in town, and I haven't been to one in forever. When we passed by the other night, the lights got Lilah's attention, and she begged Jackson to take her.

When we finally get there, the parking lot is full. Parking is pretty much park where you can and hope no one blocks you in.

Once we walk into the fair, Lilah doesn't know where she wants to go first. So she leads Jackson to the stuffed animals, jumping up and down, telling him she wants a big pink bear.

Of course not one to tell her no, he wins her the pink bear. I shake my head because she has him wrapped around her little finger.

"Momma, look, I got a pink one!" she tells me happily, hugging it close to her chest. "It's my faborite," she tells us.

We walk around, going from one ride to the other. She has the most fun on the carousel where she rides a unicorn. Jackson straps her in and stands next to her while the ride turns in a circle.

I look at all the families around us, and I feel that anyone looking in would think we are just another happy family out and about.

When the ride stops Jackson carries her off, joining me at the exit.

"Momma, ice cream." Lilah points to a picture of an ice cream cone.

"You want some ice cream, sweetheart?" Jackson asks.

"Who are you asking, me or Lilah?" I laugh, leaning into him, making his arm fall across my shoulders.

He brings me closer to him, kissing the side of my head while Lilah hugs his neck from his other side.

"Two girls. Ackson habe two girls?"

"My two favorite girls," Jackson says while laughing. "Now let's go get some ice cream." He leads us over.

Standing in line, I look around for the bathroom. Seeing there is almost no line at the bathroom, I turn around to them and say, "I'll be right back, okay? Momma has to go to the bathroom. Do you need to potty?" I ask Lilah.

She shakes her head no. "Okay, stay here. I'll be right back."

I turn to walk away but am pulled back by my hand. Jackson looks down at me. "Give me a kiss."

"Are you asking or telling?"

He doesn't bother answering, just leans down, taking my lips in a soft kiss.

"You want ice cream?" he asks while I'm pressed against him.

"No, I'm good," I answer with a smile. "I'll be back."

After washing my hands and drying them, I make my way out of the bathroom. I have one step out the door when I'm pushed to the side.

My arm is grabbed, and I'm dragged to the side. The shock of it causes my whole body to shake, making my hair fall in my face.

I don't know what is going on. I stumble over my feet, trying to right myself and see who is holding my arm.

The minute I'm no longer being dragged, I push the hair from my face as I look up. I'm face to face with the devil.

I gasp out in horror. My stomach reacts. My heart beats once, twice, and then it's beating so fast I can't even keep up with it to calm it down. My breathing picks up, coming faster and faster. I'm ready to scream. Ready to run. Ready to fight. But first I need to yell.

I finally look into his eyes, and I can see plainly he's high. There is no talking to this Adam. His once white shirt is a filthy gray with dirt. His jeans are tinged brown from how dirty they are.

"Ad—" My voice is shaking, but I don't even get his name out before he backhands me so hard my head bounces off the concrete wall.

The shock of pain causes my cheek to throb. The pain from my head is making me dizzy. I go to cup my face, leaving my stomach open for the punch he lands there.

I go down and curl up into a ball, landing on the floor.

"You thought you could leave me!" he yells at me while crouching down and spitting at me.

"Adam, please," I whisper, the bile from my stomach making its way up my throat. I throw up next to my head. I can't move my head up because he's now grabbed a handful of my hair, turning my head to look at him.

"Thought you could fuck me over!" He squeezes my face with his hand. The tears flow freely down my face. My hands try to make their way up to protect myself, but he grabs one hand, twisting it so roughly I hear it snap.

Crying out in pain, I'm trying to keep my eyes open. I'm trying to concentrate on just surviving. I'm pushed onto my back, and he straddles me. Trapping my arms to the side, he gives me no chance to protect myself from what is to come.

My white shirt is now brown with dirt. I feel a cool stickiness dripping from my head to my ear.

"You're a whore, but you're my whore." He smacks my face. "I say who else you fuck besides me!" He delivers a punch to the side of my head. I feel a pressure building in my ear, and my hearing is blocked.

I try to buck him off, try to move my head to the side. He lands three more punches before I give up.

I can barely see out of one eye. I'm going to die here on the floor in an alley. I'm going to leave my baby girl. I'm going to leave my life. I didn't get to kiss her one last time. I didn't get to tell Brenda that

I love her. I didn't get to tell Jackson that I want him. That I love him. That I've loved him from the minute I knew what love should be.

The blows keep landing.

"You fucking bitch!" He strikes me again and again. "You said you would never leave me!" He pulls my hair and screams, "Look at me, look at me when I'm talking to you!"

He lands one more blow and it's then the blackness comes to take me. It's then I let go. Hoping one day Lilah will know I did this all for her. I'm waiting for the final blow, when all of a sudden the pressure of him sitting on me is gone.

Is this it? Is this the end? Am I floating?

22

Jackson

It's been a good five minutes, and Bella hasn't come back. The ice cream cone I got Lilah is dripping all down the sides of the cone straight to her hands.

Her nose is full of ice cream, and her mouth is covered in it. She tries to stop the ice cream from dripping, but it's so hot outside nothing will stop it.

"How about we walk to the bathroom and catch up with your mom so we can see if she can clean you up?" I pick her up, the ice cream now dripping all over my shirt.

This plan wasn't thought out. I obviously didn't think this through. Maybe this is why Bella left at that moment.

We walk to the bathroom, waiting outside the door. I see the same woman go in and come out a couple of minutes later.

"I'm sorry. I'm waiting for my girlfriend. Could you go inside and see if she's there?" I ask the woman who has just walked out.

"There is no one in there. I was the only one," she tells me while walking away from me.

"It's impossible," I tell her retreating back. "Let's go and see where Momma is," I tell Lilah, who isn't even paying attention to anything but her ice cream.

I walk to the door, knocking twice hard. "Coming in," I say right before entering the bathroom.

There is one stall in there, the door half open, showing the dirty toilet. The sink faucet is leaking so much there is a rust stain in the bottom.

The hair on my neck goes up. I feel something is off.

I walk back outside, my eyes scanning the area. I'm about to walk away when I hear a male voice screaming around the corner leading into an alley.

The scene I walk into makes my heart stop and my blood boil.

In the middle of the alley, right in the back of a garbage container, is a man sitting on Bella. His fist lands blow after blow on her. I'm stuck in place. Lilah sees what happens and drops her ice cream to the ground.

Her hand goes straight to her ears as she lets out a blood-curling scream. It's a scream that brings me out of my shock.

I put her on her feet and run to grab this animal by his shirt. I rip him off Bella.

Her face is a bloody mess. Her one eye is sealed shut. Her blonde hair is matted red with her blood that has seeped out from somewhere.

Her right hand is distorted in such a way I already know it's broken. But it's her body that makes my blood run cold. It's lifeless. I don't see her chest moving up and down. Her shirt is covered in blood and dirt, but she isn't moving.

I turn around to grab the man I just ripped off her. I see black. I see nothing but rage. I see nothing but the monster that Lilah keeps talking about.

I lean down, picking him up by his shirt with both hands, ready to toss him against the wall.

The minute that I'm face to face with him, I stumble back. It's the eyes that have haunted me for the last seven years. "Adam?" I take two steps back, shock setting in, making me frozen to my spot.

The eyes staring back at me aren't the ones I knew. But I know that face. The face belongs to my brother. A brother who ran away from home seven years ago. The face haunts my dreams. That is the face of the first person I wasn't able to save.

"You and her?" I ask him, not sure I want the answer to the questions I'm asking.

"Well, if it isn't the favorite son. The golden boy. He who could do no wrong," he sneers at me.

He turns his head in response to the screams still coming out of Lilah. "The kid never shuts up. Lilah, stop screaming. Listen to Daddy for once," he yells, turning to move to her.

The minute he takes one step toward her is the minute I decide the brother I knew and loved is dead.

His bloody fist catches my eyes, and it's the final snap I need. Charging him back toward the wall, I land my first punch to his jaw.

Blow after blow, I swing. "You are a worthless piece of shit." *Smack, smack, smack.* My fists pound against his face. "Fucking scumbag. Brother no more. Dead." He falls down, but before he hits the ground I pick him up again and continue to deliver blows to his face. "You will never touch them again." I land my final blow to him before someone grabs me by the back, pulling me back. I don't even care I could have killed him in this dirty alley.

I hear screaming and crying. Looking over, I see it's Lilah in the arms of the security guard.

My chest is heaving, my hands raw and swollen. "Call nine-one-one, we need an ambulance." I rush to Bella's side.

I sit down next to her. My training tells me I'm not supposed to move her, but I cradle her head in my hands. "Bella, sweetheart, wake up." Her face is unrecognizable. Tears roll down her face, which is caked with blood and dirt.

"Please stay with me." I sob out. "Please don't leave us. Lilah needs you." I push her hair away from her face. My fingers search her neck for a pulse.

It's faint, but it's there. I'm shoved aside when the ambulance and first responders get there.

"Sir, please step away from her so we can work." How many times have I said those exact words?

"I'm not leaving her." My back goes straight, my shoulders square.

"Sir, we need the space to help her. Go tend to your daughter while we work on your wife."

I look over at Lilah, who is fighting to get to me, to get to her mom. Meanwhile, another ambulance has arrived for Adam, along with the police.

I look at Chris and Thomas, who are the police officers on duty. "Jackson, what is this?"

I shake my head and grab Lilah before I answer anything.

"It's okay, baby, it's okay. Mommy is going to be okay." I try to calm her down, but she's crying for her mom. Her sobbing is gutting me. I hold her tighter, hold her closer,

whispering words of love, promising her everything will be okay. They might be empty promises, but it's the only thing I can do right now.

Thomas makes his way to me. "That your woman?" he asks, and I just nod. My woman isn't the right word for her. She's my everything.

"You know that guy?" He nods to Adam, who has now been put on a stretcher.

"He's my brother, Adam Fletcher," I grit out while I watch Bella being loaded inside the ambulance.

"Wait a second." It finally dawns on Thomas what this means.

My missing drug-addict brother, who ran away from home at sixteen, is no longer missing. He is also the monster the two most important people in my life have been running from.

23

Bella

"Sir, you need to step away. Let us help her." I can hear someone say something. I can feel hands probing me. The pain is too much. I want to yell at them to stop.

Lilah, where is Lilah? Oh my God, he's going to hurt her. He is going to get her.

"I'm not leaving her." I hear Jackson say.

Jackson. I'm yelling, but no words are coming out. Nothing is coming out. Jackson, protect Lilah. Jackson.

Blackness takes me.

24

Jackson

Once they load her into the ambulance, I run to my truck with a sleeping Lilah in my arms. The crying and shock of what she saw overcame her, and she passed out.

I buckle her in, and she doesn't move. Putting my truck in reverse, I speed out of there.

I grab my phone, dialing Brenda.

"Hello," she answers, chipper as always.

"Brenda, I don't have time, so you have to listen and not ask questions." She must sense something is really wrong.

"Jackson, where are they?"

"We went to the county fair today, and Lilah's father found them. He beat her, Brenda, he fucking beat her." The tears I pushed aside start to fall.

"Where is she, Jackson? Where are they?" I hear the tremor in her voice, knowing she is crying. I hear things being knocked over in the background.

"I have Lilah. We're making our way to County Memorial. I need you to come take Lilah. Brenda, I need you to get in your car and come and get Lilah." I don't even finish the sentence.

"I'm leaving now." She hangs up without another word.

I look in my rearview mirror, seeing Lilah still sleeping. The dried ice cream is crusted on her face now. Her hair is all stuck together in clumps because of it.

The next call I make is to Mick. He doesn't even get to say hello. "I found him, Mick, I found him, and now I'm going to kill him."

"Whoa there, hold on, what are you talking about?"

"Adam. I found him. I found him while he beat Bella," I say through clenched teeth. My jaw is so tight I think my teeth will crack.

"Where are you? Jackson, where the fuck are you?" I hear his voice ask urgently.

"I'm with Lilah on my way to County Memorial. He beat her. He would have killed her," I whisper just in case Lilah wakes up.

"Jackson, listen to me. I'm on my way, okay? But you need to back up a second and think. You need to take care of Lilah, man. Think about Lilah and Bella. They need you now. Don't fucking do anything until I get there, yeah?" Mick tells me. When I don't answer after two seconds, he's at it again. "Jackson, you go into the ER, and you wait for me. You talk to no one. No one but me, got it?"

"Okay." It's all I can say. I hang up, and in no time, we're pulling into the hospital.

By the time I unbuckled Lilah and I'm walking in, Brenda arrives. Her face is pale and cheeks stained with tears.

"Jackson, oh my God," she says, hugging us both, shaking as she pries Lilah away from me.

"Ms. Brenda, I want my momma. Ackson, Momma," she says, leaning forward to go to Brenda, who takes her in her arms and holds her to her chest.

"I know, little heart, I know, but why don't we go wash your hands, and then Jackson can go find Mommy? How is that?" She nods to me while she turns around and walks to the bathroom at the end of the hall.

I turn and head to the desk. "Sorry, excuse me," I tell a nurse who is working on the computer when she looks up. "I'm looking for someone who was brought in by ambulance. Her name is Bella. Bella Cartwright."

"Are you family?" she asks.

I'm about to tell her no when Mick slams his badge down on the counter.

"Official police business. What is her status?" he asks and just knowing he is here, I feel a little bit better knowing Lilah will be safe.

"She is in exam room number three. The doctor is in with her now, so you can't go in there regardless of your business." She looks at us over the rim of her glasses.

"You can't do anything, you just have to wait," Mick says to me, and I look around to see where Brenda is.

When I see her walk into the room with Lilah curled up in her arms crying, my heart stops.

"What's with the tears, baby girl?" I grab her from Brenda, holding her close to me so I can feel her heart under my hand.

She curls her head into my neck. "Ackson, I scared. I want Momma." She balls her little hand in my neck next to her cheek.

"I know, baby girl, but the doctor is just going to make sure she is okay. Momma wouldn't want you to cry."

She just nods her head as we sit in the waiting room.

What feels like forever, but is maybe twenty minutes later, the doctor comes out.

"Family of Bella Cartwright? Well, the good news is that she's alive. The bad news is she's got a long road ahead of her. She has four broken ribs, a broken wrist, a broken nose, a fractured cheekbone, and a concussion. Now we're taking her for an MRI to see if there is any swelling on her brain. She needed some stitches for a contusion on the back of her head. Also, we think one of her eardrums was ruptured, but we will know more if she wakes up."

"If she wakes up? What are you saying?"

"She's in a coma. The next twenty-four to forty-eight hours will be important. I can't tell you what will happen after that. Only time will tell. We're keeping her comfortable, she'll be monitored closely, but I don't have more answers." With that, he nods and walks away.

The quiet sobbing of Brenda makes me close my eyes. "Someone needs to call my mother." I look over at Mick, and he nods his head, walking out of the room.

"She's going to be okay."

I look at Brenda, hoping against hope she's right.

Mick walks in, saying, "Your mother is on her way. She wanted to know if you had any update on Adam."

"I hope he's dead," I say, looking down the hallway that leads to the woman who has captured my heart. The woman who I want to make a life with, the woman who I would protect with my own life. The woman who is fighting to come back to her daughter. The woman who, I hope, after all this, is fighting to come back to me, too.

25

Bella

I hear beeping, but I'm not sure where I am. The pain in my body is too much. It hurts to move. I want to open my eyes, but I can't.

I hear voices. "It just takes time. Her body is healing."

Who are they talking about? Is it Lilah? I want to open my eyes. I try to speak but nothing comes out. I feel the blackness coming again.

I feel my hand being kissed. "Please, sweetheart, just wake up, please. I need you. Lilah needs you."

I try to squeeze his finger so he knows I hear him, but I can't get anything to move.

The blackness keeps taking me in. I try to fight it, but it's stronger than me. So I just go with it and let it take me away.

26

Jackson

I sit by her bed, holding her hand. The machines beep all around us. I haven't moved from this room in over a week. I haven't left her side in case she wakes up.

Lilah comes every day. We sit and read to her. So she knows she's okay. The sight of her curling up to her mother's side while she looks at her books and talks to her is too much.

"Please, Bella, come on. You need to open those beautiful eyes for me. I have so much to tell you." I place my head down next to her hand, closing my eyes, thinking about the hell of the past week.

The minute my mother found out Adam was alive, she rushed to the hospital. She came flying in, her face pale, tears streaming down it.

"Jackson, where is he? Is he here? Where can we find him? Where was he? Oh, Jackson, he's alive," she said while she clung to me, grabbing my shirt as she sobbed for her other son.

I couldn't even think of consoling her. I said nothing until Mick came in the room. She took in the both of us, looking from one to the other.

"What happened? Why aren't you with him? Oh my God." She placed her hand on her mouth.

"He's not dead." Were the only words I could say right then.

"Mick," she asked, stepping away from me, her hands falling from my chest, her arms hugging her stomach.

"Nancy, he's being attended to. But you can't see him right now." He looked down at the floor. He knew he had to tell her. I couldn't let him do it.

"It turns out Adam is Lilah's father," I said quietly. Her shocked gasp didn't stop me. "We were at the fair when Bella went to the bathroom. He pulled her into an alley and was beating her to death."

She shook her head, not wanting to hear the words.

"He is the one they've been running from. He is the reason she is so scared. He is the reason that little girl is afraid of closets."

Tears fell down her face, but I didn't know if they were for her son or the two women who'd come to mean so much to us.

"I want to see him," she said. It was the last thing I heard before I walked out of the room, leaving her with Mick.

That was five days ago. I haven't seen her since. Mick comes in every twelve hours and brings me food because he knows I won't leave her.

I don't ask him anything, and he doesn't tell me anything.

He knows when I'm ready I'll talk, so he does what I would do for him. He waits for me.

"It's been seven days, angel. You need to open those eyes. Please." The last word is a plea. The tears fall from my eyes, landing on her skin.

I kiss her fingers. Turning her palm over, I kiss her there. I make promises to her in my head. I make promises and say prayers, hoping someone answers them.

"Come back to me," I say, hoping anyone is listening. "Send her back to me. Please."

I fall asleep with my head resting on her bed while I hold her hand, hoping she takes my strength. Hoping what I have to offer helps to heal her. Hoping all of it is enough for her to find her way back to me.

27

Bella

Everything hurts. I can't move my arm. It's so heavy. Something is holding my right arm down. I want to yell out to Lilah. I want to yell out to Jackson so he knows I'm here. *I'm right here!*

"Adam, Mom, Adam did this to her." I hear Jackson say. "My brother almost killed her. Your son almost killed her."

What is he saying? Who is he talking to?

"Jackson, Adam is your brother. You can't just turn your back on him. He's sick, Jackson. This isn't him."

Wait a second, Jackson and Adam are brothers.

No, this can't be. Jackson isn't like him, is he?

I fight to open my eyes, fight with everything I have. I fight until I'm so tired. And the blackness comes to take me again.

Jackson

When the door opens and my mother steps in, I know it's going to end badly.

Her eyes go straight to the bed where Bella lies. Her face is pale and bruised, tubes all around her. A tube in her throat. Her blackened eyes are still swollen shut. The bruises are still so purple and angry looking. The stitches on her lip make her lip swollen.

Her casted arm lies on one side while I hold the hand on her other side. Her small frame looks even smaller in the bed.

"Jackson." She enters quietly, trying not to make noise.

"She won't wake up," I say to her while I touch her cheek.

"She's healing. The doctor said this is her healing."

I look at her sideways. "You spoke to the doctor about her?"

"Jackson, she's my daughter-in-law. She is the mother of my granddaughter. Of course I asked about her."

"They weren't married," I say through clenched teeth. She was never married to that bastard. He will never get close enough to her ever again.

"Adam, Mom, Adam did this to her." The anger comes out of me. "My brother almost killed her. Your son almost killed her."

She takes a step toward me, holding out her hand to hold mine.

"Jackson, Adam is your brother. For seven years, we thought he was dead. You can't just turn your back on him. He's sick, Jackson. This isn't him. You know him."

"I know I would've killed him with my bare hands. I know if they didn't pull me off him, I wouldn't have stopped until he was dead, brother or not." I look at the horror on her face. "You should go. I don't want to argue in front of her."

"Jackson, please don't shut me out."

"Mom, I can't do this right now. I can't stand here and argue with you. I can't stand here and listen to you make a case for him as if being sick was an acceptable reason to do this to her. I can't do anything. I don't want to do anything until she opens her eyes."

She nods, turning around and walking out. The breath I was holding leaves my body on a harsh exhale.

The door opens again, but now it's Mick, looking like he is fighting his own battles. "I need to know where your head is at," he says, standing by the door like he is guarding it.

"What the fuck are you asking right now?" I let go of Bella's hand, turning to look at Mick.

"Where the fuck is your head right now?" His stance sets off warning bells in my mind.

"Mick, cut the shit."

"He's gone. Slipped out during shift change. Cameras caught him walking out. Dressed in scrubs. Stumbling."

My hands clench into a fist. The hatred makes my body shake, the anger making me see black. I start for the door.

"Your head better be on straight right now. You have one girl fighting to come back, and you have another girl hoping you bring her momma home, so lock that shit down. And lock it down now." Mick doesn't give me a chance.

"I want security on Lilah and Brenda. I want guards outside this door twenty-four seven. I don't give a shit if I have to pay for it. No one touches her. No one gets close to her. NO ONE!" I yell out the last words.

I hear groaning coming from the bed, and we both turn our heads to Bella. I see her hand twitch.

I rush to the bed while Mick yells, "We need a doctor in here!"

The nurses rush in, pushing me away from her side.

"Bella, Bella, I'm here, angel." I hold her hand while the nurses work around me.

The doctor walks in. "We need you to step outside, Jackson, just for a minute, okay?" Charlene, the head nurse, tells me.

I shake my head no, so she grabs me by my shoulders. "I promise you I will not let anything happen to her, but you need to let them do their work, for her."

Mick grabs my shoulder, turning me toward the door. "Just let them work. We will stay right outside this door."

My eyes never leave her as they close the door. My heart is pounding, hoping, praying.

I lean against the wall to hold me up for support. I can't lose her. I can't and I won't.

I ask God or whoever is listening to not take her from me, to bring her back to me. I close my eyes, leaning my head back when the door opens and the doctor steps out.

"She's coming around. She opened her eyes. We're taking the tube out of her throat. It will be sore for the next couple of days. We are going to monitor her vitals for the next forty-eight hours. We will also start weaning her off the morphine. It's a good day, Mr. Fletcher, it's a good day."

He turns and walks away, leaving me feeling lighter than I have in a week. She's back. She's come back to me. She's come back to us.

I laugh finally, a nervous laugh mixed in with tears. "She's going to be okay." I look at Mick, where he just nods and smiles at me.

"Your woman is the strongest woman I know."

I just nod in agreement. She is the strongest woman, she's the bravest, and most importantly, she's mine.

29

Bella

The light is shone bright in my eyes. "Ms. Cartwright? I'm Dr. Robinson. Can you hear me?"

I turn my head, trying to get away from the light, my throat burning. The movement of my head makes me groan out loud.

My head hurts. I gasped when they removed the tube from my throat but then I'm finally able to lick my dry lips.

The first thing I feel is the stitch in it. "Water," I whisper hoarsely.

I raise my hand to touch my lip, noticing one arm with a cast on.

"Lilah?" I'm trying to get someone to answer me instead of poking and prodding.

"You've been through quite an ordeal, Ms. Cartwright," the doctor says while continuing to examine me. "You have a concussion, and you were in a coma. Do you understand what I'm saying, Ms. Cartwright?"

I nod, the movement making me want to vomit. "Lilah? Please, my daughter?"

The nurse with the blonde hair looks at me. "Your daughter is fine. Your husband hasn't left your side." The minute she says those words my heart rate spikes. The machines start alarming.

"Ms. Cartwright, you need to relax for a bit. Someone get Jackson!"

I hear the blonde-haired nurse say.

I see someone walking to the door, opening it, and saying something, but I can't hear. The next second, I feel a hand holding mine.

Turning to look at him, all that plays in my head is the dream I had. Adam and Jackson are brothers. It isn't a dream. It's a nightmare.

"Angel." He leans down, kissing my forehead. "You had us so scared. Don't you ever do that to us again!" he says, trying to smirk at me, but my eyes are watching his.

The blue eyes that kept me safe all this time are the blue eyes I have to run away from again.

"Lilah, I want Lilah," I ask him, closing my eyes, trying to stop the tears from falling for him.

"I'll call Brenda, and she'll bring her, okay, angel?" He leans in, kissing me on the lips, careful not to rip my stitch.

He steps back, taking the cell from his pocket. His eyes have circles around them. His face is rugged with a beard. He looks exhausted.

Was it all a ploy? Was it all a ploy to catch me? Was anything real? One thing is for sure. I'm not going back to hell. I made it back once. Except, this time, losing Jackson might just be something I can't come back from.

30

Jackson

As soon as I walked in, I knew something was wrong. Her eyes were void.

I sat next to her holding her hand while they did their work around us, waiting for Brenda to bring Lilah in.

The minute I said she was up, I heard weeping and keys jingling in her hand.

My thumb rubs the top of her hand, limp in mine.

I'm waiting for everyone to leave before I talk to her. There are things she needs to hear from me. Things we need to discuss. But all that will have to wait because at that minute the door opens up.

Brenda walks in with a big smile on her face. Her eyes are still wet with tears, her hand holding fiercely onto Lilah's hand.

As she walks in, Lilah runs to me, and I catch her right before she jumps in my lap.

"Momma." She looks over at her mom. Bella's eyes open, looking at her.

Tears start pooling in her eyes. "Baby." She tries to hold out her hands to take her, but she can barely get the strength to lift her hand, let alone hold her.

Placing Lilah on the bed next to Bella, I tell her to be careful of the wires and tubes all around her.

She curls up into her mother's side, careful to not touch anything.

Bella's good arm holds her close. "I'm so sorry, baby, so, so sorry I left you." She rubs her back while speaking with tears leaking into her pillow. "I promise to never leave you again."

Lilah looks up at her, nodding.

I don't even think she knows why she is agreeing, but just knowing her mother is here is good enough for her.

"I miss you, Momma." Her little hand is lying on her mother's stomach to not hurt her.

"I know, baby, I missed you so much." She tries to bring her other hand over to hug her. "Did you have a sleepover with Ms. Brenda?"

"She sure did," Brenda answers, coming close to the other side of the bed, taking her casted hand in hers.

"Thank you for taking care of her," Bella says, looking at her.

"None of that." She shoos away with her hand like it was nothing. "You scared me. You scared all of us," she says, holding her hand in both of hers. Tears escape the side of her eyes, which she wipes away with her thumb.

"Jackson, why don't we let these two talk? Little heart, I'm going to be right out that door, waiting for you when you're ready, okay? You can tell Mom all about the special dollhouse we just ordered."

I follow her out of the room while I hear Lilah talk about her dollhouse.

Once the door closes, Brenda turns, her hands going to her hips. "What is going on? What happened? Is she sick? Why is she so vacant? That isn't Bella in there. I know that look," she tells me.

I haven't had the full discussion with Brenda, but I have no choice but to do it now.

"Her ex, Lilah's father, it's Adam."

Brenda pales. "What do you mean it's Adam? Your brother ran away. We thought..." She doesn't finish that sentence because we all thought he was dead. We just didn't have the body.

"My brother did that to her. My brother is the reason those two are broken. Because of—" Before I can say more, Brenda holds up her hand.

"Don't you dare blame yourself for this, Jackson. I have watched you, ever since I met you, for the last five years blame yourself for not saving him. I will not stand here and watch it anymore. He did this, not you, not Nancy, not anyone but that bastard," she says loudly, shaking her head. "How is your mother?"

I shake my head no, hoping she doesn't push the topic. She must feel my need to drop the subject.

"I don't know what this is going to do to her. I don't know how she will get back from this, Jackson." She wipes the tears away from her face before they fall.

"I love her. All of her. The broken pieces, the whole pieces, the good, the bad, the ugly, everything. I love them. I'm not letting them go," I tell her, hoping I have the strength for the battle I'm up against. Come hell or high water, I'm not giving up.

"She is going to fight you all the way," Brenda says to me sadly, and I know she is.

This fight will be the fight of my life. But in the end, I'll walk away with my heart full. I'll walk away with the person I've learned that I can't live without. The person I want my tomorrows and forevers with.

Leaving Brenda in the hallway, I make my way inside to Bella and Lilah. I walk into the hospital room, and all I see are the two small figures curled up in the bed.

Both of them are lying, looking toward the door. She will never have her back toward the door. I never noticed she did that before.

I have to step aside and calm down the anger that is running through me.

The images of her lying there in that alley bruised and beaten are something I can never erase from my mind. It's also something I will never ever fucking let happen again.

I don't know if she senses me or hears me, but her eye flutter open.

The swelling on her face has gone down, but still only one eye can open.

Her lips are also swollen, and she has one stitch on her lip with dried blood caked on it. I want to walk over there and take her in my arms.

Hold her, cherish her, promise her it will never happen again. But that look in her eye, I've seen it, it's her hollow look.

She's gone. The spirit that was slowly coming out is not there anymore. In its place is the same person who opened the door that first day. My vow to never stop pushing till that girl was gone for good is another reminder I failed her, again.

"What are you doing here?" she asks me in a whisper, trying not to wake Lilah up, who must have fell into a slumber as soon as she got to her mom. Brenda told me she wasn't sleeping lately.

"I haven't left your side since you came in," I huff out, running my hand up my face through my hair, holding my neck after.

"I don't want you here," she says to me in a voice that is devoid of emotion. "I want you gone. I want to never see you again. I messed up my life once by falling in love with a monster, and I will not mess it up again by falling in love with his brother," she says louder this time while she tries to sit up, but the pain must have been too much as she grimaced.

"We need to tal—" I walk toward her to get to her side, to touch her. Hold her hand, anything.

"We need to talk about *nothing*. You need to turn around and walk away. You need to forget we ever met. You need to pretend we don't exist." Her face is angry and hurt.

"No fucking way in hell is that happening right now or ever," I say to her, holding my stance at the side of her bed. She needs to hear my words. She needs to see I'm not leaving without her.

"You can't be a fucking hero to everyone. You can't fucking save us. You can't fucking change anything." Her tone is hard, vicious, upset. One tear falls out of her eye. One lone tear. "Get back on your horse and leave us alone. You want to pretend to be a hero, make sure your brother never sees us. Make sure he forgets we are *his.*" She hisses out the last word. She's a warrior and she geared up for war.

"I'm no one's fucking hero, but I'm going to be yours. I'm going to make you safe again. I'm going to make sure Lilah never has the fear in her eyes that you do right now. I'm going to do that, and then we are going to get back to where we were headed before all of this happened." My heart is pounding. The thought of never holding her again is too much to bear. The thought I could never hold her hand and just watch television is making my chest tight, making breathing hard.

"You're a LIAR!" she yells out and sits up, no matter how much it hurts her. "You probably knew all along who I was. Did you know when we met I didn't know he was an addict? Had no clue what drugs even were. Did you know the first time he hit me was because Lilah was crying too loudly for him, when he was trying to smoke crack? Did you know he sold *MY BODY* so he could get his next fix? Did you know the last time he did he tied me to the bed, after he had already landed seven punches to my face and five to my head? Did you know he then turned to his dealer and told him to have fun with me? Did you know before the dealer raped me, he hit me? Did you fucking know he locked my daughter in the closet where she heard her mother being beaten and raped while he stood in the corner with his crack pipe to his lips? Did you know I stopped believing in dreams? Nothing, *nothing*, is going to change that, nothing. Nothing. So please leave me to my hell. Leave me to deal with whatever God throws my way. I don't have the energy to fight anymore, but I'll die fighting for her to not follow into my footsteps." Her chest is heaving, and the machines are starting to beep again.

The nurses along with Brenda rush in and take in the scene. "Bella, are you okay?" Brenda is the first one to ask.

"I'm fine, but I want him out of here." She turns and looks at the nurse. "Call security if you have to, I want him out of here."

Sharon, who has been the one holding my hand the whole time I sat next to her bed, turns with a sad face. "Jackson, perhaps you could come back later. Just let her rest. She needs rest."

Looking over at Bella, I see Lilah has opened her eyes and is staring at me with a confused look. She doesn't need this right now. None of us do.

"I'll give you this, Bella, but just so you know, this isn't over."

It's all I can get out before I leave, collapsing on the wall. My hand on my knees, my breathing coming in hard like I just ran a marathon.

I can't fucking lose her. I won't fucking lose her.

31

Bella

My heart hurts more than my body with all its broken bones.

The pain in my chest is like my body is burning on fire. I sent him away. He lied to me this whole time.

"Bella, you don't understand." Brenda comes to sit in the chair that, apparently, Jackson has been sitting in.

"I don't want to hear it, Brenda, not now, not tomorrow, not ever." I look at her so she sees I'm not backing down.

I'm not going to be the girl people walk over anymore. No way. I'm taking it back.

"Okay, fine, we will talk about this when you calm down and not in front of Lilah," Brenda says while she holds my hand.

Brenda does her best to take my mind off of everything that just happened by telling me stories of her adventure with Lilah.

My eyes never leave my girl and her smile while she chimes in with her side of the story.

The knock on the door has us both turning to look at the door where two men walk in.

I don't recognize them, but Lilah sits up, waving. "Hi, Mick, look, Momma is up."

"I see that Miss L," the man Mick says. "Hi, we haven't met yet, but I'm Jackson's partner, Mick, and this is Officer Chris. We are actually here to ask you some questions about what happened."

"Why?" I'm confused. They know who did this to me. Everyone knows it was Adam.

"Ms. Cartwright, my name is Chris. We have a general idea of what happened, but because no one saw you before Adam attacked you we don't know what happened." He takes out his notepad and pen. "Did Adam approach you or did you approach him?"

"I went to the bathroom. When I came out, I was grabbed by my arm. I didn't see who it was till I was already in the alley."

"So you didn't go willingly, is that right?" he asks again.

"I'm sorry, did you think I willing went into an alley to get beaten? Why are you asking this? Where is he? Where is Adam?"

Chris just looks down at his feet, but Mick speaks up, "He got away." The minute those words are out of his mouth I try to get off the bed.

"I have to get out of here. We aren't safe. Lilah, we need to go." My voice is rising. The panic is setting in. I look around to see where we can escape from. I look around to see if there is anywhere he can be hiding. The minute I try to swing my legs off the bed, my ribs feel like I've been stabbed.

Mick gets to me before I fall off the bed taking Lilah with me. "You are safe here. Jackson hasn't left your side. Plus, he has security guards standing outside as well as at your house. No one is getting to you." He places me back in bed, picking up Lilah, and holding her in his arms.

"That's what I thought till I woke up in a hospital bed."

"You're safe, Ms. Cartwright," Chris finally chimes in. "But we need to build a case to make sure he pays for this."

I laugh out loud. "A case against him? You can't even find him." My body is starting to shake. The nerves racing through my body are too much for me. "You had him, and you lost him." I shake my head.

"Why, why me? Why us? He doesn't even give a crap about us. Why would he bring me back?"

I don't even think I want them to answer me. No, in fact, I don't want them to. No one can answer that except Adam. The one thing I know is I'm not going to let him get close enough to us to answer that question.

"Just so you know, Jackson is having an alarm system set into place. As an extra precaution. We aren't letting him near you guys again," Mick says.

"I have more questions if you are up to it?" Chris says, looking at his notepad.

"How long were you and Mr. Fletcher married for?"

"I'm not married to him. We never got married." I think I should thank my lucky stars we never actually went through with it.

"Is Mr. Fletcher Lilah's father?"

I don't have to say anything because Mick clears his throat, making Chris raise his eyes. The look he gives him lets him know that question isn't going to be answered.

"Was this the first time Mr. Fletcher put his hands on you?"

"No," my voice whispers out. My eyes go to Brenda. Her eyes fill with tears, but her hand is squeezing mine tighter.

It is one thing to know what they think of you; it is another thing to actually admit it to them.

"Has Mr. Fletcher ever harmed his child?"

"He never touched her. He did lock her in a closet once and only once. I left the day after." I hang my head down in shame.

I let this happen to my daughter. I let him do that to her because I didn't leave at the beginning.

"Would you be willing to file for a protective order against Mr. Fletcher? It will help in the future if he ever comes back. Now it'll be on paper that he isn't allowed near you,"

Chris says, waiting for my answer.

"I'll sign whatever you want me to sign." I look at him, then at Brenda. "I'm not the victim no more."

"No, sweetheart, you aren't," Brenda says.

All this is too much for me. I'm so tired. I lay my head back on the pillow, just thinking I'm going to rest my eyes.

Till the blackness comes and takes me again, but this time I can fight it and open my eyes but only for a minute before Brenda tells me she is going to take Lilah home so I can rest, and she'll be back tomorrow.

I feel Lilah kiss my hand then hear the door close. I don't know if it's a dream or not, but I feel a hand holding mine.

My hand turns over and a kiss is placed right on the inside of my wrist.

When I open my eyes, darkness has taken over and the room is empty. It was a dream, all a dream.

32

Jackson

It's been a week since I sat by her bed. Actually, that is a lie. Every night I go in there when I know she's sleeping to hold her hand. To touch her, to whisper to her, to see her healing.

The nurses have been good with not telling her about my nightly visits. Mick has been calling me a stalker. I don't give a shit as long as I can sit with her.

Her bruises have faded, the swelling is down. The stitch in her lip has been removed. The cast is supposed to come off in another month. But she is set to go home tomorrow.

She is going home where I won't be able to touch her every night.

During the day I sit outside with whoever is on duty, only leaving to bring Lilah home or to take her to eat.

I'm flipping through the newspaper when my cell rings. Seeing my mother's name on the screen makes me groan.

We haven't seen each other since that day in Bella's room.

"Hello."

"Jackson, honey, how are you?"

"I'm good, Mom, what can I do for you?"

"How is Bella, how is Lilah?"

"She is getting better, but she isn't talking to me, so I haven't seen her, but I heard she looks better."

"Jackson, why don't you come over for lunch? I can whip something up real fast."

"I don't know, Mom, I don't want to leave her ju—"

"She'll be fine. Come on, sweetheart."

Looking up, I know this is a showdown that has to happen.

"Fine, Mom, but I only have about thirty minutes."

I leave my chair in the hallway, letting the nurses' station know I'm leaving for thirty minutes and if there is anything to call me.

They just smile and nod. I'm wondering if they have a bet going on for the sappy dude sitting in the hall.

Making my way over to my mother's, I think about how hard it will be not to see Bella. To not be able to touch her. I don't even want to think about it.

Pulling up into my childhood home, I notice it looks the same. Just new flowers have been planted.

Walking up the stairs to the door, I open it without knocking like I always do.

The living room is in disarray; there are photo albums everywhere.

Photo albums of my childhood, photo albums of Adam's childhood.

I walk over, picking up the album that is open to the last photo Adam ever took with us. Three weeks before he went missing.

You wouldn't know from seeing the picture of us laughing on the front lawn with Mom in the background. It was the family BBQ and someone had just said I was pumping so much muscle I would soon blow up like the Pillsbury dough boy. Adam thought it was hilarious and poked me in the stomach, asking me to "ho ho ho."

My mother must have heard me come in because she walks in, wiping her hands onher apron.

"What is all this?" I look around. Every single picture Adam ever took is in this room.

"Jackson, he is my son. I can't turn my back on him."

I throw the book against the wall. "He beat her." I don't stop or sugarcoat this shit. "He fucking beat her and watched as his dealer raped her while he got high. He stood there and watched." The tears stream down her face, her hand in front of her mouth.

"Jackson, please."

"Please what, Mom? Tell you it isn't the truth? He threw Lilah in a closet, did you know? The whole time they beat and raped her mother, that beautiful little girl was huddling in the closet scared and confused. She listened to her mother cry and beg all night to stop. Your son did that."

"Jackson, you don't understand. I can't. I thought he was dead." Her tears silently fall down her cheeks.

"I don't understand? Did you just say that to me? Let me tell you what I understand. I sat at a table with a three-year-old, and she told me she doesn't like being locked in the closet in the dark. What you don't understand is I will protect them with everything I have. You have to know that given the choice, I choose them over him. I'll choose them each and every single time."

"Jackson, he needs help. That isn't him. You know him, he isn't this person. We need to find him so we can get him help, so he can get better," she says, pleading with me.

"I hope I find him. If I don't kill him when I do, then it'll be to arrest him so he can pay for what he did to them."

"Jackson, please don't do this." She walks to me, but I hold my hand up to stop her.

"I'm not doing anything. I didn't do anything, *he did*. He did this. He chose to do this. I'm taking care of what is mine, and they are mine. From the tips of my toes to the top of my head, they fucking own me. All of me." And with that, I walk out of my childhood house, slamming the door behind me.

I walk away from the house that holds all my memories of my brother. I also walk away from the house that holds all the misery that came after my father's death, after Adam ran away. After we searched high and low for him, coming up empty each and every time.

I remember the day he went missing. Instead of taking care of my young teenage brother who was crying out for help after losing his father, I was trying to get into Kendall's pants.

The signs he was using drugs were all there. I just refused to believe my brother would stoop to that. To get mixed up with that.

Money started disappearing. Little things here and there went missing. Mom would turn a blind eye, trying not to see what was right in front of her face.

The first time I came face to face with a high Adam was a day before he went missing.

The bathroom door was supposed to be locked, so I just walked in. There, sitting on the toilet with a plastic rubber band tied around his arm and a needle in his vein, was my brother.

He didn't even notice I was watching because his head was back, his eyes closed. I waited for him to open his eyes to yell at him, but when he did, I could see he wasn't even there.

His body may have been there, but he was gone.

I waited for him to go out the next day before I searched his room. I found everything I was afraid to find. Used needles and syringes, little ziplock baggies.

When he came home, I waited for him in the kitchen with all his shit in front of me. His face went pale when he saw everything on the table.

"What is all this?" he asked while pointing to the table.

"Oh this," I said, "all this is from your room. You can't tell me you don't recognize it."

"What the fuck are you doing snooping in my room? Don't you have something better to do?" He walked toward the table.

"What the fuck am I doing? What the fuck are you doing? Have

you lost your mind?" I was talking to him, but his eyes were on the table, scanning the items.

"Where is the rest of it?" he whispered through clenched teeth.

"Oh, you mean the white powder in the baggies you had hidden in your room? Those would be in the toilet. You didn't think I would keep them, did you?" My body was wrung tight. I was waiting for that fight. The more time passed, the angrier I got. "Why are you doing this, Adam? Why?" I pleaded with him, almost begging him to tell me.

"Why? Why the fuck do you care now? Ever since Dad died, you've checked out. Your dick is so fucking mesmerized with pussy!" He threw it in my face.

Yes, my father dying in the line of duty rocked our worlds. Yes, I'd been doing everything possible not to come home and cope with it, but never did I think I was neglecting him.

"How many fucking times did I ask you to stay home, ask you to hang out? Not today, Adam, maybe later, Adam. Well, guess what, big brother, I don't need you anymore. I have my own friends now," he told me while pushing around the paraphernalia I found in his room.

"I would never push you to this. You need to stop doing this. Think of Mom." I tried begging him. "She would die if she knew you are doing this to yourself."

He started throwing around the stuff on the table. "Where are they, where are they?" he kept asking.

He was looking for the three pills I found hidden in his pillowcase.

"Adam, I flushed them. Please, we can get you help, we can tak—"

He finally snapped, throwing over the little dinette table. "FUUUUCCCKKKK! I don't fucking want help," he yelled so loud, I was surprised the windows in the house didn't break.

In that minute, my mother walked in the kitchen holding four grocery bags in her hands. "What is going on with you two? I could hear you all the way to the car." She took in the table that was turned over. She took in the needles that were now all around the room. She took in the burnt spoons and his rubber band along with the empty plastic baggies.

The look of horror crossed over her face. "What is all this, Jackson?" The bags fell out of her hands with a huge thud.

"Oh, this, Mom? This would be what Adam's been up to with his new friends," I told her, looking straight into my brother's green eyes.

She turned to look at Adam, who was looking like he could breathe fire at that point. "Adam, what's going on here?"

The question loomed in the air, the tension so thick you could cut it with a knife "I get high, Mom, all the fucking time," he said, laughing at her. "What does anyone care? No one cares!" He threw his hands out to the side. "You"—he pointed to my mother—"are so sick with grief from losing Dad and trying to make everything perfect when it's not. And you"—he pointed to me—"are too busy burying your cock in a puss—"

I didn't let him finish his sentence. I punched him right in the mouth. He turned his head to look at me, blood leaking from the side of his mouth.

He bent his head back and laughed again. "Is that all you have, brother?"

"Adam." My mother stepped to him to try to help him, but he pushed her away.

"No! I don't need this from the both of you."

"I don't give a shit if you want or need it. You aren't doing this shit here."

"What about you, Mom? You going to let him kick me out of my home?" He turned and looked at our mother's grief-stricken face.

"Adam, you can't do this to yourself. You are better than this. Your father would be—" She tried to talk to him.

"My father is dead, so he can't be anything." He smirked at her, a shocked gasp making its way out of her mouth before she covered it *with her hand.*

"Watch it. You will not talk to her like that. You aren't happy here? Then take your shit and leave." I practically dared him, hoping it was the push he needed.

"Fuck this, I'm out." He turned around and headed to the door with my mother trailing behind him, pleading with him to stay.

I watched the whole thing without saying another word. Watched him jump into a run-down Civic as my mother begged and cried for him to come back inside.

I watched her almost run after the car. But what stuck with me most of all were her eyes when she turned around. Eyes filled with sadness, regret, and sorrow.

"He'll come back, Mom. Come inside."

We waited all night, then the next and then the next, and he never came back. The guilt over my part in that whole scene ate at me every single day since.

33

Bella

The door to the hospital room is open for the first time since I opened my eyes.

I'm always scared that Adam would walk by and see me. But the last nurse who was in here just forgot to close it. In front of my door sits a man who looks like The Hulk with all his muscles.

But I'm not looking at him. I'm looking at the guy sitting in the chair next to him. The guy I kicked out of my room and my life.

He looks worse than me, and I have broken bones. He looks at me, but his eyes are no longer crystal blue. They're more of a cloudy gray.

I turn away, breaking eye contact, hoping someone else comes in and closes the door so my eyes don't go there.

It is easier to ignore him when I can't see him.

I can't wait until tomorrow when I'm released and don't have to see him or know he is so close.

Every night I feel him close to me, but when I open my eyes I'm always alone.

"Ackson!" I hear my daughter's sweet voice calling to him with obvious affection.

Looking over, I see him smile, holding out his arms as she jumps up into them. The flowers she is holding in her hands get squashed between them.

"Look what I got for Momma. Ms. Brenda says they are pretty just like her."

"No, sweetie, nothing is as pretty as your mom," he tells her while looking at me.

I blink away the tears and turn my head, ignoring the pull to him. Ignoring the need to call him over to hold my hand.

"You go give your momma her flowers." He kisses her head and places her on her feet.

"You stay here?" she asks him.

"Always." Again he is talking straight to me.

"Momma! Momma! Look, flowers," she tells me, skipping and then jumping on my hospital bed near my feet, handing me the crushed bouquet.

"They are so beautiful." I bring them to my nose, inhaling the fresh smell of the daisies.

"You more beautiful. Ackson, come sit with Momma." Lilah waves her hand at him, while I hold my breath.

"Not now, sweetheart, you visit with Momma. I'm going to go get you some of that apple juice and cookies you like," he tells her, getting up and leaving.

Brenda comes in and closes the door. "Thank you," I whisper to her. We haven't spoken yet, but I know I owe her an explanation.

"You look like you are so ready to go home," Brenda says while she puts her purse down on the chair.

"I can't wait," I say and I really can't. I want to be able to go outside and sit on the swing. I want to be able to cook my own food—food that actually has taste.

"I suppose I should tell you someone had a top of the line system installed in your house. With cameras." Brenda sits next to Lilah on the bed.

I shake my head, not even sure how to handle the information she just told me. "I can't do this. I thought I could, Brenda, but I don't think I can. Maybe Lilah and I could start over somewhere else. It won't be easy but..." My voice trails off, Brenda leaning forward to hold my hand.

"You are not letting him run you out of your own home."

The rest of the afternoon passes as normal, Lilah practicing her coloring in the lines while Brenda reads her newest book on her Kindle.

The daytime nurses switch to the evening nurses. When Lilah starts yawning, it's Brenda's cue to start packing up all their stuff.

"We should pack your stuff up since you are leaving tomorrow," Brenda says, gathering all the little things she brought me over the last two weeks.

After she is done, there are five bags filled with stuff.

"You can't bring that to the car and hold Lilah." I look over at her from the chair I'm sitting in, holding Lilah in my arms. It's still difficult with the cast, but I need to get used to it.

"I'll manage. Little heart, why don't you go to the bathroom before we leave, okay?" Brenda tells Lilah before they hit the road.

Lilah carefully climbs off my lap, taking my good hand, and pulling me to the bathroom.

When we finally come out, I see all the bags are gone and Brenda is sitting on the bed. "That was fast."

"Jackson carried them for me." She shrugs her shoulders in a matter-of-fact way.

There is a knock on the door and The Hulk pushes his head inside, saying, "Jackson said you are all good to go." Then quickly leaves.

"Okay, love bug, come give Momma a kiss. Tomorrow I get to come home with you. Maybe we can order pizza." I know just by the way her eyes light up I said the magic word.

"Yeah, pissa," she says while running out of the door, yelling for Jackson. "We gonna get pizza, Jackson," she says when she stops in front of his chair.

He picks her up, placing her on his lap just as the door closes, leaving Brenda and me alone.

"This isn't right, Bella, and you know it." She places her hands on her hips like she normally does.

"Brenda, I..." I start to say.

"You what? You don't want him? That's a lie. You can't trust him? Another lie. I don't know what happened before, and I know it's not the time to push you. But"—she exhales—"there is no way in hell Jackson would do anything to hurt you. Not one thing. Not verbally, not mentally, and definitely not physically."

I shake my head, the tears threatening to fall. My heart beats faster, the pain so strong I have to sit on the bed.

"He hasn't left this hospital since you came in," she continues.

"He lied to me," I say. I know he really didn't because it never came up. But I can't help but feel he knew who I was.

"He sent his mother away," she states, making my head snap up, "when she showed up here looking for Adam. He told her that he would choose you over everyone else." She sits next to me, wrapping her arm around my shoulders. "He loves you. You can't just throw that away."

The tears fall into my lap, landing on my hands.

"Ms. Brenda." We hear Lilah call. "I tired."

We both laugh while I wipe the tears away. She kisses my cheek. "I'll bring you some clothes tomorrow when we bust you loose from this place."

She walks to the door, and I call out to her, "Brenda." She turns and faces me. "Thank you."

"You can thank me by doing right by her"—she points her head in Lilah's direction—"and by doing right by you."

With those words she leaves, closing the door behind her.

Everything is just too much to deal with. My head hurts, my heart aches, and when I finally do crawl into bed right after Brenda leaves, sleep takes over, dragging me into a slumber. In my dream, I feel fingertips gently stroking my hand, butterfly kisses, and most of all, an overwhelming sense of love and peacefulness.

Jackson

I sit in a chair in the dark room, holding her hand and pressing small kisses to it. People would probably look at this and say I need help, but I just need Bella.

Knowing she is going to be released tomorrow is something I don't want to think about. Even if she won't allow me in her room, I sneak in at night just to hold her hand and watch her sleep.

The bruises have faded, and her lip is almost healed with just a touch of scabbing. I would give anything to be able to get into the bed with her just to hold her. Just to feel her next to me.

After the scene at my mother's house, I've been almost lost between the two, and the only thing that really calms me is Bella.

Mick is staying close by, giving me my space, waiting for me to blow up. I know it's coming; he knows it's coming.

The door opens with the night nurse coming in just to check and make sure things are okay.

"Hey, Jackson," she whispers. "It's almost dawn. She should be up soon."

I nod my head, knowing she usually gets up at six or sixty-thirty. I just want to spend every minute with her before I'm no longer able to.

"She's going home today," she continues while she writes things down in the chart. "Did you figure out how you are going to sneak into her house yet?" She laughs silently.

I think it's a running joke with the nurses that I'm going to be like Spiderman and scale her house. If I thought I could do it, I would.

"Very funny." I laugh, also thinking about it.

When Bella starts to moan and her eyes start to flutter, we both stop what we are doing.

I quietly get up, walking into the dark corner right before her eyes open up. "Oh, hey. I thought I felt someone," she says while rubbing her face with her good hand.

"Just me checking your vitals. You excited about going home?" she asks Bella.

"I can't wait. Gotta say these beds suck." They both laugh.

"How about we check the stitches on your head? If they're healed enough, I think we could finally wash that hair of yours. Get the smell of hospital out of it." The nurse has Bella turn her back toward the door, giving me just enough time to sneak out.

"She's up early," Brian, the nighttime security guy, says. He owns the security company that will be watching Bella.

When I called him, he didn't even stop to ask questions. I met Brian four years ago when his seventeen-year-old daughter took off with her boyfriend to get married. Both high on coke, we found them in the middle of the park swimming in the fountain.

Four years later, she's done a stint in rehab and is graduating beauty school.

"Yeah." I rub my hands down my face. "I'm going to take off. Go home and get things ready. You have your guys lined up?" I ask him, but I know he's already ahead of the game.

"I got her. Go home, sleep, maybe fucking shower. It's a good thing these nurses are tripping over their tongues when they see you or they would be wearing masks."

With that, I laugh before turning around and walking out.

Six hours later, I'm rolling up to the hospital freshly showered. Brian wasn't wrong. I stunk!

I don't even think I took my shoes off when I face planted in my bed.

The minute I walk inside I see Bruno, the daytime guard, up next to his chair.

"What's the matter?" I ask him.

"Nothing, boss, just waiting for her to leave. Doctor passed by about an hour ago, signed her papers," he says, looking at his watch.

"Brenda here yet?" I ask, standing next to him, putting my hands in my pockets. Sadness looms over me.

"Yup, got here about fifteen minutes ago." Bruno isn't one to talk much and it's fine.

Mick walks off the elevator five minutes later. "What are you doing here?" I ask him.

"Nothing, just came to check shit out," he says, slapping me on my shoulder. I know he came to make sure I'm okay.

The door opens with Brenda walking out first. Right behind her follows Bella. They washed her hair, and it's now in a side braid. Not a trace of makeup on her face, and I could swear right then and there that she is the most gorgeous person to ever walk the earth.

Her shorts fit her perfectly with her tank top molding her breasts. My dick finally wakes up. She doesn't see me yet, but the minute she does, something flickers in her eyes. I just don't know what it is.

Maybe she's scared of me? Maybe she looks at me and all she can see is Adam and the hatred that she feels?

I push myself off the wall, saying hi to Brenda.

"Ackson, Momma go home," Lilah says next to her mom, smiling while holding a balloon that says 'Get Well Soon'.

"I know, I heard. Are you happy?" I ask her when she just nods her head yes.

She reaches out her hand that is holding the balloon and waits for me to hold her hand. Once I have her hand in mine, she looks at her mother. "Let's go home, Momma."

Bella doesn't say anything to me, her eyes avoiding me at all costs.

Brenda and Mick walk ahead of us with Bruno following behind us.

"We play sand castles, Momma?" Lilah looks over at her, waiting for an answer when her mother just shakes her head no.

She then turns her head in my direction, looking for me to jump on her side. "Maybe when Momma takes a nap, Ms. Brenda can bring you over so you can play." I suggest more for Bella than Lilah. "I'm going into work today, so you can go anytime."

The answer seems to satisfy her for now since she doesn't say anything while we wait for the elevator. Some nurses stop by us while we are waiting to wish Bella well.

The elevator ride down is silent, everyone on alert and unease thick in the air.

"We go Ackson truck, Momma?" Lilah asks when we make it outside.

"No, honey, we are going to take Ms. Brenda's car."

Once we make it to Brenda's car, I see Brenda help Bella into the car, then I go to settle Lilah in her car seat "I'll see you later, princess, take good care of your mom." I kiss her on the nose and close the door the same time Brenda closes the front door.

"Give her time, Jackson, but whatever you do, don't stay away."

With those parting words, she gets in her car and drives off, leaving Mick and me standing in the parking lot.

"Let's go get you something strong to drink. Fuck, I think I need it more than you do after that scene," he says while walking away.

We end up at our favorite watering hole where I nurse a beer for six hours while Mick drowns himself in a bottle of Jack.

The messages I receive from Brenda have my mind at ease. They are both home. Settling in. Brian is outside, sending me hourly updates.

By the time we make it out into the darkness, I carry Mick into my truck and dump him off on his couch while he keeps talking in his sleep. No idea what he's saying, but I'm sure he obviously owes someone an apology since he's been muttering 'I'm so sorry' over and over.

By the time I park my truck in my driveway, I look over at the house that is pitch-black.

I know the alarm is set since it sends my phone a notification when she turns it on and off.

I wave to Brian, who sits in his car while I go sit on the swing outside of her house.

I can't even explain what is going on; my feet just led me here. So here I sit outside, knowing just inside those doors lies the woman who has taken over my mind, heart, and my fucking soul.

35

Bella

I lie awake, staring outside while Lilah sleeps next to me.

I know I should be sleeping, but it's almost like I'm so excited to be home that I just can't turn it off.

As soon as I stepped into the house, I knew things were different. The first thing was the alarm beeping while Brenda put in her code. She turned and looked at me. "We each have our own code so they can see who turns it on and off."

I looked around the house, taking in the alarm panel at the door as well as all the cameras in each and every single corner.

Brenda walked over to the computer screen right next to the television and switched it on. The screen filled with small squares from every room in my house. Lilah must love this because she ran over to the middle of the room. "Momma, watch me on the television." She then squatted down, shaking her bum while trying to dance.

I sat down on the couch when the front door opened again and it was followed by a ding dong. "What is that?"

"Every door has its own sound so you know where it's coming from," Brenda explained while telling Hulk to put the things on the table. "If you go out the back door, it does this." She opened the back door to a sound of beep beep.

I looked around at all that and waited for someone to jump out and tell me they were kidding.

"What is going on right now?" I asked more the universe than anyone else, but Lilah climbed up next to me.

"Ackson make me safe, Momma, for you," she said almost matter-of-fact.

"Yes, baby, he made you safe," I said to her. The love she had for Jackson was apparent, and let's face it, he was her family.

"There is also a sound when you open and close certain doors that lead outside," Brenda continued saying, "and there are panic buttons in every single room. They're silent, by the way." She looked over at Lilah. "She tested them yesterday. You would think the President of the United States was coming with all the cars that got here."

I looked over at her with my mouth open. "What do you mean?"

"Jackson may have gone a little overboard, but he has it hooked up to every single law enforcement agency in the area. He also included the fire department and paramedics." She looked at me like that was normal. "Oh, and of course, the security detail that's surrounding you."

The police, a security detail, firemen, paramedics...he had lost his mind.

I let out a yawn while listening to Brenda speak about everything. I may not be in tip top shape, but I was still worn out.

"Lilah, why don't we take a nap?" I tried to coax her into napping with me so I could have some shut-eye.

"No nap, Momma, sand castles?" she asked me while she grabbed my cheeks so she could look into my eyes.

"Oh, you go on up there and take a nap. I'll take her across the street so she can play," Brenda said while putting away the breakfast plates that were left drying.

"Brenda, it's too much, you must be exhausted." I thought about this woman who had stepped up and taken my daughter and me into

her life with no hesitation. Who never gave a second thought, just stepped up and took care of my daughter while I was in the hospital.

She shooed me off with a, "Please, I've never felt younger in my life." She grabbed Lilah's hat and sunscreen.

"You go nap. I'm going to go build some castles with my little heart."

With that the two of them were gone, leaving me all alone. I didn't know if it was the fact that I knew I was as well guarded and protected as Fort Knox, but I didn't feel scared anymore.

Once I made my way upstairs, I started to look for the panic button just in case.

My nap ended up being a deep, restful four-hour sleep which is probably why I'm not tired now.

I make my way to the window, looking outside. I take in the security car parked right in front of my door. I also notice Jackson is home, his truck parked in the driveway while his house sits as dark as the night.

I pull on a robe, making my way downstairs. I grab myself the throw blanket I have on the couch with a pillow. I know one thing will make me tired—watching the stars.

Making sure to enter my code before opening the door, I step out onto the porch, turning to the swing.

I stop in my tracks when I see the blue eyes I can't seem to let go of staring back at me.

"What are you doing here?" I ask him, holding the stuff to my chest to stop my heart from beating faster than normal.

"You're here," he whispers to me.

Jackson

I sit in the swing and look up at the stars as I wonder how the fuck I'm going to get through to her.

I'm on the swing for a few minutes when my phone buzzes in my pocket. I look at it and see an alert advising me the front door has been unarmed.

I don't know if I should walk home or stay and let the chips fall where they may.

As soon as I see her walking outside with a blanket and pillow, I know she was coming to lie outside.

She stops in her tracks when she sees me.

"What are you doing here?" she asks, bringing the cover and pillow to her chest.

I don't know what to say, so I say the only thing that comes close to the truth.

"You're here," I whisper to her.

"You should go," she tells me but doesn't move.

"You have to listen to me," I beg. I put my elbows on my knees and hide my frustration and nerves by running my fingers through my hair. "Please." I sigh.

"I kicked him out of my mother's house when he was sixteen," I start there, hoping she lets me continue. "For seven years, I searched for him. It's the reason I went into law enforcement. It's the reason I take every case involving missing children and drugs that comes across my desk. It's the reason I'm me." I shake my head. "I sat at the dinner table *every single night* with my mother. Looking into her sad eyes, knowing she blamed me for kicking him out and sending him away. She never said it like that, but I felt it. I vowed to find him and bring him home. For her. But I failed. I never found him."

She places the blanket and pillow on the swing, sitting on the other side of it.

"I let him down, and I let my mother down. My father had just been killed in the line of duty, and we all handled it badly. Instead of stepping up to be the man of the house like I should have, I was out doing what any other normal eighteen-year-old would do. I knew he was hanging with the wrong crowd, but I didn't realize just how wrong they were. I never, ever imagined he would get into drugs. *Ever*. I walked in on him with a needle in his arm, and the next day I chased him out of the house."

"Jackson," she whispers, shivering with either the breeze or the story, and I grab the blanket and wrap it around her.

"When I saw you in the alley with him on top of you…" Tears burn my eyes, ready to fall. "I just reacted and ripped him right off of you. When I saw his face and realized it was Adam, I thought I was imagining things. Seeing my brother, who I thought was dead, for the first time in seven years was too much. But all of that on top of what he was doing to you, who he was to you. I just snapped." The tears I had been trying to hold back start to fall down my face. "I saw your blood on his hands, and I was filled with such rage. I knew right then and there I was going to kill him." I hold my hands together to still the rage that courses through me at the memory.

She reaches over and places her hand on top of my own. "Don't say that."

"You have to know I had no idea who you were. I swear to you, on my life, I would never lie to you."

The tears flow down her face now. The blanket slips off one of her shoulders. I reach out to pull it back into place, and my fingers graze her collarbone. Such a slight, simple touch, but her body responds with goose bumps.

"I can't lose you, Bella. You own me. My heart, my body, my soul. Everything is yours. Sitting by your bed, watching you fight for your life knowing my brother did that to you, I can't tell you what it did to me. I can't explain it. It was worse than looking into my mother's eyes across the table all these years." I move a bit closer to her. "I would give my life for yours, I would give—"

She stops me by placing her fingers on my lips. "Don't say it," she softly whispers to me.

"I can't leave you. I can't walk away. If I have to sit out here every single night just to be near you, I will." Her face is so close to mine, if I lean just a bit closer to her, our lips would touch, but I don't want to push her.

I wipe a tear from the corner of her eye with my thumb. "What do I have to do to make you see I didn't lie to you, not now, not fucking ever?" I plead with her. "What is it going to take to see you smile at me again with that light in your eyes?"

"I don't know if I can do this," she says to me honestly.

"I sat by your bed all night, every night, holding your hand in mine just so I could feel your heartbeat under my fingers." I brush my fingers along her wrist to show her what I mean. "Every single night, our heartbeats would match, if only for the night."

"It was you?" she asks, a little bit shocked, but not totally surprised.

"I never left your side, not for one minute. I would never leave your side, Bella." I pick up her hand and kiss her wrist where I had been stroking it.

She moves closer to me, her crossed leg resting on my thigh. "I felt you." Her fingers trace the interlocking tattoo on my arm. "I didn't know then it was you, but I suspected." Her eyes come up to meet mine. "I felt peaceful in a way that I have never felt before then." She scoots closer as I pull my hand from hers to let it rest on the back of the swing, giving her the choice to come to me.

"I felt safe, I felt whole, I felt love. Even as I slipped in and out of consciousness, I heard you there. Felt you there. I believe you." She leans in and kisses me. Softly, gently, with love, like an angel. Like the angel she is.

37

Bella

As soon as I found him on the swing, I saw in his eyes the pain he was in.

I knew the storm he was fighting within himself. Then he bared his soul to me. Shed his demons to me, opened himself to me.

I knew in that moment I loved him. I knew he would lay down his life for mine and for Lilah's. I knew he hadn't lied to me and he never would. I knew that in his arms, I would never feel fear.

It was also in that moment I took the second biggest leap of faith in my life. For me, for him, for us.

I also knew I had to be the one to make the first move. I had to show him that I chose him. That I believed him.

The minute I felt his lips against mine, I knew it was a kiss that would seal our fate in a way. It was a promise to each other, a commitment to take this leap of faith with each other. It was a promise that when things got difficult, instead of pushing him away, I'd be pulling him closer.

I let the kiss linger for a minute or two. I grab the pillow and get up. He looks up at me in confusion until I hold my hand out to him from beneath the blanket and say, "Let's go to bed, Jackson."

Even in the darkness, I can see the relief shining in his eyes. He follows me inside, bringing in the pillow since my other hand is holding on to his with a vise-like grip.

He puts in his code as soon as the door closes. "Why am I not surprised you got your own code?" I smile at him teasingly.

"I almost had them put the camera feed on my television, but, apparently, there are laws against that." He smiles back at me sheepishly while throwing the pillow onto the couch.

I walk upstairs with him, but he stops. "What about Lilah?" he asks me.

"It's okay, Jackson. Brenda got her used to her own bed, so mine is all free." I get on my tippy toes to kiss under his chin.

"That bed will never be empty."

"Okay then. Now can we please, please go to bed? I'm so tired," I say, trying to hide the yawn that sounds exactly like Lilah's earlier.

"Go get into bed. I'm going to make sure Lilah is okay and check the doors and windows."

I look at him. "You have this place more wired than Radio Shack. She's fine."

"Let me see for myself." He walks over to her room, slipping inside, and covering her with her pink blanket she kicked off.

"She is only going to kick it off again," I tell him while he starts to check the windows.

I follow him out of the room once he does all of his security checks.

"What side of the bed do you sleep on?" he asks me before choosing his side.

I shrug. "I don't really have a side. We would just sleep in the middle."

"Okay. I would like to sleep closest to the door, just in case someone comes in or we have to bolt. I'll be able to get Lilah before you even get up," he says, throwing off the covers.

"Do you want to shower first?" I ask him just in case he's shy.

"You saying I smell, angel?" he says while he takes off his shirt. I cannot stop my eyes from their perusal of his chest and tight abs.

When we were on the couch, I never really got the chance to actually look at him. He is all hard muscle and smooth skin. His abs are flawless with those six definitions of perfection.

"You like what you see, angel?" he asks with a lightness I haven't heard from him in so long.

It snaps me back into the moment, and I realize I'm standing here gawking at him. I try to play it off, throwing the covers off my side of the bed. "No, I was just looking is all."

"Oh, you don't have to stop looking, but I have to warn you that if you do, my chest and abs won't be the only muscles hardening up for you," he says, pointing to the big bulge in his pants. "Mr. Big will definitely pop up to say hello."

"You named your penis Mr. Big?" I say while I grab a chopstick from my side table to scratch inside the cast on my arm. "I mean, what if you aren't Mr. Big? How do you know you're not more like Mr. Average?" I tease him, knowing how men get about their penis size.

"I can totally show it to you right here right now for research purposes, angel. Trust me, there's nothing average about Mr. Big," he says as he unbuckles his pants.

I turn my head, shielding my eyes. "Okay, okay! I believe you. We can save show and tell for another day, please." I crawl into bed on my knees.

"Angel, do you want me to keep my jeans on?" he asks, making sure I'm comfortable with the speed this is going.

"You would never take advantage of a one-handed woman, so you can take the jeans off. Mr. Big has to stay under wraps, though." I point the chopstick at his crotch.

"What the fuck are you doing with a chopstick in here?" he asks me.

"This cast is itchy! I can't scratch it, so Brenda brought me this. You try having an itch you can't scratch!" I tell him tartly.

He shuts off the lights before removing his pants. "Oh, trust me, I know the feeling of having an itch and not being able to scratch it," he says while he climbs into bed.

"I have to sleep on my back because of my arm," I whisper to him.

He pulls me to him, putting one hand under the pillows and throwing his other hand over my stomach. His legs intertwine with mine. "I don't care how you sleep as long as I can hold you," he says while he tries to get closer to me, but my arm blocks him.

I put my hand on his on my stomach, turning my face to look at him. "I missed you, and I'm so sorry for not listening to you at first and for pushing you away," I tell him. It's the truth. In these last two days, he was the only one I wanted here.

"Not being able to be in that room when you were awake was hard. Watching you finally get better, but not being there to hold your hand while you did it was painful, but I didn't care as long as you got better, as long as you were healing." His hand folds together with mine.

"Every time the door would open, I would force myself not to look outside just in case you really did leave me like I asked. I pushed you away, yet I was scared you would actually listen to me and go," I whisper to him in the dark, quiet room.

The only sounds in the room right now are our breathing, the sound of my heart beating in my chest, and the sounds of his soft snore as he drifts to sleep.

I lie awake again, this time because of the overwhelming peace and happiness I feel. The feel of his body next to mine, his hand in mine, his heart beating under my thumb, this is the feeling when your heart is filled to overflowing with happiness. That delirious happiness that sends people running up and down the street with their arms flailing all around them. It's a good feeling.

I feel him kiss my shoulder, his head coming almost on my pillow. He hums softly then slowly I hear the telltale signs he has fallen asleep once again.

And in the darkness of this room, which was so empty when I first got here, but is now filled with pictures, filled with life and filled with love, I finally, *finally*, let myself go and follow him into sleep.

38

Jackson

It's the second day since we finally cleared the air between us. It's also the second day I woke up with a knee to the balls courtesy of Lilah.

It seems she gets super excited when she sees us in bed together in the morning. So excited she jumps on the bed knees first right into the jewels.

I didn't realize waking up with Bella would come with an ache in my balls that didn't have to do with the woman lying next to me.

But now I stand in the kitchen, leaning against the counter drinking my morning coffee, looking at the little girl who owns the other part of my heart –Lilah.

She sits eating her waffles with extra syrup because 'Momma says it okay,' which I know is a lie.

I hear the shower turn off the same time I hear a key in the front door.

Brenda makes her way inside. "Good morning, my little heart," she says, heading straight to Lilah and dropping a kiss on her head. "Jackson." She nods at me while reaching to get a cup for coffee.

We don't say much and just enjoy the quiet. Bella comes downstairs, her hair still wet from the shower. "Good morning, Brenda." Walking toward the coffee pot, her cup is already sitting on the counter.

She stops in front of me, her eyes looking up.

Bending down, I place a kiss on her lips. "Good morning, angel."

She quickly kisses me, moving on to join Lilah and Brenda at the table.

I take my phone out and check my messages. I'm going back into work today after taking the last couple of weeks off. It's a good thing I had lots of vacation days saved up.

I get a message from Mick saying he'll be in by one. I send him back a quick text, telling him I'll already be in. Looking at my watch, I see it's almost nine.

"Okay, beautiful ladies, it's time to get back to the hustle and bustle," I tell them while I put my mug in the sink.

"Girl party!" Brenda yells and throws her hands up in the air. Of course Lilah mimics her, but with the addition of syrup dripping all over her from the fork still clutched in her hand.

I laugh at them while Bella groans into her cup. "Whatever you do, you lock the door, yeah?" I look at all three of them, waiting for one of them to answer me.

"Yes, sir," Bella says.

"Aye aye, captain." Brenda salutes me, leaning forward to snatch a piece of waffle before it falls on the floor.

I lean down to kiss Bella's cheek, and then over to the other side to kiss Lilah's head.

Brenda puts her elbows on the table, cradling her chin in her hands as she looks up at me with puckered lips and says, "Put it there, hot stuff."

Bella bursts out laughing.

"You kiss Ms. Brenda, Ackson?" Lilah asks while she tries to lick the syrup dripping down her chin.

I walk over, placing a big lip smacking kiss on Brenda's cheek. "Be good, you guys," I say as I walk out of the house.

There is a new security guy sitting in his car watching the area. I walk up to him as he's stepping out of his car.

"Morning. Anything abnormal?" I ask him, almost holding my breath. Since Adam left the hospital, it's been smooth sailing, but I'm not letting my guard down this time.

I didn't know what I was dealing with before. Now that I do, I'll be damned if I'm going to let him get close to them again.

"Nothing. I walked the perimeter and nothing seems to be disturbed. The guy will be coming by today to put in the outdoor motion detectors."

"Good. Call me if anything happens." I turn to make my way to my truck. Driving all the way to work feels good. Getting back will be good also.

Once I get back behind my desk, I grab Lori's file and see if there are any more notes that have been entered while I was away.

One more phone call, nothing traced back. I take out my phone and shoot a quick text to Mick.

What happened with Marissa?

His reply comes back fast.

Nothing happened with her. Why? Did she say something did?

His response makes me frown as I try to decipher his words.

Where are you?

This is obviously a conversation better had face to face.

On my way!

I throw my phone down, but then I see a message from Bella that came in while I was putting it down.

Missing you ;)

I smile at seeing her name. Two words from her and my whole day just got a little bit brighter.

Holding her all night. Waking up with her in my arms. Just being in her presence, it's everything.

Miss you more. Hope you're resting.

I'm still smiling when I hear whistling coming down the hall.

"Looks like you got that situation taken care of!" Mick says while he slides into his chair across from me. Our desks are connected in a small corner of the big office.

"So what's the story?" I ask him, not even bothering to take the bait on his greeting.

"No story, nothing." He leans back in his chair, folding his hands on his chest, but his eyes tell a different story.

"Where is she now?" I ask him, knowing he knows who I'm talking about.

"Got a job waitressing at the diner across the street. Phyllis owed me a favor. I cashed in."

"You cashed in a favor for someone you don't even like?"

"It was your fault she got fired, so technically I cashed in a favor so your ass wouldn't feel guilty." He points at me. "You're welcome."

I turn the subject around.

"Lori called again?"

"She did, same MO as before. Crying, asking for help, begging to come back. Lasted maybe a minute. Then nothing." He sits back up. "I don't like this shit. I think there is more than meets the eye here. Something else is going on. I just can't pinpoint it," he says, and I have to say I agree with him. This isn't just another case of a teen running away to be with friends. There's more to it. We just can't see it.

"Where was she when she got the call this time?" I ask him, trying to see if maybe there is some other similarity to the last call, hoping to find a dot to connect.

"My house, having dinner."

My eyebrow shoots up. "Your house having dinner? Do I have to say thank you for that one also?"

"Don't make it out to be more than it is. She came by to thank me for getting her the job and putting in a good word with Phyllis." He starts pulling papers out of a pile, pretending to be looking for something, but I know he's just doing it to avoid making eye contact with me so I don't see what he is hiding.

"Okay, so she came over to thank you. Did you fuck her?"

His head snaps up, an angry glare aimed at me.

"Watch it! I didn't fuck her. I ordered food, we sat down, she got the call. She obviously freaked out, made a hole in my rug trying to get Lori to talk to her. The call ended, she calmed down, and then she left."

"Just like that, she left? I saw her the last time Lori called. She couldn't stop shaking. How long did it take her this time?" I know there is more to this story. I also know he's evading my questions, and I want to know why.

"Sandie showed up. Ten minutes after the call." He finally lets out the breath he has been holding. Shaking his head, he continues, "Raincoat, naked. Marissa saw and bolted, okay? There, now you got the story. She hasn't talked to me since."

"You know we need to go see her, right? You know we need to follow up?" I don't need to tell him, but I do it anyway.

"I know," he whispers then looks up. "I didn't touch her. We just ate dinner. That's it."

"You don't have to convince me of anything. I don't think you would cross the line."

He nods his head. "Another girl went missing two nights ago." He thrusts the paper at me.

"What's this one?" I ask him while studying the picture of the blond teenager in front of me.

"Name is Jessica, seventeen. Divorced parents. One week with the mother, one week with the father. Started hanging with a new guy on the scene. No one knows him. Just his name. Robbie. Met in secret every time. Not even her best friend knows him or what he looks like. Mother found a bag of weed, punished her for the week. She left to go to the father's, but she never showed up there. He didn't notice until she didn't answer her mother two days later. Mother called the father. He said she texted him saying she was staying at her mom's for a couple extra days. Phone goes straight to voicemail, and it appears the SIM card has been taken out since she had the 'find my phone' app open and now no one can trace her."

"What about school? Any leads there? Did she start hanging with a different crowd?" I ask, looking over at all her details. Five foot seven, one hundred seven pounds.

"Nada, best friend said she met this new guy at the mall when she went shopping. Got smitten, started texting like crazy. From that moment on, all her time was spent with him. All Jessica told her was that he was older, drove a car and 'was hot as fuck,' which, by the way, was a direct quote in case you're wondering."

"Any connection with Lori?" I ask.

"Just the fact they both met a mystery guy no one else has met."

I spend the rest of the day going through the database, running different parameters, searching different names to see if maybe someone else is also working on the case. I call up the gang unit to see if maybe this is gang related. I come up empty.

After sitting and staring at the computer for more than seven hours, I look over at Mick. "Maybe we're looking at this the wrong way."

He looks up at me. "What do you mean?"

"Maybe they didn't run away at all. What if they were taken?"

He shrugs. "At this point it could be anything. We have nothing, not even a fucking description of what the guy—or guys—looks like. It's like we're chasing a fucking ghost."

I nod my head, thinking the exact thing. "What about the cameras from the mall? I know it's a long shot, but maybe we can catch a glimpse of him so we have a visual of who we're looking for."

"Good idea. I'll contact the security office in the morning. I know the exact date they met because she sent a text to her best friend going apeshit over him."

"Sounds like a plan. Any leads on Adam?" I ask, knowing I'm not supposed to, but I do anyway.

He looks around, making sure no one is in earshot before he speaks quietly. "Nothing. He's gone. I doubt he's going to come back."

"I still want to know where he's living."

"I know."

I close down my computer as I pick up my phone, noticing a couple of messages came in while I was in my own world.

The first one is from Brenda. It's a picture of Bella and Lilah sitting outside, the sun on their faces, their smiles big and bright. I save it to my pictures, making it my home screen.

The second is from my mother asking if she can come over for a visit. I pass over that one, looking at the next one from Bella asking what I want to eat. I think it's too soon to reply that I would love to eat her.

So my answer is a simple. *Whatever you want.*

I tell Mick to call me if anything comes up, and I head out to get home. I don't go over to Bella's house right away, instead going to mine.

Grabbing the mail at the door, I make my way into the kitchen, tossing it on the table, and grabbing a beer from the fridge. I pop it open and take a long pull.

I'm here maybe ten minutes, sorting through the mail, chucking a good portion of the junk. Taking another pull off my beer, I hear a knock on the door.

Going to the door, I open it to find Bella on the other side, all by herself.

"Hey." I grab her by the waist, pulling her inside. I close the door behind her, pinning her against it. Her surprised gasp gives me the opening I need.

My mouth crashes down on hers with a need I haven't felt before. I knew I missed her today, but I didn't realize how much until I saw her standing there.

My tongue slides into her mouth, and I taste strawberries as her tongue softly moves with mine.

My hand roams down to her ass. A light squeeze there communicates my intent, and she responds by wrapping her legs around my waist as I lift her up. Her casted arm lies over my shoulder while the other hand snakes into my hair, pulling on it.

"Missed you so much," I tell her as I break the kiss, slowly moving to her chin as I work my way down to her neck. She moves her head to the side, giving me complete access.

"Missed you, too. I came to ask if you are eating dinner with us."

"Mmm-hmm." I continue working her neck, biting it gently, and then I move back to kissing her.

Cradled right against her heat, my cock is rock hard and ready. I press further into her, and I feel her shudder in my arms. She pulls on my hair to look into my eyes. "I want you," she whispers and leans forward to kiss my lips. She kisses her way down my chin to my neck, mimicking what I just did to her.

Right as I'm about to attack her mouth again, there is another knock on the door. "I swear to God, I am going to shoot whoever is knocking on this door," I tell her while I set her down on her feet.

"Maybe it's Brenda and Lilah. I did say I was just coming over for a minute and would be right back," she tells me while I turn the knob and open the door, coming face to face with someone I'm not ready to see yet.

My mother.

39

Bella

When I hear the knock on the door, I want to cry or maybe scream. Either way, I'm just as frustrated as Jackson.

When the door opens, staring in at us is Jackson's mother. Adam's mother.

I knew I would have to face her eventually. I just didn't think it would be this soon. I certainly didn't think it would be as she interrupted her son kissing the life out of me.

"Mom, what are you doing here?" he asks her as the smile falls from her lips.

"I tried sending you a message. You didn't answer me, so I came to see you," she says, wringing her hands anxiously. She is obviously nervous to see her son and because she's forced that by showing up unannounced.

Looking past him, her eyes, bright with surprise, land on me. "Oh, Bella," she says, pushing past Jackson. She comes right to me, taking me into her arms for a hug.

My arms are glued to my side. My eyes find Jackson's.

She finally pulls back, holding my arms in her hands. "I was so worried about you and Lilah." When she says Lilah's name, my head snaps. My spine goes straight as do my shoulders.

Jackson must sense the change because he makes his way over to me. Putting his arm around me, he tries to give me strength.

"Mom, now isn't a good time. I don't think Bella is ready for a family reunion."

I lean into him, and he takes almost all of my weight, practically holding me up.

"I'm so, so sorry. Please, I won't take much of your time." She looks at me. It's a look from one mother to another, pleading with me to give her the time.

"Mom," Jackson starts.

"It's okay," I say. "It was bound to happen. Might as well get it over with now." My arms wrap around his waist.

"Fine, but when I say it's over, it's over." He looks from me to his mother. "She's healing, remember that."

She doesn't say anything and just nods.

We walk into his living room where she sits down on one love seat, and we sit on the other one facing her.

"I don't know where to start," she says. "I had this whole speech planned out. All the words ready, but the minute I saw you, my mind went blank." She looks around for the Kleenex box, finds it, and grabs one.

"He wasn't always a monster," she starts, and I know exactly who she is talking about. "He was a terror, that is for sure. I'm telling you, by the age of seven, he already had four broken bones. He was afraid of nothing," she says while she dabs her eyes.

Jackson pulls my hand into his, intertwining our fingers in a show of unity.

"He took his father's death the hardest. It was at a time in his life where he needed guidance, and there was no one there for him."

Jackson clears his throat, drawing her gaze to him.

"I mean, Jackson did try, but it wasn't the same. I admit I checked out a little at first. Losing Frank was devastating. He was the love of my life, and continuing my life without him was so hard, but I had no choice. I had two boys to raise. Or, really just one."

Tears fill my eyes at the sound of her voice cracking when she tells me about their father. The love they shared is clearly apparent even after all this time. Their shared devastation made them into the people they are today.

I don't say anything because, frankly, there isn't anything to say right now.

"I saw changes in him, but I ignored them. I just thought he was going through a phase. He was angry at first, so very angry. He punched a couple of holes in the wall." She looks over at Jackson, the surprise of her admission evident on his face.

"I never told you because I didn't want to make a big deal out of it." She shakes her head. "I'm not making excuses for him. I'm just trying to show you he's not the Adam we knew. The Adam you met, he isn't the sweet little boy who used to pick dandelions and bring them home and profess his love for me." The image of Adam she is painting is nothing like the man I knew.

"He's not the monster you think he is. It's the drugs that make him like that. He needs help." It's the last thing she says before I interrupt her.

"The first time he hit me was because Lilah was crying too much, and he hadn't had a hit for a few hours," I say, my voice strong. "There were a few good memories, in the beginning, but nothing could possibly outweigh the bad. I'm sorry, but there isn't anything you can say that will make what he did to me okay. There is no excuse for it, and drugs weren't to blame." I look over at Jackson, silently asking for permission to tell her why I left. He silently nods at me.

"I'm sorry, Nancy, but your son will always be a monster in my eyes, and he is a very real monster to Lilah. The night before we escaped, he was getting high, as usual. We were hiding in the bedroom, and she needed to pee. We tried to walk around him and his friends, who spent the day getting high." I look down at my lap, not sure if I can do this, but Jackson squeezes my hand and that's all the encouragement I need.

"He needed money for more drugs, so he sold me to his dealer for his next fix. They tied me to the bed, where he beat me and then raped me all night long. All the while Lilah was locked in a dark closet with no food, no water, scared out of her mind. That is who Adam Fletcher is to us. He's not the dandelion-giving, love-professing boy you raised anymore. He is the monster who terrorized me and my daughter for years."

Tears are streaming down her face, a nonstop flow that she cannot stop with the Kleenex in her hand.

"That is the man you are sitting there trying to defend to me. I was not his wife or his girlfriend. I was his victim. But no more. I have Jackson now. He is the one who fought with my demons. He showed me not all men are monsters." Looking right into his eyes, I say, "He is, without a doubt, the best thing to ever happen to me."

I don't even finish talking before he bends down, kissing me.

"I love you," he whispers in my ear. "You are so brave."

"I'm so sorry," Nancy says. "I…I had no idea what you two went through. That my son put you, put his daughter, Lilah, through that." She shakes with the force of her sobs.

I get up and go to comfort her. Not for Adam but for Jackson.

I sit next to her, and we both hug each other as we cry. She, for the son she lost, and me, for the monster I escaped.

I don't know how long this goes on, but the doorbell rings three times in a row. When Jackson opens the door, Lilah marches in grumbling. "I starbing, and Ms. Brenda says no eating till you come home." She is followed in by a smiling Brenda.

As soon as she sees my face and tears, Brenda's expression changes. She's in mother bear mode, ready to battle. She moves to stand by me, but I smile at her to let her know it's okay.

"Lilah, come say hi to Ms. Nancy." I hold out my arms for her, and she sits on my lap.

"Hi, Ms. Nancy, you hubry?"

"Umm, I am quite hungry. What did you cook?" she asks her, gently stroking her hand over Lilah's hair.

"I no cook, but Momma cooked her chili for Ackson," she says matter-of-factly.

"Really? That's my favorite. Do you think I can come over and eat, too?" She looks from Lilah to me, making sure it's okay.

I smile, nodding my head and bringing Lilah closer to me. "We would love for you to join us."

"Okay, let's go eat," Lilah says, jumping off me and heading over to Brenda to take her hand, pulling her toward the door.

I get up and reach out to take Nancy's hand. "I suggest we go before she eats all the corn bread."

She places her hand in mine, and we walk over to my house where she spends the rest of the night getting to know her granddaughter. I spend the rest of the night falling more in love with her son.

Jackson

It's been six weeks since I found her beaten in that alley, and today is the day she finally gets her cast off.

It's been three weeks of us being together whenever I am not working. I spend every night with her, no matter what time I get in. I always go straight to her bed.

I also have a serious case of blue balls. My showers have gone from warm to fucking ice cold.

Every single day is some form of torture. It's getting harder and harder not to push her. Right now, for example, we are sitting in her doctor's office. She is wearing a flowery summer dress, and I know the only thing she has under it is a lacy thong.

She is also getting more comfortable with me. Coming out of the shower in just a towel, and she's not so quick to cover up when I come in and she's changing.

The doctor calls her in and cuts off her cast. Opening it up, the powder dust is all over her legs. The doctor throws the cast in the garbage and then examines her wrist. It looks so fragile. The skin is a yellowish color from being in the cast for so long.

He makes her bend it left to right and then back and forth. His examination takes a good ten minutes before he gives her his instructions. "Looks good. It'll be sore for the next few days since it's been immobile, but you should be back to normal soon."

With a nod, he walks out of the room. Bella keeps moving it in circles, getting it working again.

"How does it feel?" I ask her from my spot against the wall so as not to get in the way.

"I don't know yet. Come here and let me try something."

Walking to her, I see something in her eyes I don't think I've ever seen.

Once I make it to the examining table, I move between her legs. I'm waiting for her to put her hand in my hair or under my shirt, but instead she palms my dick. Squeezes it just a bit, just enough he almost wakes up to a full salute.

"Umm." I look at her and now I get what that look in her eyes is. It's lust, it's want, it's need.

"Brenda is keeping Lilah tonight. They are going to visit her friend and stay in a hotel all night ordering room service and movies. Brenda was more excited than Lilah."

I swallow the huge rock that seems to be blocking my airways right now.

"We don't have to do anything you're not ready to do." I push her hair behind her ears so I can see her whole face.

"I want you, Jackson. I want to do this with you. Don't you want me, too?" She looks up at me, and I can see the vulnerability in her eyes.

"I want nothing more than to make love to you. I've dreamed about it. I've fantasized about it," I tell her while holding her face in my hands and kissing her.

"Then let's get out of here." She pushes me away to jump off the examining table as she grabs her purse and pulls me out of the room.

I'm in the car driving, and I'm a nervous wreck. It's almost like this is my first time.

I don't want to push myself on her. I want to go slow with her. I want to cherish her. I want to worship her.

We make it home in almost record time. Turning off the truck, I look over at her. "You can always change your mind."

She turns her body, putting her back to the door. "I know I can, and I know if I do you will stop. But I don't want to stop this time. I want it to be you." Without waiting for my answer, she turns to open the door and is practically sprinting into the house.

Dumping the purse at the door, she turns around. "Can you give me ten minutes, maybe fifteen, before you come up?" Then she runs up the stairs, leaving me here silently laughing.

I lock the door, close the curtains, check the windows, and fifteen minutes later, or maybe thirteen—I don't know at this point as it was the longest window check I ever did in my life—I head upstairs.

My palms are sweaty with nerves, my heart beating so fast I can hear it thumping in my ears.

Her bedroom door is closed, so I knock once, turning the handle, and walking in.

The sight that greets me makes me stop. The room is dark with candles lit everywhere on every single surface. Tall candles, short candles, the glow bathing the room in a warm yellow.

The bed is made all in white, which is different from the brown cover that was on her bed this morning. All of that takes a backseat, though, to the woman standing in the middle of the room.

Holding her hands in front of her, I can see her chest rising and falling with each breath she takes.

Her blonde hair cascades down around her shoulders. But as I take in what she's wearing, I'm almost brought to my knees.

She stands before me in white. A white lace bra holds her now fuller breasts, a tiny blue bow nestled between the soft swells of her cleavage. This bra is more like a cropped tank top, the lace extending down from her breasts and clinging to her torso, stopping just above her belly button.

A slash of skin separates the top from the panties. I trail my eyes along her tight, flat stomach and down to the matching panties. A sheer, lacy triangle is all that hides her from me.

She looks like a vision in white. She is a fucking wet dream, and she looks like a fucking angel. My angel.

I can't find the words to tell her how beautiful she is. I just stare at her, calming my nerves and barely restraining myself from picking her up and throwing her on the bed.

"Brenda bought this for me. I know I don't fill it out right." She looks down at herself, folding her arms over her stomach. "I also have stretch marks," she says in a soft whisper, looking to the side.

I walk into the room, closing the door behind me. No one will ever see her like this, except me.

"You're beautiful." I make my way to her, afraid to touch her. Afraid this isn't really happening, afraid I'll wake up, and it'll all be a dream. A fucking great dream, but a dream nonetheless.

I trace my finger along the top of the bra, and my touch makes her shiver. "You're so fucking perfect." I lean down, kissing her neck, feeling her racing heart beat under my lips.

"I don't deserve you. I don't deserve anything you have to give me," I say as I trail kisses along her neck, "but I'm not walking away from you." Her hands grab my shirt, bunching it in her fists. "You're my perfect, you're my salvation, and you're my everything."

I kiss her on her lips, dragging my tongue across them right before I invade her mouth. The kiss starts out gentle, soft, but it slowly builds into frantic, fast, hard, needy.

"I think you have too many clothes on." She breaks the kiss, sliding her hands under my T-shirt, pulling it up and off of me.

Her fingertips trace along the tattoos on my chest. My cock sprung to life the moment I laid eyes on her, and it's throbbing now. She follows her fingers with her tongue as I drop my head on a groan.

"The first time I saw you without a shirt, that night I dreamed of doing this to you," she tells me while placing little butterfly kisses on my chest.

Her hands snake to the button on my jeans, opening it slowly lowering the zipper. "Can Mr. Big come out and play?" She laughs while kissing and biting my nipple.

"Oh, he's coming out to play all right." And it's in that moment I remember I have no condoms.

I step back away from her hands before I shoot off in her hand. Her startled look breaks me. "I'm sorry. I went too fast," she stutters, shaking her hands on the side of her hips.

"No, angel, it's not that. I don't have any protection. I mean, I didn't think this was going to happen today." I grab my hair in my hands, ready to pull my own hair out.

"I'm on an IUD. I have been since Lilah was born. I know that"— she looks down at her hands clasped in front of her—"that I was, um, with that guy, but I've been tested." She wipes away a tear with the back of her hand. "I understand if you don't trust me." Another tear falls down her cheek, this one wiped away by me as I lift her face to look into her eyes.

"I'm clean. I've never been without one. I don't want to have anything between us. I want just you. I want just me. I want it to be just us," I tell her. "Is that okay, angel?"

She places a kiss right over my heart. "Yes, Jackson. That's perfect."

41

Bella

He places me gently in the middle of the bed. I sink into the fluffy, down-filled cover like it's a cloud.

The minute Brenda showed me this outfit, I ran upstairs to try it on, dreaming of the day I would wear it for him.

She knew I was ready. She knew we needed this time. So, like the fairy godmother she is, she gave me this.

Now here I lie in the middle of the bed I've shared with him for the past month where I imagined the day I would give him this last part of me.

He stands next to the bed, shirt off, pants button undone. The white boxers he put on after his shower this morning peek out over the waist.

Toeing off his shoes, he looks at me while I lean up on my elbows, watching the show before me. Watching him undress for me.

The candles make him look like a Greek god. His body is perfect. He's so handsome and his darkened, lust-filled eyes are hooded and raking over me hotly.

"I love you." I sit up when he finally sheds his pants. His cock is huge and pressing insistently against his boxers.

"I love you, always," he says, getting on the bed on his knees in front of me. "We do this at your pace. We do this on your time. You get me, Bella?" he asks.

I nod, not able to respond verbally without the tears over his thoughtful concern for me falling.

"Now I'm going to take off these sexy as hell panties, angel. This is something I've dreamed of doing, usually while jerking off to thoughts of you." He licks his lips and turns his darkened, stormy blue eyes down to the apex of my thighs.

"Okay," is all I can muster to say when he reaches to spread my knees apart.

He runs his hand down the center of the lace, through the wet spot formed from watching him undress. "Bella," he breaths out while leaning forward to kiss my stomach, making my breath hitch.

"You're so beautiful," he groans while running kisses along the top on my panties. His thumbs hook into the sides of the lace, peeling them down my legs. He throws them over his shoulder, and my instinct is to close my knees, but he stops me. "No more hiding from me."

He opens my legs further, and I'm still tempted to cover myself, but he's faster than me. His mouth hovers over me, his warm breath so close, I can feel it tickle my wet flesh.

"Watch me," he says.

He pulls my lips apart with his thumbs, opening me up. "So beautiful." Those are the last words he says before slowly licking up my slit.

His warm, hot tongue on me causes me to sink back into the pillows. My head rolls to the side, my eyes almost rolling to the back of my head.

He licks up again, slowly this time, stopping at my clit where he makes little circles with his tongue. Lightning bolts of pleasure zap straight through my core.

"Jackson," I pant out.

"I knew you would taste like this. I knew you would taste like heaven," he says while he licks up again, but this time he slowly slides a finger into me.

The gentle invasion causes my hips to lift off the bed.

"Oh, God." A few more gentle licks and soft strokes of his finger, and he pulls his mouth from me.

"Why are you stopping?" I'm ready to beg him to continue. Never has it been like this. Never has someone worshiped me.

"I'm taking my time. I'm savoring this moment. I'm doing everything I dreamed of doing to you," he says, his finger still moving slowly in me while he kisses his way up my stomach.

"Well, you were doing a great job. You didn't have to sto—" He stops my words with his mouth as he slips his tongue into my mouth.

The taste of Jackson and me mingles together on my tongue. I grab his head, pulling him closer. My kiss is frenzied with need. His fingers are still moving in me, touching places I forgot could bring so much pleasure.

The feeling of his weight on me is comforting. He breaks the kiss to trail his tongue down my chest to my heart and places a kiss there before continuing. "I want your heart, Bella." He kisses me right on the bow in the middle of my chest. "I want it all with you, and I want it forever."

"I'm yours." My eyes look straight into his. "I can't be anyone else's since my heart beats for you." It's true. I never knew love could be like this, so pure, so wholesome, so fucking fulfilling and beautiful and so, so perfect. "Make love to me, Jackson, make me yours completely."

He leans forward so he can kiss the swell of my breast. His finger leaves me, and I feel the loss. His hands go to the back of my bra, snapping it open. He pulls the shoulder straps down, freeing my breasts to his view.

Leaning forward, he takes a pebbled nipple into his mouth, turning his tongue around it while his hand cups the other. Rolling that nipple between his fingers while his warm mouth caresses the other, the feelings are almost overwhelming.

My hand runs through his hair. His eyes look up at me as he switches to the other breast.

I'm on edge. My body is tight with the urge to release. I want to groan, I want to beg, I want to scream, and I need him to help me go over that cliff.

"Jackson, please." My voice comes out in pants.

"Do you want to come, Bella?"

"Please." I'm not even sure I know what I'm begging him for at this point.

He smiles at me as he slowly moves two fingers back inside me while his lips find my clit and suck lightly. It's all I need to let go. My legs spread wider, giving his broad shoulders more room to lift my legs up onto his shoulders.

I fall over that cliff, and my back bows off the bed, throwing my head back into the pillow. My hands find their way into his hair, pulling at it to hold him in place at my core. The prickles from his beard are a delicious contrast to his soft lips and tongue and are just what I need to send me over again.

It's too much pleasure. His assault on me is overwhelming, and I cry out, "Jackson," thrashing my head side to side, my hands fisted in the sheets. "Jackson, it's too much."

But he knows exactly how to handle my rioting body as he slowly and gently brings me back down after riding out two orgasms.

"So fucking beautiful," he says as looks up at me. I'm in a Jackson-pleasure-induced daze.

He's on his knees between my spread legs. He's panting, almost pained looking. His cock is practically fighting to get out of his boxers, and he reaches down to squeeze the tip. A wet spot is evident there, and I do something I never thought I would have the courage to do. I sit up, look him straight into the eye, and say, "It's my turn to play."

I peel his boxers off his hips, his cock springing free and slapping loudly against his belly. He's so huge. He's so hard. The head of his cock looks almost painful.

I take his girth in my hand, my fingers not even close to closing all the way around him, and I stroke him tentatively at first. His moan is the only encouragement I need.

I continue to stroke him more firmly, and he throws his head back in pleasure. "Fuuuuckkkk."

It's a feminine thrill. I feel powerful and sexy in this moment. I did this to him. He feels this way because of me. Me and only me.

Leaning forward, I lick the pre-cum pearling on the head of his cock. He is wild-eyed and panting.

His hands tunnel into my hair as he grunts out, "I want to watch you take me in your mouth. Do it now, Bella."

I give him what he wants. I take him further into my mouth, wrapping my tongue around him as I slowly bob my head, taking in a little more of this monster with each pass.

I move one hand to the base of his cock and stroke up to meet my downward sliding lips. My other hand gently cups and teases his balls, which have drawn up tight against his body.

I'm in my own world at this point. My goal is singular: to make him lose it. His grunts and moans are the most erotic thing I've ever heard. Making him feel this way is the sexiest thing I've ever done, and my body can't help but respond to it.

I hollow out my cheeks, applying suction as I run my tongue along the notch on the underside of his head. He is slowly thrusting his hips in time with my movements. My hand continues to stroke at his base.

I look up at him as he pants out, "I'm going to come, Bella."

He tries to pull out of me, but I reach around him, pushing him further into my mouth and not giving him the option to pull out. I continue bobbing my head, sucking and licking, and he lets go. His salty essence dances across my tongue, and I swallow all of him.

His thrusts stop and he looks spent. I slowly work him down from his orgasm, gently licking him clean before I remove my mouth. I grin up at him and say, "That was fun. We should do it more often."

"Oh, we definitely will do that often. Maybe daily," he says, his cock still hard in my hand.

"Is this normal?" I ask him, wondering how it's still hard after everything we just did.

"Bella, I'm finally going to make love to you. I'm surprised I lasted that long, but I'm not even close to being done with you yet. We're just getting started, angel." He releases my hair and says, "Lie back now, Bella, and open yourself for me."

42

Jackson

When her lips wrapped around my cock, I thought I would shoot off like a sixteen-year-old virgin.

Jesus, she is going to be the death of me. I give her my caveman speech, and she doesn't pause, she doesn't shy away. She just lies back on the bed and spreads her legs for me.

On my knees above her, I take in her beautiful, naked body laid out for me as I lazily work my cock.

Bending her knees, I push them back a little. I rub my cock through her folds, coating myself with her wetness. She's wetter than before.

"You got all hot and bothered while you sucked my cock, didn't you, Bella?" I continue to slowly drag my cock through her folds. She nods her head in reply, her chest rising and falling with her anticipation.

I place my cock at her entrance, knowing from finger fucking her it's going to be a tight fit.

I slowly push in, looking down to watch my cock head enter her, watching us become one. I'm not the only one to watch. She's watching me take her, and it's obvious she likes what she sees. It's one of the most erotic things I have ever seen.

I slowly enter her and notice her eyes widening. Not wanting to hurt her, I slowly pull out and reenter her again, one time, two times, three times.

Her pussy grips me like a fucking vise. The third time I push in a little further, repeating the motion each time as I keep trying to enter her fully.

She's soaked, she's so wet. I reach down between us, finding her clit swollen with need. I press on it with my thumb, and she pulls her legs back more, opening herself up even further to me. On my last stroke, I finally sink in all the way to my balls.

Once I'm completely seated in her, I stop, giving her a moment to adjust to me as I'm relishing in the feeling of having her surround me.

She grips my ass to spur me on. "More, Jackson," she begs me while trying to thrust herself up.

I almost laugh at her neediness. I slowly pull out again and slam right back into her.

Her crying out has me stopping to see if I've hurt her. "You okay, Bella? Is it too much?"

"No," she groans as her pussy clamps down on me. She uses her heels, digging into my ass to drive her desires home. "Jackson, don't stop. Please."

I withdraw again and begin to pound into her, this time a little softer, waiting for her to beg for it harder.

I'm slamming into her so hard, the headboard hits the wall with each thrust.

Her pussy is gripping me so tightly, I really have to work to keep thrusting at this pace. I reach down with my hand again to rub her clit in circles. "So fucking tight, angel." My balls slap her ass, her juices coating them.

I hold on to the headboard with one hand while I fuck her. I wanted soft and smooth. I wanted to go slow, but once I sank into her and felt how hot and wet and tight she was, I couldn't hold back.

My spine is tingling, my balls are drawing up. I'm so fucking close, but I'm not going to go without her.

"I'm close, angel." I pound faster into her, her nails raking the skin on my ass. "So fucking tight," I groan, and with another thrust and one more flick of her clit, she goes off, coming all over my cock.

Her moans, her pants, her pleasure—it's all too much for me. One thrust, two, and then a third and plant myself into her as deep as I can go, and I come.

Her pussy is still clenching around me, squeezing me so hard I'm almost light-headed and seeing stars. I don't think I've ever come this hard.

I'm about to collapse, but I catch myself before I land on top of her, taking her with me.

She lies on my chest, our bodies sticky with a sheen of sweat. Our breaths come in fast, our heartbeats slowly returning to normal. My cock is still twitching and hard inside of her fluttering pussy.

"I changed my mind," she says while kissing my heaving chest. "We should do *that* more often than the other things."

I throw my head back with laughter. "Oh, we are going to be doing that a lot more before Lilah comes home. In fact, I think we should do it on every single surface that we can," I suggest.

"That sounds like a lot of fun. Where should we go next?" she asks me. It seems my shy woman has an adventurous side I can't wait to discover with her.

We spend the rest of the day and late into the night doing it all over the house, from the shower to the couch to the kitchen counter and the stairs. I lose a little bit more of myself to her each and every time.

She's already claimed my heart, and she's now working herself into my soul.

43

Bella

I'm asleep on my stomach when I feel little kisses start at my shoulders. It's been a month since we finally had sex.

Every night, I fall asleep curled up to him after he worships my body with his. I had no idea such pleasure existed.

Most mornings, he wakes before Lilah, and in turn, finds a creative way to wake me. I love waking up already panting with his mouth on me. But, I love waking him up with my mouth even more.

"Hmmm, morning, Jackson." I turn to face him where he takes me into his arms. As soon as I'm close enough, I reach down to run my hand along his hard cock.

I push him onto his back and climb on top of him. I'm not even fully awake yet, but I know what I want and it's right under me.

I sit up on my knees, his hands going straight into my camisole. We never sleep naked because of Lilah, but we always wear things that can easily come off or offer quick access. He pulls down the straps, letting my breasts fall into his hands.

He rolls my nipples exactly how he knows drives me crazy. Moaning, I lift just enough to place his cock at my entrance.

When I rub him through my slit, wetting him just a little, I slowly sink down on him until he's buried deep inside of me.

We both moan at the sensation as I allow myself to adjust to his size for a minute before I start rising up and down. His hands are still playing with my nipples, and it feels so good I can't help but move faster.

We usually take our time at night and have more of a quickie in the morning just in case Lilah wakes up early and we get interrupted, which has happened more times than we care to admit.

"So fucking tight, angel. You take my cock every night, sometimes twice a day, and you're still so fucking tight."

Another thing I've learned is I'm a sucker for his dirty talk. Once he's inside me, it's like he can't hold his words back, and I love it.

The dirtier he talks, the hotter I get, and he knows it, too. Leaning back, I put my hands on his knees, trying to change up the angle to hit that spot deep inside of me I didn't know existed before his cock found it.

As soon as my hands grip his knees, he wets his thumb and then starts rubbing my clit in circles. Right before I'm about to come, he stops and moves his finger away.

"We don't have time to play, Jackson. She could be up any minute," I warn him as I sink down on his cock while rotating my hips to get some friction. Another trick he taught me.

"Look at my girl taking what she wants." His voice is still sleepy and rough. He grasps onto my hips, moving me on his cock at his pace and thrusting up hard on the downward strokes.

"You want it, angel, take it." He dares me as he continues to move my hips. So I do what I know I need to do to get myself there—I play with my clit myself.

He groans at the sight. "Hottest fucking thing I've ever seen is you fucking me while you touch yourself." He slams me down harder.

Two more thrusts with me rubbing myself furiously, and I'm calling out, "I'm coming, Jackson."

He continues slamming me down onto his thrusting cock, and I continue rubbing myself.

A few more thrusts and then he slams me down, holding me there while he empties himself in me.

I collapse onto his chest just as we hear little feet running for the bedroom.

The camisole goes back into place, covering my breasts. We turn like we are cuddling, Jackson whipping the sheet up over us to cover our naked lower halves.

"Morning everybody!" Lilah says while she runs to the bed and jumps in with two knees. Jackson has gotten it down now so that he blocks his balls.

"Hey there, princess, did you have good dreams?" he asks her just like he does every morning.

"I dream fairy tales and rainbow," she answers, another thing Jackson taught her.

It's been more than two months since the Adam fiasco and a lot has changed. There are no more security details watching us.

Not because Jackson didn't want it, but because I drew the line. We are fine, Lilah's fine, I'm fine, and the house is safe. It's booby trapped, for crying out loud.

He finally gave in and cut the security details, but that didn't mean it didn't come with stipulations. I agreed not to leave the house without my cell phone. He was firm on this, saying he didn't care if it was just to put out the trash. If I was going to be outside the house, my phone was in my pocket. This made sense to me, so I had no problem agreeing.

He also told me he'd put some kind of hidden app on it that would track my every single move. Two weeks ago, I forgot to take it with me when we went over to his house during the day to play in the sand.

I was there maybe an hour when he walked into the backyard with steam practically coming out of his ears.

"Where are you?" he asked, knowing full well where we were.

"Where is your cell phone, Bella?" I knew him well enough now to not poke the bear, so I just told him how sorry I was for forgetting it and promised to never let it happen again. I also had to give him extra sexual favors because 'I owed him for making him worry.'

"Okay, we should get downstairs," I say while trying to fish under the sheets for my discarded panties I know he took off.

"I threw what you're looking for on the other side of the room."

I turn to see my panties lying on the floor in front of the bathroom door.

Turning around, I glare at him while Lilah asks, "What you looking for, Momma?"

"My shoes," I answer, saying the first thing that comes to mind. "Can you check in your room to see if I left my slippers in there?"

I'm hoping she doesn't notice the slippers are right next to the panties. Instead, she jumps off the bed, giving me just enough time to pick up the panties and make it into the bathroom.

"They no here!" I hear Lilah yelling from her room.

"She found them," Jackson says, walking into the bathroom with a smirk on his face wearing his basketball shorts.

I stop from brushing my teeth, pointing my toothbrush at him. "Not cool, Jackson, not cool."

He laughs at me, turning on the sink, and putting toothpaste on his own toothbrush. "Stop wearing them, and I won't throw them," he says right before he puts the toothbrush into his mouth.

My glare stays on him until Lilah comes in, complaining she is starving.

"My poor girl, always starving," I say while I wipe my hands on the towel. "Let's go feed my starving girl and fix Jackson's coffee."

We started this routine soon after Jackson semi-moved in. He is never home anymore. He has most of his clothes here, slowly bringing more of his stuff over and never taking anything back.

Once we started mixing our clothes and doing laundry together, it was evident we lived together.

We still go over to his house sometimes to eat and play with the park that is in the backyard. But other than that, he is always here.

I'm surprised he hasn't moved his television in since he always complains ours is too small.

I start the coffeemaker brewing and begin opening the curtains since it's a nice, sunny day outside.

"Momma, I want fluffy eggs," she says while she pulls out her chair and climbs into it with her coloring book. Fluffy eggs in Lilah's world are scrambled eggs. "Wiff toast."

"Coming right up," I tell her, grabbing the eggs, milk, and a frying pan. I crack the eggs and start mixing the ingredients to make her fluffy eggs.

I walk over to the stairs, yelling upstairs, "Want fluffy eggs, Jackson?" Hoping he can hear me with the water running.

"Sounds good, angel, I'll be down in a second," he yells from somewhere upstairs.

Breakfast is almost done when he comes barreling down the stairs. "Sorry, angel, gotta go. We got a lead on Lori."

Her name makes me gasp out of shock. I met her mother, Marissa, when we went to the diner in town. My heart breaks for her. Each time Lori calls, Marissa is filled with hope and then ripped to shreds when nothing comes of it.

"Oh my God! Go, go, go!" I rush him out the door with a quick kiss and reminders to be careful and to call me later.

If I had known that was going to be the last time I'd kiss him, I would have lingered a little. Looked into his eyes longer, hugged him tighter. Told him I loved him. If only I knew.

Jackson

When the phone rang early with a call from Mick, I immediately know something is wrong.

"Hello."

"We got a lead," he says as I hear him moving around. "Some girl came into the precinct last night, spinning a tale about meeting a guy and being creeped out by him."

"Okay. You think it's connected?"

"Not only do I think it's connected, but I also think he's the guy. She kept saying he tried pushing her to take a pill to relax. When she fought him on it, he got pissed off and started yelling at her."

I start hurrying around the room, quickly pulling out the clothes I'm going to wear.

"Where was this?" I ask as I pull a T-shirt on.

"At the fucking mall. It must be their playground. Scan the area, pick out a girl, and then approach her."

"Getting in the car in five. Meet you there."

I run downstairs, looking in the kitchen at my girl cooking her eggs and buttering toast.

"Sorry, angel, gotta go. We got a lead on Lori."

My girl has the heart of a saint, more worried about anyone else but herself.

"Oh my God! Go, go, go!" she says as she rushes me out the door with a quick kiss, telling me to be careful and to call her later.

The minute I get to the precinct, I run inside. Mick is already at his desk, looking through the notes. "What have you got?" I ask him, stopping to read with him.

"Same MO as Lori. I fucking smell this shit. I feel this in my gut," he tells me.

"Where is the girl?" I ask him, looking around.

"Room one. Her parents are on their way," Roger, the desk sergeant, tells us as he walks into the office.

"What's her story?" Mick asks.

"Maya, sixteen, pissed at the world, hangs at the mall with her friends, bitches about her parents, bitches about school, bitches about other people breathing from what I could tell. Guy approached her when her friends left. Started flirting with her. Clean-cut guy, maybe seventeen or eighteen tops. Kept talking about his friends having a party and how he wanted her to go. Something about him was off, she said."

"Finally, bastard got sloppy," Mick says, crossing his arms across his chest.

I look over at Mick, watching Roger walk out. "You okay to do this?" I ask him, knowing he's emotionally involved even if he wants to deny it. Marissa has got under his skin, but I'm not sure he even sees it yet, let alone will admit to it.

"What the fuck are you asking me, Jack?" I know I hit a nerve when he uses my nickname.

"I'm asking you right now if you are okay to do this."

"I'm getting her back. You can do it with me or you can watch. Either way, you let me know what you are going to do."

I nod my head, knowing he is okay with this but most of all I've got his back.

"Let's bring her home," I tell him, then follow him into the room.

I enter the room and immediately take in the hot pink-tipped, blonde-headed girl. Her brown eyes are bloodshot and puffy from crying. She has a blanket wrapped around her, and she's rocking back and forth. Her adrenaline is finally crashing. My first thought is this could be Lilah in a few years, which makes me clench my fists.

I sit down across from her. "Hey, Maya. I'm Jackson. This is Mick. I know someone was in here earlier asking you questions. Mind if we go over a couple of things?" I ask her.

She nods her head yes.

"Can you tell me this guy's name?" I ask her.

"Called himself Ryan," she whispers.

"What did he look like? Any scars? Tattoos? Anything special about his appearance?"

"He had brown hair, brown eyes, shaved sides and longer on top. He was wearing cargo shorts and a plain white T-shirt." She closes her eyes like she is trying to picture him. "Oh, and he had a tattoo." She opens her eyes. "I just remembered. It was a diamond with the word Peace under it on the inside of his right wrist. I remember it now. I saw it when he grabbed my wrist and squeezed me."

I look over at Mick, and he walks out of the room. He's going to be checking the database for the tattoo.

"Did he tell you where he wanted to take you or what he wanted to do?"

"He said his friends were having a party, so he wanted to bring me to show off how hot I was." She looks down at her hands, which start shaking again. "I almost went. Then I remembered hearing a story about some missing girls." She looks up at me. "I don't know what it was, but it didn't feel right. I didn't want to be another one of them."

Before I can answer her, there is a knock on the door, and Mick comes in with a silent nod, followed by Maya's parents, who both rush to hug her.

We step outside to give them some privacy. I look at Mick, waiting for some answers. "What did you find?"

"Name's Ryan King, calls himself Diamond Boy. We have an address, and an undercover is heading there now to see if we can pick him up."

"So we wait?" I ask him.

"We wait." He turns, walking to his desk as I walk to my computer to search anything else I can find on this Ryan King. Nothing really pops up. Semi-decent family, a couple of misdemeanors, but as a minor, they'll be sealed as soon as he turns eighteen in three days.

The phone on Mick's desk rings, and he picks it up. His answers are curt. Hanging up the phone, he looks at me as he says the words that will change the course of the next couple of hours. "We got him."

I nod at him and begin getting ready for when they bring in Ryan King. It takes about twenty minutes to bring him in and install him in a room on the other side of the building so Maya won't see him.

I look over at Mick, who is practically bouncing on the heels of his feet like a boxer getting ready to enter the ring.

"I think it's safe to say I'm going to be the one doing the talking. You should sit back and listen. Yeah?" I ask him, opening the door, and coming face to face with our first real lead in these cases.

He sits there in baggy sweats, tight T-shirt, and one of those stupid flat-billed baseball hats with diamond logos all around it. He looks like the punk that he is.

"Hey, Ryan, thanks for coming in." I'll start easy with him.

"Well, I didn't really have a choice since they cuffed me, put me in a car, and brought me here." I sit back, throwing the pen on the table, already knowing this little shit is going to push me to my limits.

I'm also hoping he doesn't push me so far that Mick has to take over.

"All right then, let's cut the bullshit. Where were you yesterday afternoon?"

"Out and about," he answers with a smirk.

"You go to the mall yesterday?" My voice is calm and even as I wait for him to dig his own hole.

"Yesterday? I don't really know. Maybe I should check my calendar." Such a wise-ass. I can feel my blood pressure ticking up.

"No need to check your calendar. You see, we have video." It's a stretch. We haven't seen the video yet, and I have no idea what's on it, but Ryan's expression immediately changes.

His smirk gone, the vein in his neck starting to pulse faster.

"What video?" His face pales as he asks the question.

"Come on, Ryan, smart guy like you? You have to know there are cameras all over that mall. It's all going to be there, my man."

He swallows, his leg starting to bounce. "I was told they weren't working," he mutters.

Bingo. "Who told you that? Dude, you got played. It's all there. Gotta say"—I shake my head at him—"you had us going there for a bit, but it was only a matter of time."

"I didn't do anything." He pushes himself forward, placing his hands on the table.

"See, Ryan, that's where you're wrong," I tell him and when he doesn't say anything further, I continue. "I gave you a chance to tell us your side of the story, but you think you're smarter than us." I lean back into my chair while Mick is leaning against the wall with one foot folded over the other.

"I did nothing wrong." He looks at both of us, trying to convince us.

"That isn't what the video shows. You know it." I point to Mick. "We know it."

"Listen, I don't know what you have, but I did nothing wrong."

"You baited them." Short and sweet, I tell him, "The video shows you even slipped them something."

"That's bullshit! I didn't give them shit till after we left!" And just like that, he buried himself. He knows it now just like I know it.

"Really? Then it's my mistake. You drugged them after you left, took them to wherever it is you took them, and now you are going to go down for drug possession, kidnapping, assaulting, and I gotta be honest with you, Ryan, no one in jail likes someone who drugs helpless women. Let alone sex offenders. They get the worst treatment in jail."

"I didn't kidnap anyone. They came with me willingly."

"Where are they then?" I ask him. "Give me a location."

"I...I..."

This is when I snap. "You what? Did you kill them?" I raise my voice.

He just shakes his head no.

"You drugged them, lured them out, raped them, and then killed them." My voice gets louder. "Then you disposed of their bodies. Where are they?" I slam my hand on the table, making him jump. "Pretty boy like you in prison, going to be rough keeping the boys at bay. Tell me what you did with them. TELL ME!"

"I get paid to find the girls and drop them off. That's it!"

"Who pays you?"

"No clue. Calls himself Chucky, like the Chucky doll. I bring them to him. He pays me ten grand per girl."

"How many?" I ask him, hoping he isn't going to stop talking.

"Three so far." He looks at us. "I wanted to stop, but he wouldn't let me. He kept calling, said he'd dump them off at the cops and all they'd have was my name."

"Where did you drop them off?"

"Some cheap motel off the interstate. I walked them in pretending we were going to a party, and then once we were inside, I just left. He had his guy waiting for them there."

"So you brought those three innocent girls to the devil's doorstep."

"I did nothing wrong."

Mick finally snaps. "You lured three young girls away from their families through the use of an illegal substance. You then brought them to someone who rapes and probably beats them, while you walked away with thirty grand. And you think you didn't do anything wrong here, Ryan? If any of those girls are dead, you will be charged with accessory to murder."

Mick leans over the table, looking him in the eye, and says, "And you better fucking believe I'll be the one to put you in there. I'll lead you in there like you led them in there. How is that?"

He doesn't get to answer before my cell phone goes off with the alarm company name.

Getting up, I answer the phone. "Hello."

"Hey, Jackson. It's Brian. Are you home?"

"No, I'm at work. Why?"

"The silent alarm was just triggered. We called the house and nothing. Tried the cell phone and nothing," he says and the hair stands up on my neck.

"What about Brenda?" I ask, running out of the room to get my keys.

"Nothing. We called everyone. I have someone arriving right now. I'm sure it's nothing. He's calling in now. Give me a sec."

"Mick," I yell for him, and he comes out of the room, slamming the door shut behind him.

"Silent alarm was just triggered at Bella's. Someone is on the scene, but I'm waiting for an update from Brian." I put him on speakerphone so Mick can hear.

"Jackson, where are you?" His voice is tight. It's curt and angry.

"Give it to me."

"They have an ambulance going there now. Brenda has been beaten pretty badly. Lilah was the one who ran and hit the alarm."

"Where the fuck is Bella?"

"Jackson." He exhales a deep breath. "She's nowhere to be found."

And in that minute, my phone flies across the room, my knees buckle, and I almost fall down.

Mick looks at me. "We will get her back."

I look at him, trying to wrap my head around all this.

"We will fucking get her back." He grabs me by the shirt, shaking me. "You need to snap the fuck out of it and help me find your woman. You need to lock your shit down and fucking focus here, Jackson."

I know who took her, just as I know I will find him and I will kill him myself.

45

Bella

Our day is just like any other day: eat, clean a little, and play. It's our normal routine. Sometimes we also add a walk, an errand or two or some other activity.

Brenda usually joins us on the walks. Depending on Lilah's mood, we'd either put her in the stroller or one of us would hold her hand as we walked. Our route is pretty much the same, though—just a leisurely walk around the neighborhood.

Sometimes we would stop at the big park where Lilah would sit on the swings. She could be pushed on them for hours if I let her.

But, today, we sat in the backyard at the little table I picked up, drinking some lemonade Brenda brought over.

Just watching Lilah run around, chasing bubbles from the machine Jackson hooked up.

Her giggles are so loud. So carefree.

"You did it," Brenda says, breaking our comfortable silence. I look over at her, knowing exactly what she is referring to. "The first day I met you, I was afraid it was too late. I thought you had already given up." She takes a sip of her lemonade. "But then I saw you fight your way back. Not only for yourself, you were fighting for her." She points to Lilah, who is now skipping after the bubbles.

"You helped me." I grab her hand and squeeze it. "You wouldn't let me give up. You were my fairy godmother."

She laughs at me. "Nope, just wanted to show you that life, it can be beautiful. It can be so wonderful, and it is worth fighting for."

We are both looking at each other, and we don't see Lilah has stopped skipping. Her giggles have stopped. We don't notice her standing in the middle of the yard or that she has just wet herself.

Turning my head, I'm faced with the horror of my past.

Adam.

But not just Adam. Chuck, his dealer, is with him, and he's got a gun aimed straight at my little girl.

I get up but can't move. "Adam," I whisper.

"Bitch, you do not talk to him." Chuck turns the gun to me, then to Brenda.

"Just, please, put that away. We won't fight. I'll give you whatever you want," I tell them while I try to shield Brenda behind me.

"DON'T FUCKING MOVE!" Chuck yells, halting us.

I look at Adam, hoping a tiny part of him would not actually be okay with this man killing his young daughter. I can see his dilated, black, soulless eyes, and I know he's high. He probably doesn't even realize what's going on.

"Go get the girl." Chuck gives him an order, but Lilah quickly runs to me, and I scoop her up in my arms.

Adam walks over to us, reaching out to rip her from me, but Brenda steps into his way. She isn't there for long before he backhands her across the face, sending her down hard.

Lilah and I both yell out in horror.

Adam turns to look at us. "Shut the fuck up, you two. Pains in my ass, that is what you guys are."

I hold her closer to my chest, whispering to her to be quiet. Her sobs gut me. Her tears fall onto my skin.

"Give her to me, Bella, NOW!" he yells in my face, his spit landing on us.

"Adam, don't do this. Don't take her. Take me." I stand here, offering my life for my daughter's, praying they'll accept. Deep down, I always knew someday I would have to do this.

Adam turns around to look at Chuck, who is still holding the gun at us. "We should just take Bella. Sell her off."

Chuck smiles at us. "Good call, Adam. Let's take the other two inside." He turns the gun sideways, aiming a sadistic smile at me. "Walk, bitch."

I look down at Brenda who has a swollen eye, but she rolls onto her hands and knees and manages to get up. She reaches her hand out to us.

We walk into the house. I'm hoping I can slip away and press that button, do something that can help us.

We walk over to the couch, all three of us with tears running down our faces.

"Old bitch, get over here," Chuck says once he closes the door behind him.

Brenda looks over at us, then at him while he waves the gun at her. When she doesn't move he yells, "NOW, BITCH!"

I try to get her hidden behind me, but she walks over to him with her head held high, her shoulders straight.

The minute she's in front of him, he takes the gun and points it right at her forehead. "I'm going to blow her brains out if you don't drop that fucking brat and get your ass over here."

I put Lilah on the couch, kissing her before I turn around and make my way to him.

When I'm close enough, he turns sideways and hits Brenda with the back of the gun right on the side of her head.

She falls down, blood seeping out from where the gun struck her.

I cry out in shock as I fall to my knees next to her.

"Get the fuck up, bitch! NOW!" His hands are now shaking.

I stand up and look over at Adam. There is no way for me to adequately capture the hatred I feel for him.

He walks over to the fridge where there is a picture of Jackson, Lilah, and me taken at an ice cream store two weeks ago. All smiling for the picture Jackson snapped.

"Look at this bullshit. You fucked my brother." He throws his head back, laughing. "You give that pussy away for free." He walks over to me with the picture in his hand. Getting into my face, his nose almost touching mine, he growls, "NO MORE, BITCH." And he strikes me fast and hard.

Lilah is on the couch watching this, rocking back and forth, hands over her ears. We don't notice that Chuck has turned around to kick Brenda while she lies unconscious on the floor.

"Enough, please." I try to talk despite the taste of metal in my mouth. "Just take me. You came for me, take me."

This is like walking into a lion's den wearing a meat necklace. I am so scared, but I'll be damned if I let them see it.

He points his gun down and fires a shot right at Brenda. The wails coming from my throat are hoarse and burn my throat as they leave my mouth.

I did this to her. I brought this to her. All of this is my fault. I won't let it fucking hurt anyone else.

"You came here for me. Now you have me," I say to them.

"This is how it's going to go. We are going to walk out of here and you don't try to be a fucking hero. You walk to my car, get in, and if you listen like a good little girl, I'll fuck you once more before I sell you. How'd you like that? You miss me?" Chucks says to me.

Adam grabs my arm, almost twisting it. I cry out in pain but not for too long since I feel the gun in my backside.

I have Adam on one side, Chuck on the other, both holding my arms in a death grip.

I look over at Lilah, her eyes wide with fear, with horror.

"I love you, baby girl," I tell her right before they push me forward. Right before they close the door on Brenda lying there, probably dead, and Lilah watching her mother being ushered to her own death.

Jackson

Mick does the driving, and we make it to my house in record time. By the time we get there, two cop cars are already parked at the curb, their lights blaring, along with an ambulance.

I run inside and the sight before me is like a sucker punch to the gut. The EMTs are working on Brenda, who is lifelessly lying in a puddle of her own blood.

I scan the room. Nothing seems to be out of place, no signs of a struggle. I continue scanning the room looking for my girls. Lilah sees me first, and she immediately jumps off the police officer's lap and runs right to me, crying.

I scoop her into my arms as she wails out her terror. "Ackson, they take Momma," she says between sobs.

"Who, baby girl, who took Momma?" I ask her. "Who?"

She hiccups, her sobs, her breath coming out in choppy pants. "Daddy and his briend."

I look over at Mick, who is texting the security guys we called on the way here.

Brian arrives and comes straight to us. "So, he came in the side gate from what we could tell by the censor times." He looks at his phone. "Front door censor indicates it was disengaged and reengaged twenty minutes ago. The silent alarm was activated about twenty seconds later."

I look down at Lilah. "You did so good, baby girl. Just like we showed you." I kiss her stain-streaked face. "So brave, my baby girl."

"I want Momma, Ackson," she says as her eyes start to close as the trauma of today finally hits her.

"We got the name of the hotel. We are sending two cruisers there right now."

I look at him, about to ask questions, when my mother runs into the house.

Her eyes are open wide with fear as she scans the area. Tears start falling when she sees Brenda being lifted on the stretcher.

She sees me sitting on the floor holding Lilah. "Jackson." She gets on her knees next to me, stroking Lilah's hair softly.

I look at her straight into her eyes. "He did this."

Her hand covers her mouth, and she gasps in horror. "He came here, into her home, and he took her. He beat Brenda, badly as you can see. And he did this in front of Lilah."

"Jackson." That word is ripped from her, pained, but it's all she gets out before Mick steps forward, drawing my attention.

"Jackson, Bella has her phone on her. We have a location."

I hand Lilah to my mother before I get up.

"You aren't going to like this," Mick says.

My fists clench at my sides. "Tell me," I say through gritted teeth.

"Same motel Ryan sent us to."

I look at my mother. "I have to know if you will keep her. If anything happens to us, to me, to Bella, you will keep her."

"Jackson, get Bella and just bring her home. Both of you just come home to Lilah."

I nod my head, looking at Brenda, who is being wheeled out on a stretcher. She's hanging in there, thank God. She's been shot in the side, and hopefully nothing vital was hit. Her eye is swollen, and there's an egg-shaped bump forming on the side of her head. Clearly, she was whipped with a gun.

"Mom, I need you to promise not leave her sight. Do not leave Lilah alone for a second, not even to go to the bathroom. I'm going to have someone staying with you both, but I still want you to promise not to let her out of your sight."

"I promise, Jackson. Go get Bella."

I nod at her, looking over at Mick as I turn to walk out of the house for the second time today. I pray the next time I walk back in, it will be with Bella.

47

Bella

They toss me into the backseat, closing the door right behind me. Looking at the door, I notice the door's handles have been removed.

I quickly scan the area, trying to see if I can escape. Chuck must see what I'm doing because he turns around and points the gun at my leg.

"I would hate to fucking shoot you in the leg before I fuck you, but I will. Make one move, bitch, I'll go back and get that little bitch we left behind."

I sit up straight, looking out the window at the houses while we pass through. My hands are shaking in my lap.

We pull up to a rundown motel, and my heart starts beating faster. The motel's sign is only partially lit.

We pull up in front of room number eight. The door opens, and Adam grabs my arm to yank me out. I look up at the motel's worn exterior, and I absently notice it must have been brown at some point, but years of not performing routine maintenance and weather have faded it to a dark, dingy tan. Each door is supposed to be white, but like everything else covered with dirt and grime and faded from the sun, they look dirty and yellowed. The number on the door is gold-plated with pieces of the gold chipped off. Each window has those plastic vertical blinds covering it. Some are missing pieces and some are closed.

I try to talk to Adam before Chuck gets out of the car. "Please, Adam, don't do this. Think of Lilah," I whisper to him.

Chuck closes his door, pulling out the key to open the room. Adam drags me right in with him.

I look around, taking in the filth of the room. The smell of urine is so profound, my eyes burn and I can't hold back the gag. It's unbearable.

There is one bed in the middle of the room, dirty sheets askew, half on the bed, half off. One lone chair in the corner of the room is blue with obvious blood stains on it. Carelessly discarded, used needles litter the floor all around us.

An old television sits on a cheap, dusty stand facing the bed. The television is on, tuned to The Shopping Network.

I continue scanning the room when my eyes land on three teenage girls huddled in a corner of the room and chained to the wall.

All three are wearing sheer camisoles, with no bras and sheer underwear, leaving little to the imagination. All three are filthy with greasy, stringy hair, and it's obvious none of them have bathed in quite a while. Their eyes are puffy and closed, like they are napping.

Their arms show round, fingertip-shaped bruises, but it's the swollen, red needle marks along the inside of their elbows that have me gasping aloud.

Their hands are clipped with a chain to the wall. I can see the dirt under their chipped fingernails. My heart aches for these young girls as I take in what appears to be dried blood crusted over on their inner thighs. Their panties are almost non-existent, brownish reddish stains covering them in the front.

One of the girls must hear the commotion of us coming in and rolls her head in our direction and opens her eyes.

They are vacant, like she's here but she really isn't here.

Chuck walks over to her, nudging her leg to the side, squatting down next to her. "Look at this, Lori, we brought you another bitch to train."

The minute he says her name, I know she's the girl Jackson is looking for, Marissa's daughter. Clearly, she didn't run away. She's been kidnapped.

These girls were taken from their families and have been forced to stay here.

She doesn't say anything. Only a groan escapes out of her mouth as her head lolls from side to side against the wall.

He leans down, pinching her nipple. A pained whimper escapes her. She tries to raise her hand to slap him away, but it falls limply down with a thud.

"Jesus fucking Christ, Adam. How much shit did you give them?" Chuck asks, looking over at Adam, who stands next to me.

"Just enough to last the night. It's Friday night. We already have eight guys lined up."

I turn around to look at him, and that's all I can take. I heave and vomit bile all over the side of me.

I don't even stop when Adam kicks me, sending me flying across the room. I lose my balance, hitting my head on the corner of the one nightstand in the room.

I land face down on the wet, urine soaked carpet. I reach up to touch my forehead and wipe at the blood dripping down the side of my face.

"Don't fucking touch her face. She's going to be our money cow." Chucks leans down, gripping my hair, and pulling me up.

My cries of pain fill the room. Adam ignores it as he goes looking for his next fix.

Chuck grips my chin, squeezing it so hard I think he might crack my jaw.

"Did you miss me, Bella?" he asks while he pushes me against the wall by the bed. The paint has started chipping off of it, and there are dirty, yellowed streaks where water must have run down the walls at some point.

I look away, trying to block out what is happening. Chuck has me boxed in and is dragging the gun down the middle of my chest, bringing the V of my T-shirt down with it, exposing my white bra. "Hmmm, look at these tits. They filled out good," he says while he takes the barrel of the gun and rubs it over my nipple.

A sob rips from my mouth before I can stop it. "Don't worry, beautiful Bella. If you don't want me in that pussy, I'll take your ass." He goes to the next nipple.

Chuck turns around and looks at me. "You're not worth all this fucking bullshit." He slaps me across the face, and the stinging pain rattles through my skull.

"Get a needle ready. Someone is going to fly with unicorns," Chuck tells Adam as he throws me onto the bed like a rag doll and begins roughly ripping off my clothes.

"Hurry the fuck up, Adam. I want to fuck her before the johns get here and we sell these bitches tonight." Chuck has ripped off my shirt and bra, leaving me just in my shorts.

Adam walks out of the bathroom, syringe filled with a brown liquid. I try to block myself, but Chuck yanks my arm back, twisting it.

"Hurry up and shoot her up," Chuck says while untying my shorts button.

Adam comes over, gripping my hand. "Please don't do this, Adam, please."

Chuck sits on me so I can't move while Adam ties an elastic band around my arm.

"Don't worry, Bella, you'll love it." He smiles at me as he grabs my arm, tapping on it, looking for a vein. He roughly shoves the needle into my flesh and shoots the liquid into me.

It burns at first, the liquid warming up my veins. It takes about five seconds for me to feel like my body is disconnecting from itself.

It's like I'm here but my mind is going away.

I can't fight off whatever is going on. I don't think I can move my hands. I just close my eyes, letting the feeling of being able to fly run through me.

I feel my shorts being ripped off my legs and then I hear a thud.

"What the fuck is this? FUCK! FUCK!! FUCK!!!" Chuck yells.

"Turn it off. It could be tracking our location," Adam says.

I guess they must have found my phone. That's right. Jackson must know where I am. I just have to hold on. He's coming to save me. This will be over soon. I hope.

I hear a phone ringing somewhere in the room. "FUCK! FUCK, FUCK, FUCK!!" Adam comes running out of the bathroom, whipping off the elastic band, a drop of blood coming out of the vein he just shot up in.

Chuck turns around to look at him. "It was Jasmine at the front desk. She said the cops are on their way up. They're here. They fucking found us." He is pacing the room now.

That's the last thing I hear before I think now is a good time to just take a little nap.

48

Adam

This whole fucking day has been a clusterfuck. Starting with the phone call from Ryan telling us the cops were at his door.

Then we put our plan to grab Bella into motion. If anything just to fuck with Jackson. Finding her was so fucking easy. All I did was watch my mother's house.

She led me straight to them. She's a fucking fool, that woman. I sat there laughing as I waited for the right moment.

What I wasn't counting on was her having company. The fact Chuck was slowly fucking losing his mind didn't help matters either.

The second I get the needle in my vein, I close my eyes to savor the fucking feeling. Those eight to ten seconds are the fucking best. Just letting it flow through me, getting lost in the nothing.

The phone in my pocket starts ringing. Jasmine's name comes up. She's the clerk at the front desk. She turns her head and ignores what we do. We give her blow. Easy as one, two, three. Sometimes if I'm in the mood, I even let her suck my cock.

"What?" I answer her.

"The cops are here. I saw five cars zoom by the front desk heading your way." The needle drops from my hand.

"FUCK! FUCK, FUCK, FUCK!!" I run out of the bathroom,

whipping off the elastic band, vaguely noticing the drop of blood coming out of the vein I just shot up in.

Chuck turns around to look at me.

"That was Jasmine at the front desk. She said cops are on their way up. They're here. They fucking found us." I start pacing the room now.

I pace back and forth in front of the blaring television. Chuck gets off the bed and buttons up his pants. Bella is passed out, naked on the bed.

He walks to the curtain, pulling it aside to peek outside.

"What the fuck?" He turns, looking at me. "It's fucking surrounded. How the fuck did they find us so fucking fast?"

I shake my head, grabbing and pulling the hair on my head. "How are we going to get out of here, man?" I ask him, while he turns and looks wildly around the room.

"There is no way out. There isn't even a fucking window in the damn bathroom!" He keeps looking around the room for an exit that just isn't there.

"This is all your fault!" Chuck looks at me. "All your fault and that bitch's." He points to Bella.

"I fucking told you not to take her. I told you we were going too fast." I shake my head. I can't stop pacing, and I can't stop the shaking that is wracking my already tweaked body.

I look over at Chuck. "I fucking told you it was a bad idea!"

Those were the last words I ever said. In the next instant, Chuck raises his gun and fires it at me.

Once, twice, three times, and I'm finally, *finally*, fucking free.

49

Jackson

I jump in the passenger seat of the car since Mick is driving, and I immediately call for backup.

The address they gave us is about twenty-five minutes out, but with the way Mick is driving, we should get there in about ten, maybe fifteen minutes max.

There are five undercovers on-site, waiting around the corner, scoping the place out.

There is a black Honda parked right in front of room eight, which is the room we think they are in.

We let the on-sites know when we are two minutes out. I want into the room the minute we get there.

"You loaded?" I ask Mick, knowing he understands I'm asking if he has more than one gun on him.

"Got two on me. A couple in the back, locked."

I nod, preparing myself for the war that is about to be waged at the motel.

The moment we get there, I walk in the front door and straight to the reception desk. "Adam Fletcher, what room?"

She looks at me, smacking her bubble gum. "Who are you?"

I take my gun out and place it on the counter, her eyes going as wide as saucers. "You really want to do that right now?"

She shakes her head. "Room eight."

I don't even wait to hear her finish before I walk back out, talking to the team that has gathered. I open up the trunk so Mick and I can grab our vests and put them on.

"Room eight confirmed. We know they are armed. Brenda has a bullet hole to prove it."

I look around at the twenty officers who have showed up, plus the ten of Brian's guys, all waiting for the war to start.

"We just saw movement," Brian says while looking over at the room.

"It's go time. Seems they know we are here." I turn to walk away from the car to attack the door from the side.

We're a few feet from the door when we hear a shot fired. My stomach drops, and I rock to a halt as my feet stop moving. Two shots and my breathing stops. Three shots and I brace myself on the wall outside room seven.

I hear shouting all around me. The door is kicked in. I snap out of it and run through the door where my past is holding my future.

"Drop your weapon!" Mick commands, upon entering the room. "Drop the fucking weapon now!" he warns again right before he fires a shot at the man's leg. The man cries out in pain as he drops the gun to staunch the blood flow in his leg.

I enter the room, taking in the scene before me.

Bella is on the bed naked, and three young girls are chained to the wall and clearly drugged.

My brother is slumped on the floor in front of the television, which probably fell over when he was shot. I see three bullet wounds in his chest.

I rush to the bed, checking Bella for a pulse. It's there, thank God.

I cover her with the filthy sheet and gather her in my arms to walk out of the room. I look down at Chuck, who is cuffed in the middle of the room, blood seeping out of his leg.

Brian, Hulk, and Roger are all working to remove the chains from the three other girls in the room.

I make it to the car just as the ambulances start to arrive. Six in total. I run with Bella to the closest one. Placing her on the stretcher, they start asking me questions I don't have the answers to. The one thing I know is there is a puncture wound in her arm and her head is bleeding.

"Sir, we need to know what she is on," one of the paramedics asks as the other starts taking her vitals.

"I don't know. We just found her."

"We need transport. I'll draw her blood for a tox screen. They'll run it when we get to the ER, and we'll know in about thirty minutes," he says to me while gathering up the items he needs to draw her blood and his partner heads up front to drive.

I look toward the motel room and see Mick walking out holding a girl who is so jaundiced, she looks yellow. Her blonde hair is stringy with filth, and if I didn't know better, I would assume she's a junkie.

"I need help," he calls as he places her on a stretcher right outside another ambulance.

He looks over at me and calls out, "It's Lori. We found them."

I don't say anything more because the door to the ambulance I am in is shut, and we are rushing off to the hospital where I hope and pray we are in time and they can wake her up.

50

Jackson

As soon as we arrive at the ER, the paramedic hands off the tubes of blood and a nurse rushes off to get them to the lab. Another nurse and an ER doctor run alongside the stretcher as the paramedic rattles off her vitals and what he knows while he moves it into an exam room.

Mick arrives in an ambulance with Lori about ten minutes later. He runs alongside Lori's stretcher, keeping pace with the paramedic, the doctor, and the nurse.

The doctor stops him before he can get into the room.

Dread and fear are written all over his face. "Her pulse is weak. So weak. At one point, they couldn't find it." He looks toward her room, absently swiping at tears on his face I'm not sure he even realizes are there.

I don't have a chance to ask him anything else before the door bursts open and Marissa comes running in looking frantic.

As soon as she sees us in the hallway and she sees the tears falling down on Mick's face, she stops in her tracks. Her knees give out, and the wail is ripped from her, shaking me to my core.

Mick moves so fast, I don't see him move until I notice him at her side. He picks her up, sitting on the floor with her cradled in his lap as he slowly rocks her to calm her down.

"Baby, she's a fighter," I hear him whisper to her. "She is going to pull through. She didn't survive all of this to die this way."

Marissa doesn't reply. She just holds on to him like he's her anchor, her lifeline.

We both sit in that waiting room, waiting for news.

The minutes feel like hours, the hours feel like days. Each time someone comes out of those doors, we all look up hopefully.

The other girls have also been brought in, and their parents are here waiting just like we are. They are going through drug screening and rape kits. It's a fucking parents' worst nightmare.

Marissa has calmed down a bit, but she hasn't moved from Mick's lap, nor has she lessened her grip on his shirt. Her head is resting in the crook of his neck, like she was made to fit there.

The doors open again and in walks my mother holding Lilah in her arms.

Looking around, she spots us and hurries over to us. When Lilah sees me, she wiggles out of my mother's arms.

"I couldn't stay away knowing what's happening." She sits next to me and holds my hand.

"The doctor just came out to tell me about Brenda. She just got out of surgery. She lost a lot of blood and her spleen, but she's going to make it," I tell her while Lilah sits on my lap facing me, her legs wrapped around my waist, her arms around my neck, her cheek pressed to my chest. She's holding on tight.

"Jackson," my mother starts, and I know she doesn't want to say his name, but she doesn't know how else to ask about him.

"We couldn't save him, Mom."

She nods her head while she cries silently next to me.

In the end, she's a mother who just lost her child. A child she never thought the worst of and tried to see the good. A child she brought into this world and raised. A child she thought she could save.

I wrap one arm around her shoulder, pulling her close to me while she cries on my shoulder.

"Nana, you sad?" Lilah asks her. The fact she called her Nana surprises us both.

"Only a little sad, my beautiful girl," she tries to reassure her.

The door opens and the doctor walks out. "Mr. Fletcher, Bella is awake and asking for you."

I get up, bringing Lilah with me, and follow the doctor into Bella's room. I'm holding my breath, bracing myself for the worst.

"She has heroin coursing through her body, and I'm not sure how much. She's on an IV to keep her hydrated as her body works to metabolize it and rid the drug from her system," the doctor advises. "She's got two stitches on her temple, but other than that, she'll be fine."

He turns and walks out of the room. I sit next to her on the bed, reaching out to hold her hand.

Her eyes flutter open, a bit surprised and confused.

"Jackson?" she whispers, blinking her eyes more in an effort to keep them open.

"I'm here, angel. I'm right here." I lean down to kiss her on her lips.

"You found me. You saved me just like I knew you would." She lifts her hand to touch Lilah's head. "Jackson found Momma. Isn't he the bravest?" She smiles at us with a tear running from the corner of her eye.

Lilah nods her head and looks up at me. "He da brafest of da whole world."

We both laugh at Lilah's "da whole world." I correct her, but she just shrugs at me.

Bella opens her arms so Lilah can crawl into them and hug her. "Momma, I so scared. Ms. Brenda went bye bye."

Bella immediately sits up in her bed. Her eyes fill with big tears that spill over. "I need to find her," she says, trying to get out of bed.

"I have to be there with her." She is sobbing and trying to get out from under the covers I'm sitting on.

"Angel, she is going to be okay." As soon as I say those words, her body stills. "She lost a lot of blood and her spleen, but other than that, she is fine. I swear to you, angel, she's okay."

She looks at me as the tears continue rolling down her beautiful face, the emotions of the day—fear, loss, relief—clearly playing out on it.

"I have to see her," she whispers to me. "Please, take me to her."

"I don't know if I can make that happen, angel. You have to rest."

She shakes her head insistently. "I need to see her." She pushes the emergency button by her bed about fifteen times before a nurse races in the room.

Once she sees everything is all right, she jokes, "Where's the fire, hot stuff?"

Bella squares her shoulders, preparing to battle. "I called you." She sits up a bit taller, her voice stronger. "I need to go and see another patient here in the hospital."

The nurse looks at her like she has grown a second head. "You do realize you just suffered a trauma?" she asks while she walks over to the IV machine to check the bags.

"I have to see Brenda Barette. She came in earlier," Bella starts out loud but ends on a whisper. "Please."

The change of tone coming out of Bella causes the nurse to pause. "I'll be right back," she tells us and leaves the room.

"Jackson, you need to bust me out of this joint." She points at me. "You have a badge. You need to use it and tell them you are taking me."

I can't hold back my laughter. She is totally serious. The funny thing is I would do whatever she wanted me to do.

I don't have time to answer because the door opens and the nurse comes in pushing a wheelchair.

"Okay, this can totally get me fired, but I know if I don't do it, that hunk of a man will find a way to take you there without me," the nurse says while taking the IV bags off the stand to help Bella move off the bed.

"You do realize he's my boyfriend, right?" Bella tells her as she literally kicks me off the bed.

"Ouch!" I say as I rub the spot on my back where she landed her kick.

"Is that so? You and him are dating? It's not like I could tell from the loving looks of adoration he aims in your direction whenever he looks at you. Besides, my girlfriend, Sherry, is the one watching Brenda. So technically, you're doing me a favor," she says with a wink at Bella.

Bella is speechless. Her mouth is opening and closing, but no words are coming out. Never one to admit when she's wrong, she glares at me. "This is your fault. If you weren't such a hunky man, I wouldn't have to keep staking my claim over here."

I throw my head back with the force of one of the biggest belly laughs I've ever had. It is in this moment I know for certain my girl is going to be fine. She *is* fine. The thought I could have lost her again almost broke me. But even more upsetting, thoughts of what she could have—what she would have—endured will haunt me for quite a while.

51

Bella

I settle into the wheelchair and ask Jackson to put Lilah on my lap. The nurse wheels me down a couple of hallways and stops at a room with the door closed.

I look at Jackson. "Can you take Lilah and let me go in alone for a few minutes?"

There are things I need to say, and I don't think I could do it with Lilah on my lap.

"Come here, princess. We're going to let Momma go see Ms. Brenda first. Then if she is up to it, we can go in after." Lilah wraps herself around him, laying her head in the crook of Jackson's neck.

The door opens, and on the bed in the middle of the room lies the woman who has been my rock since the first day she laid her eyes on me.

She is hooked up to so many different machines, I'm almost afraid to even touch her hand.

When I finally do reach for her hand and grasp it with mine, I see how pale it is, I feel how cold it is, and I am overwhelmed with how much this woman has been through for me. For us.

The minute I bring her hand to my lips, the sob I was holding comes rushing out.

"I'm so sorry. I'm so very sorry. I can't begin to thank you." My tears fall, hot and fast, landing on her hand. "You were so brave, and it was your strength in those hellish moments that got me through it. It was because of you I found the courage to do what needed to be done to keep Lilah safe. I'm just so sorry my courage and Lilah's safety came at such a high price for you." Another sob breaks free from me, making it hard to continue, but I take a few deep breaths, and I continue on. It's the least I can do.

"You love my little girl as if she were your own. I can't tell you how much it means to me that she has you and your love in her life, Brenda. It means more than I could ever find the words to explain. You love me unconditionally, with your whole heart, and other than my Nan, you're the only person who has loved me like this." I lay my head next to her hand. "I never said goodbye to her. I never got a chance to thank her for loving me like she did. But then I come home, a broken shell of a woman who had nothing but the love of a little girl." I bring the back of my hand to my face. "Then almost as if we were meant to meet you, you were there and took one look at me, at us, and instead of turning your nose up at us, you held out your hand and gripped mine. You never let go, Brenda, not once."

My breath is catching in my throat, and my words are punctuated with hiccups. "I'm a mother, so I know, I can recognize it. You love me like a mother loves a child. You love my daughter like a grandmother loves a grandchild. You love us so much that you didn't hesitate to put yourself between us and our monster, to put your life on the line for ours. I know why you did it, but I'm so mad you did that." I lick my lips and continue, "You can't leave us now. You can't leave your little heart. Please, Brenda. Please don't go."

I lay my head back down on the bed next to her, and I break down. I cry for her, the woman who I consider a friend, the woman who is the only maternal figure I have left in my life, and I cry for the woman I pray will be here by my side, guiding me and cheering me on.

I feel fingers in my hair, and at first I think it's my imagination until I hear a whispered, "Don't cry, Bella."

I raise my head to see the eyes of the woman I just poured my heart out to. "Oh my God, oh my God. My God, Brenda." I wipe my nose and try to stand, but my legs are still like jelly from the drugs in my system.

"Was..." She tries to speak, but she's so weak, it's a bit of a challenge for her. "...so scared. Little heart?"

This woman went through the same terrifying experience as we did, but she was the one who was shot. She lost a lot of blood and had to have major surgery. She just woke up in the hospital, and the first thing she asked wasn't what happened or where she is, but how Lilah is.

I look over my shoulder at the door, knowing Jackson's right on the other side of it waiting for me. "Jackson." I raise my voice a little to call out.

Just like I knew he would, Jackson opens the door and walks in with Lilah still wrapped around him like a monkey.

"Lilah." Brenda tries to open her eyes and sit up, but she moves too quickly and cries out in pain.

"Don't you move!" I practically yell at her.

"Ms. Brenda, you have big ouchies?" Lilah asks.

"No, little heart. I'm okay, this is nothing."

It doesn't surprise me Brenda tries to pretend this isn't a big deal. "Lilah, Ms. Brenda was very brave," I tell her.

"Braber dan Ackson?" she asks.

"Just as brave as Jackson. She loves us very, very much." I squeeze Brenda's hand, watching the tears now fill her eyes. "She loves you like Nan loved me." I turn to look at Brenda. "Right?"

Brenda doesn't say anything, instead just nods her head in agreement.

"I think it would be very special if from now on we call her Nan. So she knows we love her just as if she were our Nan." Looking at

Brenda, I ask her, "Would that be okay?"

"I lobe you, Nan," Lilah says, not even giving her the chance to say no.

"I love you, too, little heart, so very, very much."

"Ackson, I have a Nan and a Nana," she tells him like she just discovered the secret to a Caramilk bar.

"That is because you are so very loved."

"She is. Now I'm just going to rest my eyes a bit, okay?" Brenda says.

"We should go, but I'll be back as soon as I can."

I bend down, placing a kiss on her hand because I can't reach her cheek.

52

Jackson

Two weeks have passed since that fateful day.

Our physical wounds are healing, but it's our emotional ones that cut the deepest. Those are going to take some time to heal.

Mom claimed Adam's body and had a funeral for him. Not wanting to upset us, she did it by herself.

But when Bella found out about it, she forced me to put on a suit and be the man she said she knew I was.

Even with the sun shining, I couldn't help but feel the sadness around us when we got to the cemetery.

I saw the coffin, white flowers lying on top of it, poised above the empty grave. But it was my mother who really got to me. Standing there alone beside her son's coffin, dressed all in black, head bowed, and crying.

I parked the car, and we got out. United as one family.

Me on one side, Bella in the middle, and Lilah holding her mother's hand.

As we approached the gravesite, my mom's head turned to us, the tears not stopping. We gathered around her, offering her the comfort of our presence. I may not have shared in her grief, but I held her hand as she said goodbye to her son.

It's not something I thought I would be able to do, but Bella said it wasn't for Adam, it was for my mother, and she was right.

Watching the coffin being lowered into the ground, I had an epiphany. With my heart beating hard and fast, I realized I couldn't save Adam. He didn't want to be saved. This was the freedom he was looking for all along.

But I did save someone. I saved Bella, and in doing so, she saved me. My mother spent the rest of the day with us, her family, soothing her pain by spending time with Lilah, the only piece of my brother she has left.

In the end, the only good that was left in him will live on. Together in my childhood home, we explained to Lilah that Adam was my brother. Something tells me she didn't really understand what we were saying because her only response was to look at me and ask, "You my daddy now, Ackson?"

Skirting around her question, no one really replied. My mother just wrapped her up in her arms and held her.

It's been a crazy two weeks since then. Not only did we close our case files on the missing kids, Mick was in his own personal hell.

While he was trying hard to give Marissa and Lori some space, she was widening that space. She was packing up to move.

Walking into the office last week and seeing Mick, his face white, his eyes bloodshot, I didn't know if it was from Jack Daniel's or from lack of sleep or a combination of the two.

"S'up," I said to him as I sat down to finish closing out all the files so I could take a nice, extended fucking vacation.

"She's leaving," he said, staring out the window at nothing. "She says they have to leave this place behind to heal."

I was about to say something to him when the phone on his desk rang. The caller ID indicated it was Sandie.

He didn't answer it. He just looked at it.

"I don't know what's going on, but if you really want what I think

you want, you need to put things in order."

"Yeah, Jackson?" His voice void of emotion, he asked, "Like what?"

"I'm not telling you what to do, Mick. You need to figure that out all on your own. Just know"—I indicated toward the phone—"that is the cancer in your life." Pausing for a second to gather my thoughts, I looked him in the eye and told it to him straight. "A man knows heaven when he finds it. Now you know what heaven feels like. You also know what isn't heaven."

He shook his head, saying, "She doesn't want me."

"If you really think that, then let her walk away. But know this, you don't fight for her, you don't tell her where you are at, you'll let heaven slip through your fingers, and you'll always regret you didn't even try. But even more, man, you have to be free and clear to accept heaven. You need to cut that other one out, because no woman, especially one who is your heaven, will accept sharing you with someone who makes your life hell."

I continued laying it out for him, "You need someone who will fight for you, too. Fight just as hard as you fight for them. I don't know Marissa, but I do know she is a fighter. You just have to show her you are worth fighting for."

With that, he got up before I had a chance to say anything else and he walked out, leaving his phone behind.

Now I'm in the car, listening to Lilah talk about all the things her and Nan will do now that she is finally coming home.

The excitement over Brenda coming home has been contagious. My mother is planning a big welcome home and we love you so much BBQ.

She and Bella have gone crazy with the food and decorations. I'm afraid to see the end result.

We don't even make it two steps into the room before Brenda is on her feet, purse in hand, ready to leave. She takes one look at the wheelchair I'm pushing and glares at me. "Jackson Fletcher, don't make me hurt you."

She walks up to Lilah, grabbing her hand in hers. "Let's go party, little heart."

Bella leans into me, trying to hide her giggles. "I told you so," she says before she jogs to join the other two.

I pull into the driveway and look around. There is practically no parking.

I hear music coming from the backyard. Making our way into the backyard, I take in the scene. These two have lost their ever loving minds.

It's like we've walked into a fucking carnival. There are so many balloons, I feel like that guy in the movie *Up*.

The backyard is packed with people. Family members, neighbors, acquaintances. It feels like my mother put up a sign and everyone just showed up.

There are circus clowns, popcorn machines, hot dog carts, jugglers, a cotton candy machine. All that's missing is the goddamn lion.

"What in the world did you guys do?" I hear Brenda ask.

Lilah is so excited, she jumps up and down yelling, "Surprise, Nan!" Her little hands clap out their excitement.

"It's your very own carnival." My mother looks at her, placing an arm around her shoulder. "It's your happy place."

Brenda also claps her hands in excitement. She doesn't get much time to look around before people approach her with their well wishes.

I hear shrieks of laughter, giggles, and many, many 'oh my gosh, you shouldn't haves' coming from Brenda. Bella stands right next to her the whole time. I look around the yard as my eyes land on Kendall's.

I make my way to her standing beside the lemonade table.

"Hey." I lean down to kiss her cheek. She places her hand on my chest, and it's then I realize it was never supposed to be her. "You look nice." And she really does.

"You look like you always do," she says shyly. "I heard about Adam. I'm so sorry, Jackson."

She was with me when I went through that whole thing. She saw the guilt eat at me. She felt me slipping away, felt me push her to the side.

I'm not sure what to say, so I say what she expects me to. "Thank you." I turn to look around to see if I can spot Bella, and I find her sitting with Lilah on the grass near a clown making balloon animals.

"She makes you happy?" Her question breaks my trance.

"I never thought I deserved to be this happy." I'm trying to find the right words, but I don't get them out before I hear Thomas speaking to her. "Hey, baby, I've been looking everywhere for you." He slings his arm around Kendall's waist, and her eyes light up when she looks up at him.

"Hey, Thomas." I reach out my hand to shake his.

"Ackson, Ackson, look, it's a cat!" Lilah says, running to me with her animal balloon.

I bend down to pull her into my arms, and Bella walks up beside me, wrapping her arms around my waist. "Hey," she says softly, and I lean down to kiss her on her head.

"Bella, right?" Kendall asks.

"Yes. Hi, we met once before. I brought over cookies," Bella says.

An awkward silence grows until Lilah pipes in. "I so hunbry."

We all laugh.

"Excuse us, you two. I gotta get my girls fed." I smile at them and say, "It was nice seeing you." I turn to walk away, but Bella smiles at them.

"We should have you two over one of these days. That would be fun."

I think to myself that would not be fun at all.

Thomas, who is clearly not feeling the 'hell no' vibes both Kendall and I are throwing off, actually agrees with Bella. Giving them a polite nod, I pull my girls to the hot dog stand.

"I hope you realize that is never going to really happen," Bella says quietly as we walk away.

I have no answer, but I am in full agreement, so I just laugh at her.

53

Bella

We walk into the house with Lilah passed out on Jackson's shoulder. It's way, way past her bed time.

She didn't even open her eyes when I unbuckled her from the car seat. She is down and out for the count.

Making my way upstairs, I walk into her room, watching him place her on the covers. "Undress her or leave her?" She wore her best dress for her Nan today. It's a long, flower print dress that matches her doll's, with black ballerina shoes.

"Angel, the house could shake right now around her, and she wouldn't notice." We both lean down, kissing her goodnight before turning on the night light she sleeps with.

"I can't believe we just left Brenda at her house without forcing our way in," I tell him while taking off my shoes.

He looks at me with one eyebrow cocked up. "Angel, she said she would shoot me with my own weapon if I walked into her house." He laughs and adds, "I don't know about you, but I'm pretty sure she would do it, too."

I let out a little laugh, rolling my eyes at him. "Like you can't defend yourself." I walk to him, placing my hands on his chest, getting up on my tippy toes. "You're so big and strong." I continue to joke with him.

He rubs my arms with his hands, and just the feel of his hands on me makes my heart beat faster each and every single time.

"I'll show you big and strong." He picks me up and my legs automatically wrap around his waist.

"Yeah," I tell him while one of my hands snakes around his neck and the other one strokes his cheek. He hasn't shaved in two days, so his stubble is long. I lean in, placing a kiss on his lips.

His beard pricks my lips like little needles. "You really need to shave. It's starting to get dangerous to kiss you." I rub his beard with one finger.

"You know you love my beard," he says as he kisses my neck. The sensation of his beard along my skin is rough and tingly, a sensation I've come to love a bit more each time I feel it.

"Hmmm, really?"

"Remember the last time I ate your pussy? Your thighs had a lovely razor burn, and every time you saw those marks, you jumped my bones," he reminds me, and he isn't lying. The thought of being marked by him was a huge turn on.

"It's not my fault. You made me into this." I laugh at him.

He places me on my feet, and I look at him in confusion. "I thought we were going to have a repeat of the performance." I'm almost whining like Lilah does when she doesn't get her way.

"Wait here," he tells me before walking over to the closet and pulling out his duffle bag.

I can't see what he's doing, but he comes back with a smile on his face. He pushes me until I'm sitting on the bed and then kneels in front of me.

"My sweet, Bella," he begins. My heart starts beating just a bit faster, not sure what he is going to say. Did seeing Kendall make him change his mind? What if he doesn't love me? That thought alone has tears forming in my eyes.

"Did you know I watched you that first night you went outside to watch the stars with Lilah?" I shake my head no, because I had no idea, I thought I was invisible.

"I watched you from my house, darkness all around me, all around you, but even then I knew I was watching an angel."

He grabs both my hands in his. "I kept thinking I had to meet you. I kept wondering who you were. Then you opened the door the next morning." He laughs at the memory. "I only saw your head. The rest of you was hidden behind the door. I remember thinking you really did look like an angel."

"You were very pushy," I add in, thinking back to those first days.

"You were a pain in my ass, even then. I came home and you were doing the one thing I asked you not to do. I remember thinking, *of course I'm going to fall for someone who would bust my balls.* And I sure did."

I glare at him. "I don't bust your balls, Jackson."

"I fell in love with you while I made sand castles with your daughter. I fell in love with your daughter the minute she asked me to save her from monsters." His voice is rough, husky. "From that moment, I vowed to always do what I could do to protect and care for you both." He reaches into his pocket and takes out a black box.

He raises one leg off the floor. "Bella Cartwright, I never want to know what a tomorrow will be like without you in it. I never want to wake up in a bed without you in it. I don't want to go through this life without you by my side. I want to love you. I want to cherish you. I want to honor you. I want to grow old with you sitting next to me in that swing watching stars."

A tear rolls down my face, which he wipes away.

"Marry me?"

I look at this man with the crystal blue eyes, who has personally chased off every single one of my demons. The man who showed me what it was like to love and to be loved. The man who shows me tomorrow will be better than today.

"I used to watch your house after that first day, too, just to get a little glimpse of you," I tell him shyly.

"Before I even knew you existed, though, I used to dream of a man with blue eyes who would chase away the bad that was in my life," I tell him. "I fell in love with you as you built sand castles with my daughter. I fell in love with you when you told her you would build it so high no monsters could get her."

I lean in to kiss him, because I can't not kiss him. "If I say yes, does this mean you'll actually move all of your stuff over here?" I ask him with a sly smile.

"Angel, I'm already moved in. You just didn't realize it," he jokes, and looking around, I actually see all of his stuff is here. Even his television. "Well then, I guess we have no choice."

"You got that one right. You're stuck with me," he says while slipping the ring on my finger.

Tears of joy run down my face as I look at the ring that will show the world I am his. Knowing everyone who sees it will know I'm his, but more importantly, they'll know he's mine.

I kiss him with everything I have and wind up knocking him down to the floor.

"When can we get married?" I ask him, not even interested in waiting.

"How is next week?" he asks me while tucking the hair behind my ears.

"Perfect."

It really is fucking perfect.

I'm in the middle of the house that was just a shell when I moved in, but it's a loving home for our family now.

We have both been to the gates of hell, but together we fought our way back.

Back to life, back to happiness, back to love.

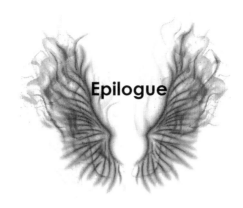

Epilogue

Seven years later

"DDDDAAAAAAADDDDDD!!!" I hear being yelled as soon as I walk into the house.

It's like they have a tracker on me. I throw my keys on the table by the door and make my way in the direction of the noise, to the kitchen.

"I'm home," I say, walking over to the sink and kissing my wife on her neck as I wrap my arms around her.

"You guys are gross!" I hear from the table beside us. Lilah is doing her homework at the table while her brother tries to color next to her.

Lilah is now ten going on twenty, and Frankie is almost five.

Little Frankie, as we call him, is named after my dad and is the spitting image of me. "Yeah, Dad, you gwoss," he says while coloring his picture, his tongue sticking out of his mouth in concentration.

Lilah's iPad beeps with a notification of a message coming in. She quickly reads it and then erases it. I look at Bella, who just shrugs then looks away smiling.

"Who is that?" I ask, pointing to the iPad.

"It's Jeremy," Frankie says, not taking his face off the picture he's working on.

"Who is Jeremy?" I ask Lilah, then look at Bella for the answer to my question.

The iPad dings again. This time Lilah gathers all her stuff up, placing it in her schoolbag. "Okay, I'll be back."

"Where are you going?" I ask her retreating back.

"Over to Nan's. We had the S-E-X talk today, so Nan is going to go over it with me. Later, Dad."

I don't have a chance to say anything. I'm looking around, wondering when they started talking about sex. "Bella, you need to call that school and tell them we do not want her taking that class."

Bella laughs at me while she checks the food in the oven. "Oh, please, it's normal stuff. We all learned it," she says while she saunters over to sit on my lap.

"I did not learn that in school." I shake my head. "Fine, I'll just go there myself tomorrow and take care of that, and while I'm at it, I'm going to find out who this Jeremy kid is."

"Jeremy is da boy, Dad, da cute boy." Frankie looks up at me while picking up another color crayon. "Da really cute boy," he tells me. He repeats whatever his older sister says.

"You seriously have to talk to her, Bella. No boys. I'm serious."

"I have to talk to her? Why do I have to talk to her? You should talk to her." Bella is still a pain in my ass.

"I liked it better when you agreed with me," I tell her, nipping her earlobe.

She places her hand on mine on the table. Our matching rings shine under the light.

"In ten minutes, dinner will be ready, so go wash up, Frankie."

He puts all his things away, jumps down from the table, and runs to the bathroom to wash his hands.

"Is that a pencil in your pocket, Mr. Fletcher?" Bella asks me as she grinds her ass down on my cock. My hand moves up her thigh, sliding under her skirt, finding her bare.

My head snaps up.

"I missed you," she tells me while she leans down and kisses my neck, tracing it with her tongue.

"Frankie, go next door to Nan's house. Tell her Mom and Dad are talking serious," I yell at him while he is coming out of the bathroom.

"Okay, Dad." He doesn't question it, just runs right out, slamming the door behind him.

"Your mother is supposed to come over," she tells me as I'm unbuttoning my pants to pull my cock out.

"What time?" I ask her while pulling her skirt up and placing her right on top of my hard cock, reverse cowgirl style. She hovers over me before slowly sinking down.

"So fucking wet," I tell her, holding her hips to control her movements. If you walked in right now, you wouldn't be able to tell because her skirt has fallen down to cover her.

Her moans, though, are getting kind of loud. Turning her face to mine, I kiss her mouth. Our tongues roll with each other. Her pants are increasing, but at least she's not loud anymore.

I trail my hand under her skirt, heading straight for her clit, wetting my finger as I slowly make circles around it. Her hips start to rise and fall faster. I pinch her clit, knowing she's almost there because her pussy is practically strangling my cock, it's squeezing me so tightly.

Fuck, it never gets old with her. It just gets better and better.

"I'm going to come," she says two seconds before she slams down on me. Riding out the wave of her orgasm, her pussy contracts around me and I can't hold back.

I come hard, emptying myself inside of her.

We sit here for a minute more, catching our breaths.

"Why is my mother coming over?" I ask her.

My mother sold our childhood home and moved into my old house.

Between Brenda and Mom, the kids can come and go as they please.

"We need to tell her she's going to be a grandma again," she whispers to me.

I look over at my wife, who has given me everything. Placing my hand on her still flat stomach, I hold her and the child we created, thanking God for sending me my angel.

The End

ABOUT THE AUTHOR

When her nose isn't buried in a book, or her fingers flying across a keyboard writing, she's in the kitchen creating gourmet meals. You can find her, in four inch heels no less, in the car chauffeuring kids, or possibly with her husband scheduling his business trips. It's a good thing her characters do what she says, because even her Labrador doesn't listen to her...

You can find/stalk her here:

https://www.facebook.com/AuthorNatashaMadison/

https://twitter.com/natashamauthor

https://www.instagram.com/natashamauthor/

ReadersGroup https://www.facebook.com/groups/1152112081478827/

Goodreads:
https://www.goodreads.com/author/show/15371222.Natasha_Madison

Other Books by Natasha Madison

Something So Right

ACKNOWLEDGMENTS

This may take a while so sit back.

Crystal: My hooker. Thank you for holding my hand. Thank you for cheering me on even when I was overly dramatic. Just thank you for being you and loving me!

Rachel: You are my blurb bitch. Each time you do it without even reading this book and you rocked it. I'm really happy I bulldozed my way into your life.

Aly: I think you'll be in every single book I write because I HATE YOU, BUT I LOVE YOU.

Kendall: You have become a special part of me. The nice part, of course. You pumped me up when I get down, you pushed me to be better, and you made me cry. Your friendship is better than chocolate.

Lori: I don't know what I would do without you in my life. You take over and I don't even have to ask or worry because I know everything will be fine, because you're a rock star!

Beta girls: Teressa, Natasha M, Lori, Diane, Sian, Yolanda, Ashley, and Jamie. You girls made me not give up. You loved each and every single word and wrote and begged and pleaded for more. HOLY SHIT THIS IS HAPPENING. You can never leave me. EVER.

Danielle Deraney Palumbo: I don't think I could have done this without you. Thank you for taking the time and reading it and sending me your notes. I don't think I could release a book without you!

Madison Maniacs: This group is my go to, my safe place. You push me and get excited for me and I can't wait to watch us grow even bigger!

Lauren: You are my go-to what should I do and you answer it each and every time. I'm forever grateful for you!!!!

Mia: I'm so happy that Nanny threw out Archer's Voice and I needed to tell you because that snowballed to a friendship that is without a doubt the best ever!

Emily, my PR Guru: You saved my butt big time the first time, and this ride has been awesome!

Emily, my Editor Extraordinaire: Thank you for not tearing my book to shreds and for loving it with me.

BLOGGERS. THANK YOU FOR TAKING A CHANCE ON ME. EVEN WHEN I HAD NO COVER, NO BLURB, NO NOTHING! FOR SHARING MY BOOK, MY TEASERS, MY COVER, EVERYTHING. IT COULDN'T BE DONE WITHOUT YOU!

My Girls: Sabrina, Melanie, Marie-Eve, Lydia, Shelly, Stephanie, Marisa. Your support during this whole thing has been amazing. GUYS, I WROTE A BOOK AND THEN ANOTHER ONE!
Lastly and more importantly to Tony, Matteo, Michael, and Erica, who have to put up with Mom sitting at the table listening to country songs and serving you frozen pizza or McDonald's. You encouraged me, you pushed me, you support me, and I am utterly and forever grateful for all of that. Well when you weren't complaining you want real home cooked food, which was often.

Made in the USA
Columbia, SC
23 July 2024

39224883R00146